To Catie
Thanks! Enjoy

Robert Dean Anderson

AA

Aux Arc Novel
(Ozark Novel)

Hahatonka

ON TRIAL

Robert
Dean
Anderson

Cover Art: Beth Mix

For Beth my lovely daughter—Because of who she is,
Because I love her

Introduction

In the early 1930's, three stories dominated the news in the state of Missouri:

(1) The Snyder brothers, owners of an unusually beautiful and naturally pristine estate in central Missouri known locally as Hahatonka, (generally spelled as one word, but at times as two or three words prior to becoming a Missouri State Park, afterwards designated by three words—Ha Ha Tonka) filed suit for a million dollars in damages against the Union Electric Light and Power Company of St. Louis that had just constructed Bagnell Dam, the largest dam in the state, creating the largest man-made lake in the country.

(2) The Snyder brothers hired three-time U.S. Senator James Reed to convince a jury in federal court that the dam had ruinously damaged the estate's scenery and that lost scenery can be worth a million dollars. Reed was known as the best trial attorney in the state, if not the entire country. He welcomed the challenge and he needed the money for a run for the Presidency against Franklin Delano Roosevelt.

(3) During the trial in Jefferson City, Missouri's capital, the best known woman in Kansas City, Nell Donnelly, owner and manager of the largest garment manufacturing company in the country and one of the most wealthy women in the state, was kidnapped and held for $75,000 ransom. Reed interrupted the trial to use his influence with the Boss of Kansas City, Tom Pendergast, to return Nell Donnelly, his next door neighbor and his lover, to her home and her four-month-old

son who was secretly his son. Both Donnelly and Reed were married to other people and had been in an affair with each other for four years.

As an author of a number of novels and several works of non-fiction, my mantra in writing has always been the words of Novelist Somerset Maughan: "History tells us what happened, fiction tells us how it felt."

Faced with the decision of telling these three intriguing tales in one book, my dilemma was: History or Fiction; Facts or Feeling.

When listing the historical events, where is the emotion, the heartbreaks, the agony, the suspense and the anticipation? Where is the love and the sorrow? All elements of a good story, but missing from a mere listing of historical events. What has been presented here are the events chronologically from notes I have researched and gathered from a collection of newspapers, magazines and historical documents; notes I have bridged with those elements I felt necessary to tell the complete story.

I owe my appreciation for all those documents I have listed in the note section at the back of the book. Thanks to the assistance I received from the Camden County, Missouri, Historical Society, from the Missouri Historical Society, from the Missouri State Archives, and from all the named media. My special thanks to Daphne Jeffries of the Camden County Historical Society, to Nancy Masterson of the Ha Ha Tonka Missouri State Park, to my wife, Carol, for her support and inspiration, to my daughter Beth Mix for the cover art and to my daughter

Gwen and my son-in-law Richard Zetterlund for their help and support.

I didn't invent the word, "Faction," but I chose that route to present these three great stories of what really happened. No one involved in the drama that ensued is around to tell us exactly how it felt to them as these events played out. All we have are snippets of their conversations with others, legal documents, and abundant news clippings. It is my sincere belief after studying them in great detail in the resources I have listed, that the characters in this story would have said and done pretty much what I have them saying and doing.

I have included a listing of notes in the back of the book containing the material I have used in the compilation of this book. These notes identify sources of direct quotations and of any facts or opinions not generally known or easily checked. They are by no means a complete record of all the sources I have consulted, however, they do indicate the substance and range of reading upon which I formed my ideas and how I replicated the character and the action of the people depicted.

These notes are offered as a convenience for those who wish to pursue the complete study of the history of events this book is based on. You will find that many of the written materials you study in connection with these stories conflict with one another in minor detail. I have chosen versions I thought most likely, others may differ with me.

My hope is that you find my rendition of these three outstanding stories both entertaining and informative. That is what writing should do.

Robert McClure Snyder Sr. and sons, LeRoy, Kenneth, Carey and Robert Jr.

I
October 27, 1906

ROBERT SNYDER SR left his office at 316 American Bank Building a bit after 6 pm on October 27, 1906 to meet his chauffeur, Frank Schroeder, in Snyder's green, 40 horsepower Royal Tourist automobile. One of the two Royal Tourists he had purchased from his brother-in-law, Kansas City's dealer for Royal Tourists.

Schroeder held the door open for Snyder who seated himself behind the driver's seat on the right side of the automobile.

"Rather late tonight, Frank," Snyder told the chauffeur. "Let's get along lively."

Schroeder complied and they moved quickly through the city toward Snyder's Independence Boulevard residence.

Snyder had a busy day that included a round of golf and some more time dealing with the gas situation. Oh, yes, the gas situation. He'd been working that for more than ten years now and it was starting to pay off handsomely. And he had some help now, he'd assigned his son Robert Jr to handle the gas distribution end down at the source in Independence, Kansas. His son did not have the business acumen Snyder possessed, but he needed the training, the exposure. For Snyder, business was a challenge, a pleasure. He derived as much enjoyment from business as he did from fishing. From catching the largest tarpon ever caught off the Texas coast.

Snyder thought of what a writer friend of his told him once about writing. "Show me a story and I'll write it for you. It's a matter of confidence."

That's how Snyder felt about business, show him an opportunity and he could show you a business success. He hoped his sons would succeed in their field of endeavor as he had in his. Robert Jr showed promise—notwithstanding his passion for books and historical documents—and LeRoy was schooling in Harvard University while Kenneth finished prep school.

For just a moment—one fleeting moment—his thoughts went to the sadness that lay in the far reaches of his memory. Two wives dead, an only daughter dead at an early age, and what seemed like just days ago word from the state of Oregon about the death of his son, Carey. Carey, the black sheep he had never been able to reach in spite of the hundred thousand dollars or more he had spent in his attempts to do so. Carey, once again accused by the authorities there in Oregon of being involved in a series of robberies.

Enough of that. He leaned forward and asked Schroeder what he thought his wife might have ready for his dinner, the twenty-year-old chauffeur's wife working as a maid in the Snyder household.

"Why, I don't know," Schroeder said over his shoulder. "Maybe a nice trout from down there at that Hahatonka place you own."

"That would be good," Snyder said in Schroeder's ear. Hahatonka, what a joy the place was to him. An exquisite wilderness. Maybe he could get down there next weekend to check on the huge stone structure that locals insisted on calling a castle. The workmen should be putting the roof on the huge three and a half story structure. What a pleasure the place was going to be when the big house was completed and the garage and stable, large enough to hold a hundred horses, and the water tower that would hold enough of the clear, cold water piped up from the ever gushing spring 300 feet below the cliff that the buildings sat on. Just thinking about the place put him in an expectant mood.

As Schroeder steered the ton and a quarter luxury vehicle along Admiral Boulevard, onto Grand Avenue, on to Woodland to meet Independence Boulevard, they passed another automobile Snyder recognized as the Steven-Duryea auto owned by his neighbor on Independence, Harry Loose. He took a bit of boyish joy in the speed of the Royal Tourist overtaking the lesser powered auto of his good neighbor's.

As the gliding Royal Tourist neared Park Avenue, practically in front of the Bonaventure Hotel, lives of every person in a nearby radius changed abruptly. Frank Schroeder, struck with shock and terror, saw a boy drawing a small coasting wagon across the boulevard in front of the auto he was driving. Schroeder would later tell the police it happened this way:

"I saw the boy in plenty of time and sounded my horn. The boy heard it, for he hesitated and stopped. I pulled farther toward the curb and had nearly reached the boy when he started again right in front of the automobile. I turned more sharply to the right and struck the curb as the machine hit the boy. The machine struck the boy in the body and his head hit the radiator. I don't think the wheels passed over him, for he was lying alongside the machine when he was picked up. Mr. Snyder was thrown outward by the jerk of the machine and his head struck the iron post."

Richard Andrew watched the green Royal Tourist approaching the Bonaventure Hotel where he clerked, saw the automobile strike the boy, saw his body fly into the air so quickly it could hardly be realized what was happening until the car shot past and he saw the boy lying, bruised and bloody, in the gutter. Andrew ran to the boy, picked him up and carried him in his arms into the nearby drug store.

Drug salesman Fred Davis along with his wife in their third floor room in the hotel saw the accident, saw the boy tossed a dozen feet into the air, heard his wife exclaim that a runaway car struck the boy and Davis ran from his room down to the street to help.

A man named Morgan, a clerk in Finney's grocery store fronting the street saw Snyder slide from the back seat of the Royal Tourist onto the floor while the others who had rushed to the scene of the accident were gathered around the boy.

"A man's been hurt here in the automobile," he announced loudly. Snyder's neighbor on Independence Boulevard, Harry Loose and his passenger H.C. Edwards had reached the accident in Loose's Steven-Duryea and they rushed to help with Snyder now half lying, half sitting on the floor of the back seat of the Royal Tourist.

"I saw them sliding on the street," Edwards said. "They just oiled the street. It's slick."

Snyder's head lay upon his breast and his face and the left side of his head showed massive damage. As Edwards, Loose and Morgan were helping the chauffeur Schroeder extricate Snyder from the automobile, Dr. Smith who owned the Bonaventure Hotel had come to help. He noticed wounds to Snyder's left side of his face, noticed the trolley pole on the curb now behind the Royal Tourist and said Snyder must have turned his head to look back at the boy and was struck on his head when the auto swerved close to the pole.

Mr. Edwards held Snyder in his arms and Schroeder turned the automobile around in the street and drove to nearby Agnew Hospital as fast as he could get the Royal Tourist to go. At the hospital three doctors rushed to help bring Snyder inside and up to the second floor. Dr. Eldridge examined him, found that his collar bone was fractured in multiple places, the lower jaw was crushed and a serious contusion on the left side of his face looked ominous. Snyder breathed with great difficulty. He died within minutes after he was laid on the bed.

While Snyder was being rushed to the Agnew Hospital, the other people who had witnessed the accident had rushed to help the boy lying in the gutter bleeding from both ears, unconscious as Andrew carried him into the Haller and Beck drugstore in the Bonaventure Hotel building. Dr Smith and two other doctors who had come to the scene tried to help the boy. The police and an ambulance had been sent for and while waiting for them to arrive the people now forming a small group around the boy tried to ascertain who he was. Professor Charles Reynolds, principal of the Garfield school was sent for, but he was unable to identify the boy. A number of boys and girls were brought into the drugstore to see if they could identify him. Finally one young girl said, "I know his name. It's Arthur. He takes German from Miss. Andrews."

Someone thought to pick up the coaster wagon the boy had been pulling and on the bottom was painted, "Arthur Rodell."

After the boy was taken to Agnew Hospital his parents name and address was found and they were sent for. The boy's injuries that included a skull fracture and numerous bruises along with internal damage was treated but he died about four hours after Snyder.

Mrs. Snyder arrived at the hospital and was notified by Reverend Combs that her husband was dead. She was greatly grieved and was attended by Dr. Eldredge. Frank Schroeder did not realize Snyder had been killed in the accident until the prosecutor I.B. Kimbrell told him after Patrolman Briny Underwood arrested him.

"Oh, no, not my Mr. Snyder," Schroeder said and burst into tears. "What shall I do? What shall I do?"

Kimbrell decided Schroeder was not at fault and let him go until an inquest could be held.

Mrs. Snyder asked that Snyder's sons be notified along with her family back in Boston. She told Mrs. Schroeder, the chauffeur's wife and her household maid, that she had dreamed that very morning about the one son LeRoy, called Roy by the family, came home from Harvard University where he was attending college, and she was troubled by the dream.

Snyder was buried in Elmwood Cemetery in Kansas City with three ministers helping in the funeral services that were attended by most of the dignitaries and major business men in the city.

Standing by the open grave, the son Roy asked Robert Jr, now in charge of Snyder's business interests, how he was going to manage the responsibilities and was he worried about the situation.

"Yes," Robert Jr said. "The gas business is coming to a head with the pipeline nearly finished that will deliver gas from the wells to Kansas City homes and businesses. And there's the cattle and land in Texas and Oklahoma. I'll need plenty of help."

A long pause and an expiration of breath later, Robert Jr said, "What I'm really concerned about is Hahatonka and the big house there. What's going to become of it."

II
April 22, 1929

KENNETH SNYDER handed the April 22, 1929 issue of the *Kansas City Times* To Robert Jr and pointed to the headlines: TO BUILD HUGE DAM. Union Electric Light and Power Company President Louis Egan announced that their company had signed a contract with Stone and Webster of Boston, MA, to build a 30 million dollar dam at Bagnell on the Osage River creating a lake 125 miles long that would flood the Niangua River in Hahatonka.

Robert took a long time reading the entire article. When he finished he looked at Kenneth and LeRoy gathered around the table in the huge mansion—only a few hundred yards from the Niangua River—that they had agreed to finish in 1922 after their father had started it in 1906 before his death.

"I guess we knew the dam was coming," he said. "They started working on it six years ago, right after we finished the great house here."

"Yeah," LeRoy said, "but I thought the banker and his secretary were convicted for using depositor's money and Kansas City and everyone else had backed away from the idea. If the Niangua is turned into a lake, it will overflow Hahatonka."

"You said you knew this Egan guy," Kenneth said. "Why don't you go talk with him. What I read is they have to cut all the trees and level the ground before closing the dam."

"Yes, I know Louis Egan. It's been a while since we talked. We have to remember they will have eminent domain so they can take the land if they want it."

"I don't see anything good coming out of this," LeRoy said. "Warsaw was worried about their town being flooded and the county seat at Linn Creek is fighting them in court. Sid Roach's family owned Hahatonka at one time and he's representing Linn Creek. He's a former congressman and a good lawyer."

Robert walked from the room onto the terrace that overlooked a beautiful blue-water lake several hundred feet below the castle. His brothers followed him and the three of them stood looking down at a sight no one had ever looked at and not been greatly impressed. Across the lake, leaves on oak, walnut and sassafras were now shooting from greening limbs and snow white blossoms on the dogwoods mixed with the reddish-purple blooms on the redbud trees—the Judas trees from biblical times.

"Time will tell," Robert said.

They stood silently staring at the magnificent lake and wondering what was to come.

III
March 1, 1931

TWENTY-FOUR years plus since his father died and barely a month since the gates closed on the new Bagnell Dam, Robert McClure Snyder Jr stood at the edge of the 90 acre cold-water lake, the pride of Hahatonka, full of large rainbow trout and enormous crawfish that had provided some actual—although meager—income from the large, park-like summer home for him and his family. But this week he had not prowled through the natural splendors he loved so much—the dozen or so caves, natural bridges, rushing blue, cold-water spring, and every species of trees known to the state. This week he had come to watch the horde of tree-cutters now gathered across the lake.

With his three sons—Bill, Fred and Robert III—standing beside him he watched as the men across the water paired off in twos and began sawing the trunks of the oak, sassafras and walnut trees on the gentle hillside. The noise of the saws ripping into the beautiful trees, the nauseating sound of the coarse men yelling and swearing at each other upset him.

Robert III turned to him and asked, "Do they have to cut all the trees? Is that going to be the big lake they talk about, covering all the campground?"

Where the tree cutters worked was the area used by campers during the summer when they came to visit Hahatonka and the bathing beach at the foot of Juanita Bluff.

Lakeside was the name for the area. The Snyders leased it each year to a manager who rented camping space on the beach, rented boats to prowl the blue-water lake and to fish for rainbow trout. A large dining hall was under the same manager.

"We will have to wait and see," his father said.

"Ask Ed when you see him," Bill, the tallest son at six foot six inches said. "He's working for the dam people."

Ed was the oldest of the sons. Bob, as the brothers called the youngest, looked up at Bill and said, "I'll bet it'll be over your head."

Robert Jr paid scant attention to the three sons who began recalling other summer days they had spent on this spot fishing in the lake, and like he at this time, looking up to the top of the 300 foot cliff at the large stone house designed and partially constructed under the direction of his father twenty-five years ago before the tragic accident took his life.

The noise and chatter of the woodcutters rang across the water and grated on his already bare and exhausted nerves.

Bill broke the spell his father had fallen into when it became apparent he was asking a question.

"This guy Egan, Dad, I thought you were going to work something out with him about this big dam he's building. Weren't you friends at one time."

"When he lived in Kansas City," his father said.

"Yeah," Bob said. "He's the one married to Jesse James' cousin isn't he?"

"Second or third cousins, something like that. His wife

Fannie is a sister to Mr. Dunlap's wife Helen. You should remember Mr. Dunlap, he's the one who brought the radio down here several years ago and all of you were there listening to it."

Fred was smiling. "So, the James gang has gone from robbing trains to stealing land. That's a good story. I'm working on a story for the *Kansas City Star*, I'll include that about the James gang."

"It was all legal," Robert Jr said. "The court appointed three experts to appraise the property and determine how much the acreage the electric company took is worth."

"Eminent domain," Bill said. "We just studied that in the law classes at Princeton. In 1920 Congress passed the Federal Water Powers Act, a law allowing electrical transmission companies the right to take your land for what they termed, 'superior use for the common good.'"

"Nothing common about Hahatonka," Bob said. "So what did this James gang robber say when you talked with him, Dad?"

"Started out friendly enough, he offered twenty-eight thousand dollars. That's what your grandfather paid for it in 1902, twenty-eight years ago."

"Ha!" Bob said. "Was he holding Jesse's six shooter in his hand when he made the offer?"

"The court set the amount a lot higher than that, didn't they?" Bill asked. "A hundred and forty some thousand? Has your so-called friend paid you yet?"

"The check cleared," Robert Jr said. "Now they've sent out their spoilers."

"The dam was closed in February and the water in the Niangua River is starting to back up. If it backs up to the lake it'll be ruined," Fred said. "Can't we go back to court and stop this destruction?"

"They're already objecting to what the appraisers awarded us. If we have to go to court we'll need the best lawyer we can hire."

Bill said, "Maybe we could get the law professor at Princeton. If you want, I'll talk with him when I go back to school."

"We would need someone local," Robert Jr said. "If it goes to a trial we'll need it to be a jury trial and we would want someone without a New England accent. Someone who would understand the people in the jury."

Bob, with a grin, "What was that man's name that shot Jesse James?"

"I heard them talking one day in the newsroom at the *Star*," Fred said. "The name that came up the most was the former senator, Jim Reed. He just got some woman off on a murder charge. She fired four bullets into her husband over a card game they were playing and she claimed it was an accident. That took some pretty good lawyering. Even Pete Wellington, the editor at the *Star* said Reed was the best lawyer in Kansas City. When he was the prosecuting attorney he won something like 255 cases and lost only two."

"That was thirty years ago," his father said. "Reed's nearly seventy years old now."

"And running for President again so I heard," Bill said. "We need someone young and vigorous."

"I'm holding off going back to court if we can help it," Robert Jr said. "I need more information about where the high water point is going to be. I'll talk it over with Roy and Kenneth, they have a say in this, too. Egan didn't like the figure the three commissioners awarded us and he's waiting for a new court date. When I turned down his offer of $28,000 and took it to court he threatened to keep us in court for seven years. If they give him a date and he takes us back to court we don't have much choice but to file a countersuit."

Bob said, "Dad. Dad," and when his father looked at him, Bob pointed behind them. "Dad, what's that smoke? Something's burning."

Robert Jr looked where his son was pointing and Bill said, "That's down at the old grist-mill house."

"You wanted to talk with Roy," Fred said. "That looks like his big foreign car coming."

Robert Jr watched his brother coming from the road that passed the post office and the log house where Roy was staying. He noticed the car Roy drove, noticed it was English made, even had the steering wheel on the right side and that little bit of recognition once again shot a 25 year-old memory to mind. The green automobile his father had been killed in had steering on the right side.

Roy brought the auto to a quick stop and dismounted in haste, unlike his usual movements.

"Did you see it?" he shouted. "Did you see the mill house burning?"

Robert Jr walked to meet him and his sons started firing questions at Roy: "Who did it?"

"How'd it get started?"

"Is anyone trying to put it out?"

"The damn electric company," Roy spat out, the "damn" taking Robert Jr by surprise, not the usual language for his brother.

"The electric company?" Robert Jr asked. "They started it? How do you know?"

"Because I asked them who the hell they were." Roy was right up in his brother's face now, his own face burning with anger. "Can't we do something? I told them I was calling the sheriff and they laughed."

"Why?" Robert Jr asked, not directing the question at Roy. "Why are they doing that? That's going to allow the river water all the way to the spring."

"Oh, no," from Roy. "The river water's going to come through the trout glen. That's how the river water's going to get to the spring. Through the trout glen."

"But . . . the dam," Robert Jr said. "The water can't get past the old dam that has been holding back the river for years . . ."

"Yeah, Uncle Roy . . ." Fred said, but Roy cut him off.

"I think they've set charges at the dam," he said. "Someone put up a homemade sign to stay out, 'Dangerous Explosives.'"

Young Bob now grew more excited than even the older ones. "If the dam is gone then water from the river will run into the lake. Right here. Right where we're standing. River water in the lake means no more trout, river water's too warm."

Fred said, "Yeah, no more lobsters, either. The cold-water crayfish Ed and I used to take down to Lebanon and put on the train for St. Louis. Big ones, as big as your hand."

"Gone," Roy said. "All gone. Hahatonka will be destroyed. What was it Mr. Williams the president of the university said, 'Hahatonka is the number one wonder of the whole state.' And it's destroyed just so people in St. Louis can have more light bulbs in their homes."

They turned as one to look at Robert Jr, as if for guidance. He stood mute staring at the plume of smoke rising into the clear blue sky of the Ozarks, through majestic oaks and stately walnut trees. Agony was etched into his face and his rigid body jerked with the noise of the explosion from the direction of the dam that backed up the cold, blue water coming from the spring.

He spoke finally, determination in his words, his voice on this occasion not unlike his father's: "We're going to court," he said.

Voices of the others flowed together, warmly, relieved, charged with motivation. Robert McClure Snyder Sr. might have been smiling with them in spirit.

IV
March 11, 1931

"WHEN?" Louis Egan asked the man standing in front of him whose name he had trouble remembering. "When is the lodge going to be finished? I've been inviting people to go up and look at the work on the dam, but I continue to have to cancel. They said a year ago it was finished. How long does it take to pound a few pegs into some logs anyway? They put the thing together in Oregon, took it apart and shipped it here. Shouldn't have taken more than a month to put the damn thing together. It's been more than that."

"I'll check with them again," the man said, his voice unsure, his mind scrambling for plausible answers to the president of Union Electric Light and Power Company. "Everything is finished, they've been using it to observe progress on the dam."

"And don't let them forget to put up the sign, 'Egan's Lodge.' That's the official name. Make sure it's on the sign in front. Now, send Frank in here."

"Yes sir." The man backed slowly from the room, closed the door and exhaled a long, nervous breath.

When Frank Boehm entered Egan's office, the president was shuffling with vexation through a stack of loose sheets of paper with handwritten notes on them. Boehm wore a casual look about his features that was only skin deep. Egan glanced up at him, but continued to thrash through the papers, finally halting at one, scanned it, then looked up at Boehm.

"What are we doing on the condemnation of that place the Snyders own—what do they call it, Hahatonka, something like that?"

"The judge appointed a commission, remember . . ."

"Yeah, yeah, I know all that. We paid them a hundred forty three thousand for a piece of land not worth the twenty-eight thousand I offered Snyder. What I'm asking is when are we going to court to overturn the hundred forty three thousand. When are we getting a court date?"

"I've been talking with Brewster, Louis and . . ."

"Brewster? I want somebody better than Brewster to go to court with. Christ, look at all these damn papers I've got in front of me. Problems, all of them. For instance, here's this one . . ." Egan shuffled through the papers again, found the one he was looking for and read it to Boehm: "All those damn property owners in the town of Linn Creek that have not accepted our offer for their property." He looked up at Boehm impatiently as if he expected immediate results to come pouring out of the vice president's mouth.

"Condemnation suits have been filed," Boehm said, dismissing it with a wave of his hand. "Our immediate problem in that town is the city council passed a new ordinance placing a tax on every automobile used in business there. A tax that's clearly aimed at us. We drive a vehicle into town to any of our offices there, we pay a tax on it."

"And we're doing what about it?"

"Well, we're talking with the council members, but they're a pretty tough lot. Not making much headway."

"It's that damn newspaper man down there, Vincent, who's stirring them up. We need our own newspaper. How long would that take us?"

"Not a real possibility. We're getting our best returns out of the people we're paying real money to for a pile of rocks they can't grow anything on."

"What're we doing about those places in town we've bought and the people won't move out. Or some damn squatter that's working on the dam just moves into because it's vacant?"

"We're burning the houses."

"Burning them? Isn't that causing trouble?"

"Some. Has to be done sooner or later. Federals ruled everything has to be removed between 628 and 660 foot elevation."

"Just move our offices out of that damn town. I'm tired of messing with them."

"Have to find a place to move them to."

"Do it."

Egan shuffled through the papers again. Stopped, looked up, than back at the paper. "Here's another one. You know that prosecutor down there, Moulder? Him and Vincent and some others, lawyer named Roach, filed against us in the Circuit court in Bolivar, Missouri. Judge named Skinker ruled in their favor. Says we have to stop construction of the dam."

He flipped the sheet of paper across his desk, but Boehn didn't pick it up.

"Don't worry about what some small time circuit court judge rules. Reeves, the federal court judge has already ruled in our favor. That's all we need."

"This Reeves, he's leaning our way?"

"Seems to, yeah."

"I think he's the guy who lost the election to Pendergast's man about twelve years ago for representative or something. You think if we go to federal court about this Hahatonka thing Reeves would be the judge?"

"Probably," Boehm said.

"We have a tab on him? Laun have him in his book?"

"The man seems to be pretty straight. Have to be careful approaching him."

"Maybe we could have him down for a weekend at that log cabin they ever get it finished. Maybe with Caulfield, the governor."

"Maybe. I'll talk with Laun and Oscar Funk."

"And speaking of that log cabin, nobody knows when it'll be finished. And I just got back from a trip down to check on the progress at the dam and had to wait a couple of hours on a plane. I want to start a regular schedule on flights down there. I don't want to be wasting my time waiting for some damn airplane."

"Taken care of it."

Egan shuffled papers again, pulled one out. "Here's something else we should have taken care of by now. Those bridges across the lake that the county down there in Linn Creek wants—Christ those people down there are a pain in the ass—I thought we had that taken care of through that highway commissioner McDonald."

"He's on board."

"What do you mean, 'on board?'"

"I mean he's taken care of. Oscar's working with him."

"Oscar." Egan's voice showed disgust. "I'm not paying for two more bridges, you tell Oscar that. They're running the highway across on top of the dam. Supposed to be open in a few weeks, isn't it? The state is paying for that. See that we're not paying for any more damn bridges."

"Right." Boehm hadn't changed positions since entering.

"We got approval from the Public Service Commission for the transmission lines to the lead mines and to the Page Avenue plant. Make sure everyone knows that. We don't need approval from anyone else, town, county or property owner."

"We're already working on the transmission lines. No more problems."

Egan stacked the papers in his hands and laid them on a corner of his desk. "Anything else?"

"I shouldn't think so. They're getting ready to move the county seat now that it was passed at the election. Everyone's for that except the hardcore in Linn Creek. Man named Woodruff has everything in order since the election. Going to be a brand new town out in some cow pasture."

"I don't give a damn about any county seat. They want to they could have held their county court forty feet under water. Rassieur made a proposal to them half of what Cravens company offered for the courthouse before we bought Walter Cravens out. Then, like I said, I just got back from down there and met with their commissioners, but they wouldn't talk with me about price. They actually thought that this Judge Clinker or Stinker, or whatever the hell his name is, was going to shut us down."

"We tore their courthouse down."

"Speaking of that," Egan said, now rising from his chair to a height a half foot over Boehm, "I'm going to contest all the appraisals for sidewalks and curbs and streets in the town. They were paid for by the property owners, not the town so we don't owe the town for them."

"I see," Boehm said. "And about contesting the hundred and forty some thousands we paid the Snyders for that Hahatonka wilderness."

"You got us a lawyer?" Egan snapped. "I'm waiting."

"How much you want to reduce it so that we get a payback from them?"

Egan smiled. "The head of the clan, Robert Jr, turned down my offer of twenty-eight thousand and took it to the judge to appoint the three appraisers. I told him then I'd keep him in court for seven years and I will. Fifty thousand is going to be my maximum on that. Cut the appraisals to the town, to Snyder, to the county by thirty thousand for the courthouse and the two bridges I'm not going to build and that ought to pay for Egan's Lodge."

"Going to be a nice weekend retreat. Almost as nice as the big castle the Snyders built at Hahatonka." Boehm was matching Egan's smile.

"The lawyer?" Egan raised his brows.

"It's that man in Texas I told you about," Boehm said.

"Houston. Man named Walne. He's coming to talk with you so you can see what he's going to charge us."

"Nothing if we put the screws to them on this Hahatonka thing. Have Judge Reeves award court costs to us as well as a reduction in the appraisals."

Boehm on his way out the door, turned back. "Just make sure they don't get a jury trial."

V
March 15, 1931

"ELLEN 'NELL' QUINLAN DONNELLY stood patiently by the window, a smooth drink in her hand, clothed in a "Nelly Don" original frock, her eyes on the taxi cab that had pulled through the rocked entrance to the driveway of their fashionable house. Paul Donnelly, her husband, dismounted from the back seat of the cab, lurched awkwardly to the front door of the vehicle fumbled through his jacket pocket, pulled out a wad of paper money and thrust it through the cab's lowered window.

He stumbled then as he turned and walked toward the entrance to the house. Nell took another drink and continued to stare after the departing taxi. She heard her husband's scuffling steps into the house, his mumbling, then knew he had come into the entry room where she stood by the gilt-edged railing along the stairway.

"Thought you'd be at work," he said, disappointment in his voice. "Putting out more of those damn dresses you think are so great."

"The dresses keep you in liquor," she said, still not looking at him. "Supports the tramp you spent the night with, also."

"Huh, man can't enjoy himself once in a while?"

"Once perhaps, not every night."

He looked around the large dining room. "Where's the help?"

"I let her go for the day."

"What am I supposed to eat for breakfast? The famous dressmaker Nelly Don sure can't fix a meal for her husband."

She turned to face him then. "It's going to have to stop, Paul, this philandering. The employees at the plant know what's going on. It's starting to become embarrassing."

"Well," he said, slurring a bit, "how about the senator? Are the employees gossiping about him?"

"The senator does not go down to the Donnelly Garment Factory and walk up and down the aisles after a liquid lunch and pinch the women on their behind."

"Jealous, my dear?" Donnelly laughed, then choked and coughed. "I'm going to bed."

"We have to talk. This has to be settled."

"If I can't get anything around here to eat, I'm going down to the diner." Donnelly turned back to the door onto the expansive porch fronted by massive fluted columns. Nell stood in his path.

Perplexed, he stumbled backwards until he was against the railing. "All right, all right. Settle it, then get out of the way."

"I'll buy out your interest in the business," she said. "Name a price."

"A price? You want a price for my half of the largest garment factory in Kansas City? No, not Kansas City, in the whole damn country. No, no, wait. Not the whole country, the whole damn world."

"Come up with a reasonable offer then,"she said.

"Let me see now. Sales last year was about three and a half million dollars. So that's my price on the company I built. The company named after me."

"I had something to do with it, don't forget. Don't forget the pink checked dress I started out with making eighteen dozen and selling them to Peck's."

"Using machines I bought and paid for. Using the money from the credit line I established for you. You couldn't make eighteen dozen dresses on your home sewing machine in two years without my help, my money I got for you."

Nell said, "The Handy Dandy Apron keeps everyone working throughout the year. My design. No more seasonal layoffs in the hard times when husbands are losing their jobs. We're selling thousands of them and probably . . ."

Donnelly had a finger raised to jab at her. "Don't pull that Queen of the Company on me. You're just trying to get rid of me after all I've done, setting things up for you. I work my damn ass off for you and this is the thanks I get? No, no, no. I don't think so . . ."

"Settle down, Paul, don't go into one of your 'Poor Me' episodes. Let's settle this like two reasonable people . . ."

"Take it," yelling now. "Take it all. You and the senator. Take over everything."

He took off his jacket and slung it on the floor. He searched through his trouser pockets and came out with more paper money, then his billfold and threw everything on top of the jacket lying on the floor.

"There. There. Take it all," and turned toward the other door out of the room, stumbled part way through it, turned, slapped his head with his open palm and mumbled lowly, "Where is it? Where's my damn revolver. I'll end this thing right now."

"I took the revolver," Nell Donnelly said. "Don't threaten to kill yourself again, Paul. It's so melodramatic. We go through this every time. Please, I'm asking you, let's end this so both of us can get on with our lives."

Paul Donnelly began crying, big tears running down each cheek. "I try my best, I do everything to keep the business on top, but no, you want me out of it. Out of your life . . ."

"What is it you want, Paul? Just more liquor, more women?"

"I want some respect. Some gratitude for what I've done. What I've built. I want you to love me again, Nell. I want things the way they used to be."

He was coming toward her, his arms outstretched. She took him by his arms before he could get them around her.

"You mean before you started drinking and before you started sleeping with every woman you could get to go with you."

She paused.

"Go sleep it off, Paul. When you wake up, we'll

talk about you changing back to the way you were when I respected you, needed you, wanted you. Go on, go to sleep."

He went limp and backed away from her. He picked up his jacket and billfold and the bills he had scattered on the floor. As he was walking through the door out of the entryway she said behind him, "And take a bath before you come back down. Wash the whore off of you."

THE SUN was at work heating up the day while Kansas City humidity threatened to obscure its brilliance. Nell led her over-friendly dark brown German shepherd along the worn and familiar path between the houses, the Donnelly's and Senator James Reed and his wife Lura's. The confrontation between her and Paul had gone as she suspected it would, like it always did these days. She had a full schedule of tasks that needed her attention at the factory, but she needed some calm before going there. She had told her chauffeur George Blair to pick her up at ten o'clock. Less than an hour. She glanced toward the Reed home, hoping, wishing Senator Reed, "Jim," would show up soon with his German shepherd, Jeff. She needed to talk with someone to ease her mind. Someone like Jim. Or her niece Kate. Better to talk this over with Jim.

On her second trip along the bordered walk she heard footsteps crunching the rock-strewn path behind her. She stopped, waited for the footsteps to come up to her, looked up, smiled happily at the tall, aristocratic Senator James Reed. He bent to peck her on the cheek, stepped back and asked, "Again?"

She nodded.

"How bad?"

"It's getting repetitious," she said. "I don't know how many pistols I've taken away from him. This one was loaded."

"We can end this," he said, his voice lower than his normal resonant tone. "It needs to be ended."

"I know. Give it some time."

"Not my advice, but your call."

The dogs who had been sniffing each other began to get more familiar. Reed pulled Jeff closer to him and held the collar.

"I'm planning a trip to Europe next month," she said, watching him for a reaction. "I'm taking Kate with me."

"It would be such a pleasure if I could get away, meet you there. Or travel over with you."

They began walking now, side by side, each holding their dog on their opposing sides.

She spoke without looking at him as she plucked a bloom off the bridal wreath that grew beside the path, "I understand. How is Lura?"

"Not good," he said, disappointment apparent. "Not terribly bad, but not good."

"You're a good husband, Jim."

They walked silently for a dozen steps. "Paul was at one time. His manic depressive traits were invisible to me at the time, though looking back I can recognize them in retrospect."

"Life changes."

"It certainly has. For both of us. Just look at you, prosecuting attorney, mayor, United States Senator. Candidate for President of the United States. You could have been President, or at least, Vice President."

"I knew Al Smith couldn't win. A year later on he would have run away with it."

"How about next time? Are you getting ready to run in '32?"

He didn't answer right away. "The worst part is raising enough money to run. I think I'm in a good position in spite of the woman's suffrage thing, but I probably won't decide for another year."

"I should be mad at you about being against the right of women to vote. Have you changed your mind about that, about being against it ten years ago?"

"Yes and no. I don't like it that women think I'm against them, but I think I was right. Most women—present company excluded—vote the way their husband tells them to."

"It's democratic for everyone to vote," she said. "Even we Republicans think so."

They both laughed.

She stopped in the path. "I'd better go, George is coming for me."

"Anything I can do for you? Anything else to tell me?"

She placed a hand on his arm. "Yes there is. I think I told you that Paul and I haven't slept together for several years now."

He nodded, a question on his face.

"So I wanted you to be the first to know."

Pause.

"I'm pregnant."

VI
March 18, 1931

"JOHN MMMMMMFL" the reporter said, introducing himself to the famous Senator James Reed, offering his hand
the ex-senator took with a smile. John had heard through
a grapevine reporters maintained, about how the tall,
rugged, white-haired nationally renowned politician-
lawyer had threatened to punch ("If you publish this picture, I'll knock your goddamn head off,") a photographer
for the *Kansas City Journal-Post*, George Cauthen, if a picture
Cauthen had taken of Myrtle Bennett in the courtroom
immediately after she was acquitted of murdering her
husband, showed up in the newspaper.

John preferred the senator not to know, nor remember
his name. Just in case.

Reed had just arrived in front of the Kenwood Arms
Hotel and the busboy there who John tipped when he was
notified that guests of importance had registered, tele-
phoned the reporter for the *Springfield Daily News*.

"What brings you to Springfield, Senator?" John
asked. "By my recollection you haven't been here since
the '28 Presidential run."

"Primarily a business trip," Reed said. "I'm going with
the Snyder brothers and others up to Camden County to a
place called Hahatonka. Then on to St. Louis. Strictly
business, but I expect the trip to Hahatonka will be a
pleasant outing, considering the attractions of the place."

"Nothing to do with any further criminal cases, then?"
John asked, being careful in his wording.

"No, no. I've moved on from the practice of criminal law."

"So the Bennett case you just finished a couple of weeks ago will be your last criminal case?"

The Bennett case John referred to was the murder trial of Myrtle Bennett in Kansas City for shooting her husband, John Bennett, (Uh aw, another John) during a bridge game they played with their neighbors. Reed, in a spectacular defense, had achieved freedom for the woman by claiming self-defense and an accident.

"I thought this girl was not guilty, more or less a victim of circumstances," Reed said. "Her friends interceded for her and I thought it my duty to help. The not guilty verdict justified my convictions."

Best to leave it there, John thought. "There's talk about being a candidate for President again next year, Senator. What are your plans on that?"

Senator Reed flashed a brief, but self-gratifying smile as he said, "I'd like to give you an interview about politics," he said, "but I have my own reason for not talking public affairs right now."

"There are a lot of people around who would welcome the opportunity to vote for Jim Reed again."

The Senator's smile increased. "I'm working very hard right now looking after my own business."

"Which doesn't include any more criminal cases?"

"I never did practice criminal law much," Reed said. "Excepting of course when I was prosecuting attorney."

Reed, who at one time had been the scourge of the United States Senate when he had taken on President

Woodrow Wilson over the League of Nations issue—which got him barred from the 1920 Democratic
Presidential Convention—moved on into the hotel lobby
leaving behind four other men at the check-in counter.

The Snyder brothers—LeRoy and Kenneth—were
willing, even anxious to talk with the reporter about their
destination, the picturesque area once the home of the
Osage tribe. LeRoy, a man of medium height in his for-
ties, maybe fities, reminded John that the United States
government purchased the area from the Osage in 1825
and the tribe moved on to the Nations, now the state of
Oklahoma. He was effusive in relating the history of the
Hahatonka area, about counterfeiters, settlers and his father who was killed tragically in an automobile accident
in Kansas City twenty-five years ago. When John asked
about the Bagnell Dam that is nearing completion in the
area, and if it would affect the wonders of Hahatonka,
LeRoy's voice level picked up and he told John how the
electric company building the dam—Union Electric Light
and Power, pronounced with distaste—had burned a century's old grist mill close to the ever-flowing, cold water
spring and dynamited the foundation.

"A month ago," LeRoy snapped, his voice rising, "they
blew up the dam that held the cold spring water in the
lake that was full of rainbows and huge crawfish. No
warning. Someone could have been killed. And they sent
in a bunch of ruffians to cut down about a thousand trees
alongside the lake. Huge oaks three, four feet in diame-
ter. And beautiful walnut trees that could have been

sawed into gorgeous wood. Instead they piled them up and burned them."

LeRoy introduced his brother Kenneth who seemed perfectly satisfied to let LeRoy do the interview. Kenneth with a slim mustache and pin striped suit looked every bit the business man. LeRoy had the reporter shake hands with Henry Bundscheu, introduced as an attorney, and with a Mister Hanley from Kansas. Both those men left promptly with Kenneth.

When the other man finished at the clerk's counter, LeRoy said, "Tell this man from the newspaper here, Ernest, about what the dam's going to do to Hahatonka. This is Ernest Howard, an engineer from Kansas City. He knows about dams and floods and such stuff."

"What's going to happen up there," Howard said, seeming quite prepared to talk about the area, "is the flood stage is thirty feet over the cold water lake level. What that means is that when the river water drops thirty feet what will be left by that beautiful lake will be nothing but mud flats."

"Are you going to court against the Union Electric Light and Power Company?" the reporter asked.

LeRoy said, "They've already filed against the appraisal the three appointed commissioners awarded us. That means it will go to a federal court because of the Water Powers Act. We'll wait and see if and when they schedule action on that matter."

"It kind of looks like you're enticing Senator Reed to take your case if you go to court," John the reporter said.

"We're seeking his advice," LeRoy said. "He's very knowledgable about the legal issues involved."

With a grin John said, "He's very good on murder cases, too."

LeRoy said seriously, "We're hoping it doesn't come to that."

STANDING IN THE PLAZA in front of the big stone house started by Robert McClure Snyder, Sr twenty-six years ago, looking out over the large lake, the spring and an island around which water from the spring flowed, Jim Reed said around an unlit cigar, "Remarkable. Truly splendid."

LeRoy said, "You can see the muddy water from the Niangua River flowing into the lake now that the dam has been blown. No more blue water. No more rainbow trout."

Reed asked, "Did you have any income from the lake? Rentals, charges, anything that brought in more revenue than the cost of upkeep?"

LeRoy didn't answer for a full minute. "Probably not. Robert would have the financial figures, but from what I remember I would have to say no. We rented boats, we sold the crayfish, we had a resort area called Lakeside that we leased. No real income, though."

"Was the area open to the public? Could anyone come into the area and fish or whatever?"

"It was open, people came here, looked around, fished. We didn't have a way to keep people out. The house, of course, was not open to the public. We use it in the summer. Robert spends a good deal of time in the house. He has his collection of books and historical matter there."

"And that's not open to the public?"

"No."

Reed turned and directed his attention to the huge stone house locals referred to as the castle. "No rentals from the big house? Would make a nice resort for weekends or short term rentals."

"Kenneth and I have tried to persuade Robert to turn the house into a resort type hotel, but he's not in favor of it."

"You've tried to sell it? To the state of Missouri for a park?"

"Every governor since father died has been in favor of turning Hahatonka into a state park for the public to enjoy. In 1909 it lacked one vote in the legislature of becoming a state park."

"When you've discussed selling the property to someone—the state, anyone—what kind of money were you talking about?"

Again LeRoy took time to answer. "In the neighborhood of a hundred thousand dollars."

Reed turned and sat at a concrete table with benches, laid his briefcase on the table, extracted a large tablet from the briefcase, took a pen from inside his jacket, unscrewed the cap and began to write, the cigar clenched in his teeth.

"All right, here's what we'll do. I'll take your case. I'll prepare a suit against the electric company. Our damages will have to be limited to destruction of the scenery. Destroying the beauty of the place. What we have to have is a jury to hear our case. We can bring in experts to tell the jury about the beauty of Hahatonka and how the dam is destroying that beauty. We can't say we've lost any revenue or any possible sale of the property. We will tell the jury the dam has destroyed the most unique and natural features in the state."

"Will the jury buy that? Damages that affect the landscape? What kind of value will they place on rocks and trees?" LeRoy looked skeptical.

"A million dollars," Reed said. He made another note on his tablet, screwed the top back on his pen and stuck it in his inside jacket pocket. He stood and looked again toward the lake and the area across from the lake where the woodcutters had removed hundreds of trees, where the mill building had once stood, where the dam had once held back the silted river water from the clear, blue spring water.

"Our suit will say their Bagnell Dam damaged Hahatonka by a million dollars," He said. He stood and turned to leave.

"Then I'll prove it."

VII
June 4, 1931

MARY BOWEN SNYDER poured tea into the three cups on the grand table in the west lounge of the 38 room grand stone house atop the cliff 300 feet above the Hahatonka lake. Her guests, sisters-in-law Mary Louise Snyder, wife of Kenneth Snyder, and Lillian Snyder, wife of LeRoy Snyder, thanked her and waited as Mary placed the kettle on the table, sat and joined the others in sipping her drink.

The table in the room was massive with square, carved legs beneath it. The central hallway, visible through the archway leading into the lounge, glowed with sunlight throughout the lower level. As usual, before seating themselves in the lounge, the three women had stood for moments in the central hallway—or ballroom as the younger ones in the family liked to call it—and absorbed the grandeur of the place, embellished by the surrounding second floor arches looking into the hallway in front of the bedrooms.

"The announcement made the *Star* several days ago," Mary said, opening the conversation. "About the trial, I mean. It's going to be next month the article said. I guess the men need time to get prepared."

She was the wife of Robert Snyder Jr, an attractive woman of medium height, dark hair swept away from her face with stylish waves. She sat at the end of the table, placing herself as the host, though the immense structure as well as the rest of Hahatonka property belonged to the

Snyder Estate, equally owned by the three brothers. It was Robert Jr and Mary along with their three sons who normally used the big house as their retreat during the summer months.

"Roy says it will be put off," Lillian said. She wore the cloth, cloche hat with fringed brim that may or may not have been slightly out of style at this time. "He doesn't think the electric company will want to go to trial that quickly. Especially since they must have been quite surprised by the lawsuit Mr. Reed filed for our side. A million dollars. That had to come as a surprise to them."

"Surprised Kenneth when Mr. Reed told them what he was going to do," Mary Louise said. "I think every newspaper in Missouri must have carried the story. A million dollar lawsuit gets attention."

"I just hope Mr. Reed knows what he's doing," Mary, wife of Robert Jr said. "I watched him at the Bennett trial. He was quite overpowering."

"You went to the Bennett trial?" Lillian exclaimed. "My goodness that must have been a real experience. I kept up with it in the newspapers. Was she guilty? What did you think?"

"I don't know," Mary said. "You shoot your husband over a card game it's pretty remarkable that the jury sets you free."

Mary Louise leaned forward as if to get closer to the story. "But didn't she shoot him four times? How could they call it self defense?"

"The whole thing got pretty confusing," Mary said. "As I recall what happened was she shot through the bathroom door twice missing him, then when he tried to run out the door to their apartment to get away from her she shot him twice in the back."

"Because he played the wrong card?" Mary Louise said. "Unbelievable."

"Mr. Reed was quite persuasive," Mary said. "When he cried along with Myrtle Bennett he convinced me. At least, right at that moment."

"What did the judge say when Mr. Reed started crying with Mrs. Bennett?" Lillian asked.

"The other man, the prosecutor, Mr. Page said, 'I don't want him trembling with tears in his eyes talking how destitute the defendant is.' And then the senator said, 'Well, you'd be trembling, too, if you knew the facts of this woman's life.' And Mr. Page says, 'I'll tremble because she shot her husband in the back.'"

The three of them smiled, even laughing a bit, and Mary said, "Mr. Page said, 'Let's pause long enough to give the counsel for the defense and the defendant time to get their cry over with,' and that caused Mr. Reed to accuse Mr. Page of being cold blooded."

Lillian said, "Some of the women in our church group said Mr. Reed was a bit of a ladies man."

"I . . . well . . . maybe, I don't know." Mary paused to think about it. "Myrtle Bennett was quite attractive."

"Some of the church women are . . . they gossip. Not me, of course." She paused. "But I listen," with a laugh.

Mary Louise asked, "What do they say about our Senator Reed?"

"That he may be carrying on with the woman who

makes the Nelly Don dresses," from Lillian. "She lives next door to him."

Mary straightened, ran her hand down the chiffon dress she wore with appealing figures printed in lines across it. "Don't tell me," she said. "This is a Nelly Don. And I wore it to the trial."

"Did he give you the eye?" Lillian asked in jest.

"Tell us again exactly how it was supposed to have happened," Mary Louise said. "It started when she got angry because he played the wrong card and he slapped her and then she got a gun somehow. How did that happen?"

"The husband was supposed to be packing his suitcase to leave and she went to her mother's room and got his gun. I never did find out why his gun was in her mother's room. When he saw her with the gun, that's when he ran into the bathroom."

"And later Mr. Reed says she dropped the gun and it went off accidentally?" Mary Louise asked.

"Yes, and then, according to Mr. Reed, Mr. Bennett grabbed for the gun and it went off killing him," Mary said. "Had me believing it along with the jury."

"But the newspaper said she told his nephew that she intended to shoot her husband, but they wouldn't let the nephew testify," Lillian said. "One of the newspapers claimed that Mr. Reed, the judge and the prosecutor all had their positions because of Tom Pendergast. Implying, I suppose, that the three of them decided how the trial would go before the trial even started."

"I don't think so," Mary said. "The prosecutor, Mr.

Page was quite adversarial and criticized Mr. Reed throughout the trial."

"Let's hope Mr. Reed has the power to convince the jury in the Hahatonka case that this is all worth a million dollars," Mary Louise said.

Lillian glanced at the sunlit central hallway, the daylight pouring through the skylights in the ceiling of the three and a half story house. "Maybe he could if they would spend the day here and see all the magnificent things there is to see."

"I'll bet Mr. Reed charges a good deal of money to take the case. He must have gotten a sizable amount from Mrs. Bennett," Mary said. "She got her husband's life insurance after shooting him. Thirty thousand dollars, I think it was."

Mary Louise, with a grin, said, "The question then did she shoot him for his insurance or because he played the wrong card?"

"I think it was because he slapped her," Lillian said.

"One of the New York newspapers said that shooting your partner for playing the wrong card could now be called justifiable homicide," Mary said.

All three laughed and Mary, in an attempt at seriousness, said they shouldn't treat it with levity as a man was dead.

"Talking seriously," Lillian said, "Does Robert think this will pay off, suing the electric company and hiring the ex-senator for the trial."

"He didn't see any other recourse," Mary said. "The electric company could have had the appraisal overturned and then Robert would be back dealing with that dreadful man Egan who offered him twenty-eight thousand dollars for the property. Robert's quite upset over the matter. He comes down here whenever we can get away and he loses himself in his books and historical matter he has collected. There is peace in that for him."

After a pause she adds, "And I enjoy the same thing. We both have great interest in books and manuscripts, especially about history of the area and of the state."

"But if Mr. Reed doesn't get the million dollars for the property, how will the estate pay him?" Lillian asked. "I don't get too involved in the financial affairs of the family businesses, Roy has a good paying job, but how much are we at risk? The estate doesn't own the gas company any longer and that's where the boys' father made most of his money wasn't it, Mary? You know more about it than the rest of us. You were there when they started pumping the gas up from where you lived."

"Independence, Kansas," Mary said. "Grew up there. Met Robert there. Got married there. An exciting time. They were burning the gas off the oil wells then. Oil was the next big thing, everyone said. The automobiles were taking over and they used oil and gasoline for their engines. Robert's father saw a good business possibility if he could get the gas from the oil wells to Kansas City and sell it there it would be better and cheaper than making gas."

"How did they make gas?" Mary Louise wanted to know. "I never did understand that."

"They made it from burning coal, somehow," Mary

said. "Robert explained it to me, but I'm no engineer so I couldn't get the details correct. Some company—Kansas City Gas and Light Company or something like that, was making the gas and selling it for a dollar sixty per unit, whatever the unit was, and Robert's father started selling it for a dollar. So the company bought him out. He made a great deal of money off of that. Then he got the idea of pumping the gas out of the oil wells up to Kansas City in a big underground pipe and sent Robert down to Independence to take care of it. Lucky for me he sent Robert there."

"Lucky for Robert for sure," Lillian said with a smile. "My big question is, what will the legacy of the Snyder women be? We know what people will say about the men's father 75 years from now, and what they will say about our husbands—depending on Mr. Reed's success, of course—but what will people say about the Snyder women?"

They sat quietly, contemplating. "I think," Mary said, breaking the spell, "they will say we took care of our men when they needed us."

After a moment she poured more tea.

VIII
June 6, 1931

PAUL DONNELLY sat immobile in the chair at the dining room table in the Donnelly home, his arms resting on the table, his hands clasped, his eyes straight ahead, his face tense. Standing by the table side by side, not touching each other, Senator James Reed and Nell Donnelly.

"Why are you doing this to me?" Paul asked, his voice firm, shaking slightly.

"It's done, Paul," Nell said. "I'm going to have Jim's baby. It happened. We moved away from each other. You began drinking heavily and consorting with other women, I gave all my time to the business, designing dresses, promoting dresses, choosing fabrics. Our interests grew apart. I met Jim, he filled a need you used to fill. So we came to this point in life. That's why we're here, to set a plan for us to follow in the future."

"Like a dress plan, huh?" sarcastically.

"If you want to look at it that way."

"Just give me my gun you keep taking away from me. I'll set the plan myself and you and the good senator can go to hell."

"I was hoping you wouldn't go melodramatic on me again, Paul. Let's treat this seriously."

Reed put a hand on Nell's arm. "Here's the way it can go, Paul. The best path for all of us. Nell goes to Europe telling whoever asks that she is going there to adopt a baby. She comes back this fall when the baby is due, has the baby and returns to Kansas City with an adopted baby. You adopt the baby in your name, the child is accepted as a Donnelly, then next year Nell buys your interest in the business, she files for divorce and you're free to conduct your life the way you want to, a million dollars in your hand."

"How very nice, all planned out for me." Paul continued to look straight ahead.

"No, you can plan it any way you want to, Paul," Nell said. "You can go to the press and tell about Jim and I. You can tell them what a faithful husband you have been and they'll start asking around because I guarantee that will be the biggest story all the newspapers, the radio, the gossip circuit will talk about. Sales of dresses will spike upward for a while, then people will look at our ads, at our models, at me and they will start to turn away. The employees will lose their loyalty, you will become the philanderer everyone will talk about and you won't be able to hit all the clubs in town the way you do now. You'll be the talk of the town. And you won't like that."

Paul snapped his head toward the two, centered his agitated look on Nell and said, "And what about the two of you? Where will you be? What will they say about you?"

"We'll be together with our child."

"I can't accept this . . . this betrayal," Paul said. He wiped at his eyes, pursed his lips, then directed his attention to Reed with scornful eyes.

"That won't go over too well with getting to be President. That's what you want isn't it? President of the whole United States? How are people going to vote for a man who lays with another man's wife."

Reed said, "I would think you should be thinking about how it's going to affect your life. I can take care of mine. Nell can take care of her life. Can you take care of yours?"

"Next year you can marry Virginia, Paul," Nell said and he quickly turned to look at her. "That's her name isn't it? Virginia George? Everyone in the plant knows about her. And about you. Isn't she the would-be actress you've been seeing. A million dollars will help her career."

Paul slumped at the table. He waved a hand limply. "You're not giving me any choice."

"It's your call, Paul. Which plan you want to follow?" Reed asked.

"Why can't we just . . . just go back?" Paul said, looking now at the table, head bent downward. He brushed at his hair. "The way it used to be."

"We're where we are, Paul. We're past the time I come home to find another woman in my bed with you and wearing my pajamas. It's like the business, you don't go backwards, you go forward," from Nell.

Reed began to unwrap a cigar, bit the end, placed it in his hand and stuck the cigar in his mouth. "We'll take your silence as agreement, Paul. Nell leaves tomorrow for Paris."

Paul Donnelly remained silent, staring at the opposite wall. Nell Donnelly and James Reed left the room holding hands.

Reed asked, "Can we trust him?"

"He's a good person," Nell said. "Gone astray, maybe. He doesn't have much choice."

"What if he finds another gun?"

Nell sighed. "I don't like to think about that. I have to go down to the plant and get things in order to leave tomorrow. What about you? What will you be doing while I'm gone?"

"The Snyders have retained me for the trial with the electric company. I expect I will be quite busy preparing for that."

"The trial is next month?"

"I think more likely it will be toward the end of the year. Judge Reeves has been assigned to the case and he doesn't have an open agenda until November. You'll be back by then. A new mother and me a new father. Quite a new experience for both of us."

"I wish you could be with me."

"As do I."

"What about the election next year? You've got that to work on. You'll be busy."

"It's quite sure to be the other man. Roosevelt has too much backing. Just like in '28, the Eastern faction pretty well controls who will be President. It won't be Hoover again, that much we know."

"But you'll have backing from Pendergast, won't

you? That should amount to something."

"Tom's going to back me as favorite son. At least for the first vote at the convention he will. But he wants a chance to switch to Roosevelt. He wants Roosevelt to owe him some favors with all the money that's going to be spread around in this New Deal thing Roosevelt is promoting."

"The country needs something, Jim. Times are getting bad out there. I've switched our employees from seasonal to full time. Quite a few of their husbands have lost their jobs."

"All the money is going one way, now," Reed observed. "And it's not toward the common man."

"Nor common woman," Nell said, looking at him, smiling, squeezing his hand. "Don't forget the women."

He removed the cigar from his mouth, leaned and kissed her cheek.

"Not likely," he said.

THE TRIAL

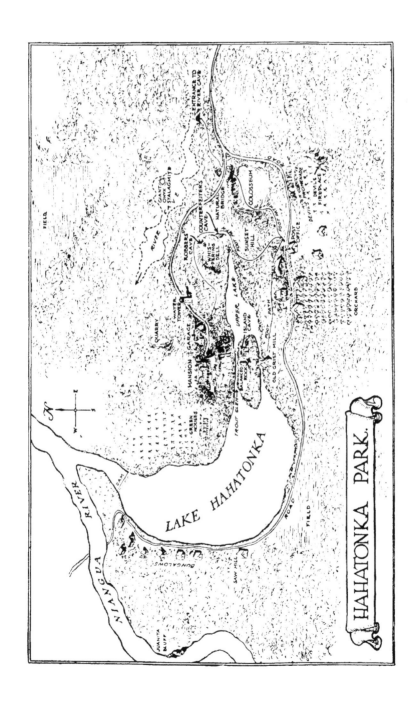

H

IX
November 30-31, 1931

WHEN THEY CAME into the courtroom the seats they passed on their way to the counsels' table were taken by people of all dress. Farmers in their denim, wives in sacking dresses, merchants in jackets and ties.

Sid Roach placed his briefcase on the counsels' table for the space he would use between John Wilson's and chief counsel's Senator James A. Reed. Sid was not well acquainted with either of them. Wilson was from a Kansas City firm chosen most probably by Reed. Or perhaps the Snyders knew him.

Sid had been chosen, he was sure, because he had been a local attorney in Camdenton, county seat of Camden County where Hahatonka was located, and because his father had been the one who sold the area in question for this trial, to Colonel R. G. Scott in 1895. Scott then, seven years later, sold the property to the Snyders' father, Robert McClure Snyder Sr.

Sid had been in conference with both attorneys several times and was well versed on what his assignment for the trial was and what subjects the other two would be responding to. Reed was positive of what he was doing in the trial and left little doubt that he expected the others to be the same.

But, Sid had some doubts. He knew Reed's reputation—getting a not-guilty verdict for a woman after she shot her husband over a card game and representing Henry Ford in a libel case. Observing Reed in the courtroom is not what had inspired Sid to listen spellbound when they had convened for preparation and the ex-senator had explained in courtroom form what he would do in the trial and how he would do it. Sid believed that he could.

His own doubts were twofold: He had seen Judge Albert Reeves—who would be the presiding judge in this case—in the courtroom. He had, in fact, argued several cases before him. A bit over a year earlier Sid had argued that Union Electric Light and Power Company should be prohibited from building Bagnell Dam for several reasons. One: the dam would restrict navigation of the Osage River against state law and, Two: the state had no right to take over schools and courthouses under eminent domain.

Judge Reeves had ruled against Sid's argument and against the county in favor of the electric company. Would the ruling in that trial be prejudicial in favor of Union Electric in this trial? And Reeves was a known adversary of Tom Pendergast, the Boss in Kansas City who had been appointed street commissioner by James Reed when he'd been mayor of the city.

Sid had brought up that possibility to Reed that Reeves might not look favorably on their cause, but Reed said it wasn't the judge they had to convince, it was the jury.

Sid's other concern was his secondary job at the trial. If you could call it that. His friend J.W. Vincent, publisher of the *Reveille* newspaper in Camdenton, had implied—not asked or demanded—that Sid should keep him informed on the trial. So when Sid returned to Camdenton over the weekend he was expected to bring J.W. up to date on what took place in the courtroom the week before.

Sid was not a reporter. Robert Snyder Jr's son Fred was a reporter for the *Kansas City Star*. Fred was covering the trial for the *Star* so perhaps Sid could get some pointers from Fred. He wasn't sure just what information he was expected to pass on to Vincent. Or what he should pass on. He hadn't mentioned this casual undertaking to Reed. The ex-senator was no stranger to the press, nor had he ever seemed to be overly hostile to the press (except for the Bennett trial). With the daily conferences Reed and Sid had with the Snyders, Fred was frequently included and Reed seemed to pay him no never mind. Sid didn't want to take any chance that he might be expected to shade the news he reported to Vincent to favor their— his, Reed's and Wilson's—side of the issue.

So he kept quiet about Vincent and the *Reveille*. Reed probably would not notice that Sid was keeping two sets of notes about the trial.

First order of business for Judge Reeves was to select the jury. Fifty-seven men had been called for duty. Reeves, the clerk-stenographer, Mrs. Anna Feltenstein, Reed and the electric company's chief counsel Walter Walne, met at the bench and went over the list. Ten names were removed for statutory reasons. Reed brought the list of remaining possible jurors to the table and talked with Sid and Wilson about them. He wanted men who would honor the intrinsic value of the property without concentrating on income or possible sale of the property. He wanted people who would not directly benefit from the new lake designated as the Lake of the Ozarks.

"You'll know these men," Reed said to Sid, meaning not personally knowing them, but knowing them by their actions, their dress, their speech, when called upon.

Small task, huge responsibility.

The day wore on, questioning continued until afternoon. Reed had some poignant questions about the men as did Walne, Sid was sure, who would be looking for jurors who might think little of scenic or artistic value of the property. Sid felt confident in this part of the trial, he'd sat through jury selection before, men from small towns and villages and men who lived off the land and appreciated it. By the end of the day he had circled his choice of men for the jury. Reed seemed pleased with his list. All of the men selected were on Sid's list: five farmers, one cattleman, four merchants, one foreman and one assistant bank cashier.

Walne struck Sid as a bit blustery. He certainly had the voice for a chief counsel, sharp, piercing, perfect enunciation. The same words you could use in describing Reed. One thing Walne did not have: Reed's reputation as a three time senator from the state of Missouri. Several of the jurors had been obviously privileged to be addressed by Reed, a fact Walne easily observed, but was unable to counter or diminish.

In Reed's hotel room the three of them along with the

three Snyder brothers and Fred the reporter conferred. Reed explained what day two was going to be. If his oratorical skills in the hotel room was an indication of how he would lambaste the electric company tomorrow, Sid could barely wait.

The other problem Sid had, or perhaps didn't have, was his dress. He had good quality suits he had purchased in Jefferson City just a few years back, starched and bleached shirts, silk tie, shined wingtip shoes. Senator Reed's dress was, at a mere glance, far more stylish, more tailored, richer looking than Sid's.

Perhaps that was what the senator wanted, a common man the jurors could associate with, while the lead counsel showed how seriously the Snyder brothers intended their case to be. Who could be a better, more impressive attorney than their own ex-senator that many of them had voted for and held in high regard.

Day two started when the three of them entered the courtroom together (stylishly late), placed their cases on their table and nodded courteously to the opposition and remained standing as the bailiff called for the court to rise. Judge Albert Reeves had not given Sid any indication that he recognized him from the case where the judge had ruled against him and that was good.

The jury was called in and all twelve seated themselves, wearing suits and ties more in common with Sid's dress than any of the other counselors. After conferring at the bench, Walne was given the floor to open the electric company's case against the one million dollar condemnation proceeding.

He wore a dark suit with vest and tie, manicured dark hair and a pair of pince nez glasses far up on his nose, which he looked down along the length of it at the jurors. Not too smart, Sid thought. Farmers and small town merchants do not forget being looked down at. Walne's coat was unbuttoned and he had his hands in his pockets in a strange manner of trying to look casual in his hundred dollar suit. He did not approach the jury, did not need to as his voice cracked the stillness of the crowded courtroom like a pool cue whacked against the end of the table.

"This condemnation suit is one involving the power of eminent domain, a part of the procedure of that power being that the government may take the property for public use when adequate compensation is paid the owner. And what is adequate compensation? The court said it was one hundred forty-four thousand dollars. A figure we know is over five times what the Snyder family paid for the property. Now if you want an exaggerated figure, listen to this:" Walne took a paper from his table, walked to the jury and leaned against the railing setting the twelve men off from the rest of the courtroom. "This is from a paper prepared by the Snyder family and presented to the court in the original condemnation proceedings. Here, the family values the estate at between three quarters and one million dollars. Talk about exaggeration."

Walne then told the jury he would prove to them that, "Not one slick dime should be paid to the Snyder brothers of Kansas City for the flooding of their property at Hahatonka by the Lake of the Ozarks."

The Bagnell Dam was actually, Walne told the jury, "A promotion for Hahatonka as it greatly enhanced the Snyders' estate, making it more accessible."

In addition, Walne said, strutting now around the counsel's table, but not approaching the jury, "This company will prove to you that these same Snyder brothers have offered this property for sale at a fraction of what they want you to award them."

Reed then rose for the Snyder Estate and strode gracefully toward the seated jury, the jacket of his classic, timeless suit of cultured fabric open to his vest, his tie correctly tied, his white hair denoting a man of distinction. When he spoke it was not with the barking, imperative voice of Walne's, but the voice of a friend come to discuss an issue of importance. Some of the jury leaned forward anticipating his words.

"The utility company says it is the United States government that created this Bagnell Lake and dam and that it is for the public use. But I think you will be convinced before we get through my statement and with the evidence, that Uncle Sam didn't build the dam and isn't going to get the profit from it.

"Now this dam was built for the benefit of Uncle Sam's water power company and by these gentlemen," (turning with authority to point to Walne and his associates including Union Electric President Louis Egan seated behind them).

"It is alleged" (emphasized) "to have been erected in the interest of navigation. That is the way they get the right of eminent domain that you're hearing about."

Turning away from the jury, his back to them, voice still strong, penetrating, "But the Osage River was already a navigable stream. You could take small boats from the Missouri River up the Osage River far above this point."

Turning quickly to face the twelve of them, voice rising, "And gentlemen, they proceed to i m p r o v e" (drawn out) "its navigability by building a dam 140 feet high and with no lock in it?"

A large plaster model of the features of Hahatonka was placed before the jury. Reed began to point out the natural scenic wonders of the exceptional display of nature. There is the trout glen, he pointed, once full of rainbow trout because the spring right here, (finger on the cliff above the spring) gushing fifteen million gallons of cold, clear, blue water into the glen as well as on the other side of the island where once sat a one hundred year old grist mill, burned for no reason or necessity by the electric company. His hand moved to point out the location of the long-ago built dam that the electric company dynamited to allow the dirty debris of the river to flow into the pristine glen, killing thousands of rainbow trout and thousands of huge crayfish that diners at expensive restaurants craved.

He pointed out the stone curved natural bridge, counterfeiters cave, river cave (lifting a cover from it to display a record sized stalagmite), chasms, winding trails, dry hollows, steep cliffs and finally the big stone castle sitting above the spring and trout glen and the 100 horse stable and garage. And the three story water tower.

Members of the jury were infatuated and many of them leaned forward to get a better look at the display.

Reed had been right when, the night before, he said he would coerce the jury members to schedule a trip to the area in their minds.

"There was in this country," Reed said, standing beside the plaster model, facing the jury, "a place that for its grandeur, its beauty and sublimity, has been known and celebrated for more than a hundred years. It has been written about and described by such authors as Bayard Taylor; it has been described in geographies; it has been portrayed by scores of writers as one of the wonder spots of the world."

Walking closer to the jury, voice lower now in volume, "This is proper for me to state and proper for you to consider because the reputation of the place constitutes an element of value in any transaction.

"On this estate was that old mill that had ground its grist for more than a hundred years. It was a picturesque old thing, ought to have been preserved for a hundred more years.

"These gentlemen, (turning to point to the electric company's counselors' table) went in and burned it down. I will show you a picture of this desecration later.

"There is also that beautiful glen which, when the backwater from the Bagnell Dam is forced into it, is a depository of corn stalks, trees, tin cans and material left by the picnickers along the shore.

"We will put witnesses on the stand who have traveled widely and have seen the glories of Europe, of all the world, and the wonders of the United States."

A brief pause before continuing, walking closer to the jury, looking at each member, "The most beautiful spot in Missouri we will show you, has been desecrated and destroyed by this dam."

Walking away again, shaking his head, "Counsel for the power company has made the statement that they have created a beautiful and glorious lake which has improved the Snyder estate.

"Gentlemen, I think the men who will come here to tell you man after man, that their eyes have never beheld any natural beauty and attractiveness equal to this place will also tell you that it is now gone."

Sid leaned forward with the rest of the jury, expectant.

Reed slashed his hand toward the floor.

"Forever!"

THE HAHATONKA JURORS were the recipients of forty thousand words of testimony in the form of photographs (assuming each of the 40 pictures was worth a thousand words) all in one day, plus several thousand more from a live witness, Ernie Howard.

Howard identified each large photograph using the plaster model of the area that Senator Reed had used to place the location where they were taken. Counselors scanned the photographs along with Judge Reeves, then handed them on to the jury who passed them from juror to juror.

Reed needed the engineer Howard to explain to the jury the damage that would result from the thirty-foot drawdown the new lake could experience. Union Electric offered photos of their own, photos tinted and expertly developed that they said showed the lack of damage to Hahatonka.

Howard told the jurors how the lake level could rise ten feet over the established maximum level of 660 feet above sea level during extreme floods and how it could recede thirty feet below that leaving mud flats. He then explained in technical detail how the electrical generating system in the dam worked and how the water level would fluctuate to keep the output at the required level of online wattage. Most of the jurors had to move around in their seats to stay awake.

Sid Roach understood why Reed had brought Howard to testify and why he needed his testimony. But, Sid also knew a large part of the expert explanation Howard was giving the jury was not being totally absorbed by the farmers and merchants sitting in the box.

Testimony excitement didn't increase any for the jurors on Friday. Union Electric's lead attorney, Walter Walne, tried to get Howard to say the dangers he had expressed to the jurors about the damages to Hahatonka during direct examination were unlikely.

Howard wasn't willing to abandon his exposé of lake damage, returning again and again to the "drawdown" of a thirty foot drop in the lake level and his growing visage to the jurors about mud flats and dead fish and turtles and snakes abandoned on those flats.

Reed rose on punctual occasion to challenge Walne's legal right to some obscure question to Howard who remained impassive while Judge Reeves, looking studious through horn-rimmed spectacles, studied Walne's words.

When Judge Reeves adjourned court on Friday he announced that court would adjourn on noon the next day, Saturday, to meet the requests of several witnesses to be allowed to return home for the weekend.

Sid arrived at J.W. Vincent's home-newspaper office Saturday evening before returning to his own house for dinner. Vincent had recently moved his newspaper office and printing equipment up the hill from the now flooded county seat town of Linn Creek to sit where the lake waters would not rise. Apparently, although Vincent had never confirmed this to Sid, the assumption was in the minds of some that the town would just move up the hill to higher ground when the dam gates were closed. Instead, the county seat had been voted to be a brand new town in a vacant cow pasture to be called Camdenton.

Sid returned Vincent's greeting and seated himself on a metal adjustable stool next to the Linotype Vincent was operating. Vincent stopped his motion, hands over the keyboard on the typesetting machine and asked Sid about the Hahatonka trial. Sid flipped open his notebook and began telling Vincent details about the trial from the notes he had taken during the court sessions. Vincent listened, then asked Sid if the case had been turned over to the jury. Sid told him that it had not and Vincent asked what exactly had been decided during the week. Sid examined his notes and found nothing in the way of a lasting decision by the judge or by either side of attorneys. Vincent asked if he had brought copies back from the large photographs that had been shown to the jurors. Sid said copies of the photographs had not been made available to either side.

Vincent asked if either Reed or the "Electric man" had made any newsworthy comments or objections. Sid said no.

Vincent turned back to his Linotype and began hitting the round keys on the machine which responded by pouring hot lead into receptacles for the letters.

Sid moved his notebook closer to the keys on the Linotype and flipped through the pages before asking Vincent if there was any thing in his notes he could use in the *Reveille*.

"No," Vincent replied. "Thanks all the same, Sid. Keep me informed."

SEVEN MEN SAT at the table Sunday evening in the restaurant of the Governors Hotel in Jefferson City. Gutzon Borglum sat at the end of the table looking every bit the self-assured artist that he was. Bald, mustache, blazing eyes, bronze skin not from a winter in Missouri for sure. As Borglum talked of the huge sculpture he was in charge of, George Washington on a mountainside in South Dakota, Sid Roach wondered how you sculpted a sixty foot head and face on a hundred foot granite mountainside. He asked Borglum that question.

"Dynamite," Borglum said. "You remove the heavy stuff with dynamite. Then jack hammers. We use drills for smaller amounts. You drill a series of holes close together and chisel chips out between them. Finish the surface with sanding."

The idea of using dynamite and jack hammers to form a sculpture silenced the table. LeRoy Snyder broke the silence.

"How about putting my dad's head on the three hundred foot cliff at Hahatonka below the big stone house?"

"No granite," Borglum said. "The rock is too soft. Even if I could get an image sculpted on the face of the cliff without it crumbling away—doubtful, of course—erosion would destroy it."

"I can't picture how men climb the face of a granite mountain and dynamite rock into the likeness of a face,"

Robert Jr said. "I would like to know more about that."

Borglum was pleased to accommodate him. He was interesting, Sid gave him that. He talked endlessly about the mountain where he planned to sculpt Thomas Jefferson's head and Theodore Roosevelt. Sid noticed an uncomfortable squirming by Jim Reed at the mention of a Roosevelt. He quickly switched the conversation to Monday's court session where Borglum would be testifying about the worth of Hahatonka after the influx of dirty river water. Borglum had during an earlier deposition placed the value of the area at a half million dollars. An amount Reed wanted him to double, although he refrained from leading his potential witness. Tomorrow would be an interesting day in the courtroom.

Borglum was still boasting about his various projects—including a bust of Robert E. Lee that he never finished at Stone Mountain, Georgia—when Sid quietly excused himself and retreated to his room. He spent some time writing instructions he planned to present to Senator Reed tomorrow when Borglum was on the witness stand and farmers and small town merchants grew restless when the egotistical Borglum went on too long. As Sid knew he would.

"ONE AND ONE-HALF MILLION DOLLARS," Gutzon Borglum said in reply to Senator Reed's question about the worth of Hahatonka before being innundated by dirty river water as a result of the newly formed Bagnell Dam.

Walter Walne flew to his feet barking, "Objection to

the qualifications of the witness to place a value on the property in question."

"We'll get into that," Reed responded, then led Borglum into naming the scenic spots of the world he had visited in his lifetime—Bavaria, the Swiss Alps, Copenhagen Bay, Rome, the Thames, White Cliffs of Dover—until Walne made the mistake of asking what those places had in common with Hahatonka which started Borglum numbering the beauty and grandeur of each place. Reed brought up the value factor again and Walne objected again, but this time Judge Reeves overruled his objection.

Reed switched the questions around to the spots of beauty in Hahatonka and Borglum went into lavish details of each spot as he frequently rose from the witness chair to point out the feature he was discussing on the large model that had remained in the courtroom. Words such as beautiful, amazing, wonderful and marvelous came with his descriptions. He frequently stood and, looking every bit the artist, motioned eloquently and spoke with conviction.

"I have never seen a place more beautiful than Hahatonka before the Union Electric company condemned part of the property for their dam," he said.

The clear blue lake that once held rainbow trout was described as, "A great emerald with nothing comparable to it in Missouri."

Sid was mildly surprised at the jury's reaction to Borglum. He was fascinating them with his descriptions of Hahatonka and faraway places. With his gestures, his confessions of love for the scenes and features of that wonderful land, each juror showed a growing interest in the artist's words.

The cutting of the trees there would, "Take all the charm, killing its life, making it valueless as a country estate."

When Borglum told the jury of the varied uses such a place could have had if the waters from the lake had not entered its boundaries, Walne objected, saying the way the property was divided would make such uses Borglum suggested impossible.

Reed asked Borglum what value he would place on the property now with the lake waters overtaking it.

"That beautiful spot is killed," Borglum said, his stark, commanding voice holding the jurors attention. "Entirely wiped out. I would not have it at any price with the water on it."

Reed frequently pulled his watch from a pocket to view it as he walked from his table of notes Sid had prepared for him to the jurors. Wondering about Reed's interest in what the time was, Sid came to the conclusion that the senator was milking the clock to leave just enough time for Walne to begin his cross examination of Borglum, but the information he would get from the witness would be forgotten by the jurors by the morning session tomorrow.

"To what purpose could the Snyders have used the Hahatonka tract before the invasion of the dirty river water?" Reed put to Borglum.

"Why it would have made a perfect game preserve," Borglum said with emphasis on the word perfect. "As part of a country estate, the value would have been immense, to the owners and to the area as a whole. Sadly, that option would no longer be possible."

With one last check on his watch, Reed relinquished his time in direct testimony and Walne jumped to his feet. With his barrel chest leading the way, the "Electric man," as J.W. Vincent had referred to him, charged the witness stand as if time was running out on him. When his voice began barking questions at Borglum, the artist-sculptor glared back at him as if Walne was one of the wild animals Borglum had said would have been inhabiting the game preserve he had said was a lost possibility for Hahatonka.

"Have you ever been to Hahatonka?" Walne practically shouted at the witness.

Borglum glared back at the lunging lawyer who leaned forward with his bespectacled face. The world famous artist who had sculpted pieces in galleries, in the capital of the United States, who had the audience of the President of the United States, Calvin Coolidge, who had spoken on the floor of the United States Senate, said to the mere lawyer from Houston, Texas, "Are you doubting my word, Sir?"

"You haven't been to all of it," Walne bellowed, shrinking back somewhat, overmatched, (Sid thought, as did the jurors, he noticed) "You only saw part of it, isn't that right?"

"I saw everything I have described," Borglum said, looking down at Walne as if he was vermin on the floor.

"But the property is so divided it could not possibly be used as a game preserve, isn't that correct?"

"I stand by my testimony," Borglum said.

Reed was on his feet. "Badgering the witness, your honor. If counsel can't show proper respect for this honorable witness, how can he expect respect in return?"

Walne raised a hand toward the judge, but Reeves brought his gavel down lightly on the bench and announced, "That will do for today. Court is adjourned. The jury is reminded that we have an evening session scheduled for the showing of some motion pictures when the light level permits. This will be movies that were shown to the bench and to both counsels this morning."

The movies were "before and after," views of the estate. All in all Sid considered it a successful day in court for the Snyders.

Who knew what tomorrow would bring.

XI

MARTIN Depew brushed the front of his only suit, a gray single-breasted worsted with a matching vest. His wife Ethel looked admiringly at him, she in a clinging, lace-adorned Nelly Don fashion.

"You need to get a job where you can dress like that every day," she told him. "You're very handsome."

He fingered his dark, center-parted hair and waved off her remark. "Can't dress like this if you're operating a steam shovel for the Marion Steam Shovel Company," he said.

"Besides, they don't need me any longer, at least that's how they put it."

"You can find something else," Ethel told him. "Go looking for something while you're dressed like you are now."

"Hmmph," he said. "Not many jobs out there, even for a steam shovel operator. They call it a recession or depression, something or other."

"Things will change," she said.

"You sound like that guy Roosevelt. He blames it all on Herbert Hoover. Wants to be President himself."

"I thought Senator Reed here in Kansas City wanted to be President," Ethel said. "I met him last year when I worked for the Donnellys. He lives next door to them. Seemed okay, but he did vote against women getting the right to vote. I don't think I could vote for him."

"Donnellys, Reeds, all rich people. We got nothing in common with any of them. Doesn't seem fair, them having all the money in Kansas City and we don't have any. Not even a job."

"They paid me well," Ethel said.

"There ought to be some way their money could be spread out to the rest of us," Martin Depew said.

"Well, I would work for them again as a nurse if they asked," Ethel said. "I think Mrs. Donnelly liked my work as a nurse, taking care of her husband and stuff around the house."

"Why don't you ask her if she needs you again, maybe full time?"

"I don't know," she said. "She knows how to contact me if she needs me."

Depew looked at his wife, a shapely brunette, her hair attractively done at a salon, shoes that cost eight bucks a pair—sixteen hours of work on a steam shovel—and considered how the dinner tonight he had promised her in the bottoms close to the stockyards (steak with all the trimmings) was going to cost him five bucks out of his last twenty and resentment rose inside.

"I read in the Police Gazette down at the barber shop last week that kidnappings were second to bank robberies that people get away with," he said. "Maybe we ought to try that."

She laughed. "Spend the rest of your life in prison if you want. Not me."

"One case in Michigan some rich man's wife was grabbed and he paid a hundred thousand dollars to get her back. What would you do if we had a hundred thousand dollars?"

"Buy me a bunch of Nelly Don dresses like this one she gave me," Ethel said.

"If we grabbed Nelly Don her old man would give a hundred thousand to get her back."

"That's crazy," Ethel said. "We're not kidnappers. You'd get caught the first day. What do you know about kidnapping other than what you read in the Police Gazette?"

"Nothing, but I know a guy that could do it. Vic Bonura. He would do anything for a buck. He runs a cafe where all the Italian crooks hang out. He told me about a couple of heists they pulled and got away with. I call Vic, cut him in for ten percent, he does the job, we get the money, turn her loose, pay Vic off and leave town with eighty, ninety thousand dollars in our pocket."

Ethel Depew looked at her husband for a full minute. "I don't believe you," she said. "Talking like that. You know better than that. We're not crooks. Besides, Pendergast runs things in Kansas City. Cops and everything else. All the crooks in town pay him off so I've heard. That's what the paper says. Every crook in town has to pay this Italian guy Lazia off for being here or Pendergast's police throw them in jail. Talk sense. Sure, I'd like to have money, but I don't want to go to jail for it."

"But we don't do it in Kansas City. We grab her, take her to Kansas someplace where Pendergast or his cops can't touch us, collect the money and leave town before they even find out about it."

"How are you going to kidnap the most famous woman in Kansas City without anyone else knowing about it?"

"Easy. We grab her, take her out to Kansas, send a note to her husband, threaten to kill her if he talks, arrange to get the money from him and 24 hours later we're out of here. Leave her wandering around in the country out in Kansas. Be days before they even find her. When they do, we're in Chicago or somewhere living off a hundred thousand dollars."

"I couldn't be a part of anything having to do with killing someone. Don't count on me."

"I'm not going to kill anyone. He doesn't know that. He won't take the chance that we might so he'll pay up. Hell, what's a hundred thousand dollars to someone who has millions?"

She shook her head. "This isn't going to work, Martin. Think of some other way to make some money."

He regarded her for a moment, dressed up and no where to go except a crummy joint in the west bottoms where they could both have a Kansas City steak for five bucks. He shook his head.

"Let's go eat," he said and led her out of the house.

XII

"TOMORROW," Senator Reed said at the table where Sid Roach and the Snyders gathered, "We begin emphasizing the valuation of the estate."

Heads nodded and Sid made a note in his ledger.

"Roy," Reed looked at LeRoy Snyder, "you start things off. You set it up for the witnesses I'm calling who will throw out the numbers. This jury"—looking at Sid now—"won't comprehend a million dollars. But we're going to keep throwing it out there. Walne will keep objecting, but he will also keep showing how valuable the property was before the dam went in and how much more valuable it is now, trying to say they didn't hurt the value. The more he talks about how valuable it is now, the better. We keep agreeing with him how beautiful it was before the dam, then we keep showing pictures of dead frogs, dead fish, dead snakes lying around in mud flats left behind from the drawdowns."

"What about the offers we made to the state for a park?" LeRoy asked. "They'll bring that in for sure and those figures aren't close to a million dollars."

"There were so many offers made over a period of years since it was first offered as a park in 1909 the jury will have a hard time trying to decide how much a 1909 offer would be today," Reed said. "We can quash that."

He looked at Sid. "Sid, you're going to be fronting the jury a lot as we go through this phase. They're your people, your farmers, your merchants. They relate to you, they understand you. When you talk of a million dollars, it's like one of them saying it and it sticks with them. First Roy brings it into discussion—Walne objecting, saying how beautiful and valuable Hahatonka is today—then I bring in some witnesses who swear how valuable and beautiful it was and how in their expert opinion that value has declined. Mister Seely, a real estate appraisal expert who knows farm values and small business values, will talk to our jury in their language, not Walne's or Union Electric's language. I'll bring in a man who owns a valuable piece of property close to Hahatonka on the Niangua River and he can convince the jury how raising and lowering the level of that river which is now a part of the lake because of the dam, can injure property there."

Robert Snyder Jr, who had been sitting passively, a three-inch stack of papers on the table in front of him, said, "Then it is my turn."

"Then it is your turn, Bob," Reed said, nodding his head. He stuck an ever-present cigar in his mouth, exhaled thin, blue smoke around it and smiled. "You're the one who is going to close the deal."

Kenneth and LeRoy Snyder looked at their older brother, a question on each of their faces that asked how was he going to do it.

He told them. "I'm going to give the history of Hahatonka from the Osage Indians to Bagnell Dam. I'm going to tell the men in the jury about the most fantastic place in the state of Missouri and perhaps the whole country."

Reed was nodding his head again. "That's the plan. First we introduce the million dollar figure to men who won't understand a million dollars. Then we tell them through our witnesses just what a million dollars is and how it applies to something very unique, very special Then Bob here tells them about a place so unique, so special they will buy into it."

It was sinking in to those around the table. By the expression on their faces they understood and they were in agreement with what the Senator was telling them. Sid pointed to the papers in front of Robert Snyder Jr.

"Don't read it, Bob. Tell it. These aren't people who like to be read to in a court of law."

Robert nodded. "Don't worry, Sid. This is all up here (pointing to his head) and here (at his heart). I don't need these notes to tell this story."

WHEN LEROY had completed listing the valuations that his family had placed on Hahatonka following the building of the castle—started by his father in 1905 and finished by the family in 1922—Senator Reed rose, paper in hand, asked the judge for permission to read the entire document to the jury. Walne immediately objected.

"What is the document?" he asked. "Why do we not have a copy?"

"But you do," Reed said. "In fact, you read from this very document when you were speaking about the condemnation proceedings. This paper was prepared by the Snyder family and you are the one who chose to introduce it to this court."

"That doesn't make the whole document relevant," Walne objected. "I strenuously object."

Judge Reeves asked for the document and Reed handed it across the bench to him. Reeves thumbed through the pages then announced a recess and he retired from the courtroom to examine the document in private.

The court waited.

Reeeves returned and announced that the court was once again in session. He handed the papers back to Reed and told him to proceed reading the document. Walne sat down heavily.

Reed looked at the jurors, one by one. They looked back with admiration for his rank and for his person who had served them well, most of them thought. There were no women jurors so no offense at his outspoken opposition on the floor of the United States Senate for Amendment 20 to the Constitution that finally passed giving women the same right to vote that Senator Reed and all the other men in the jury had.

He read:

"In contemplating the destruction of any life work, the matter of sentiment would be a strong consideration in arriving at a valuation. The esteem voiced by distinguished visitors is important in showing the beauty of the place and a question to be answered is, 'would they hold the same opinion after the metamorphosis?'"

That last word may have been over the heads of some or most of the jurors. Sid saw a few of them squirm a bit. Reed won them back when he began to read names from the paper. If there is one thing that will garner attention it is the telling of names. Whether you do it in the coffee shop, whisper it in the pews in church, tell them on the front porch with neighbors ears glued to the sound of your voice, names get attention.

He started the names with former Governor Frederick D. Gardner and followed the names with a brief description of how each of them described Hahatonka: Enos H. Mills, founder of the park system in the state of Colorado, John T. Farris, an author that not many of them had heard of, former Governor Herbert Hadley—and here he read off Governor Hadley's entire account of Hahatonka in 1909 when it had failed by one vote in the legislature of becoming Missouri's first state park.

"In many particulars," the governor wrote, "Hahatonka and the surrounding country would make a more attractive park than the National Yellowstone Park. It would be infinitely more attractive to Missourians. If the people of this state only knew of the real beauty of Hahatonka they would flock there. I had heard of the place, but was not at all prepared for the wonders of Nature that met my gaze. I was never more surprised in my life. If a snow-capped mountain could be added, there would not be another such a wonderful spot found anywhere. Why, they catch mountain trout there larger than were ever caught in Colorado and there are rainbow trout there that weigh as high as eleven pounds."

Reed paused, lowered the paper in his hand and regarded the jurors. "From one of our governors," he said. "From a learned man who appreciated the wonders of nature who actually walked the trails and the beauty of this estate. Someone who saw the marvelous trout and the cold, blue waters where they swam. Waters muddied and fouled by the electric company."

Walne, on his feet, "Your honor . . ."

Judge Reeves tapped his mallet on the bench. "Counselor, I have given my approval for this document."

"But his editorial remarks, your honor . . ."

"You're taking issue with the document?"

Walne turned his back to the judge. "Reserve my comments, your honor."

Sid noticed that the jurors were not reacting favorably to Walne and he thought Walne noticed that reaction also. The forceful counselor was too wise not to notice.

Reed, in a majestic pose, paper in hand, waited patiently for his opponent to be seated. He raised the paper slowly and resumed the reading of names: "Harley C. Gross, a magazine writer that some of the *Saturday Evening Post* and *Colliers* magazine readers among you may recognize. Bishop Quayle," Reed looked up, "He once wrote that the old mill at Hahatonka was reverent, almost holy in his book, '*God Out of Doors.*'"

Continuing, "Charles Phelps, another magazine writer. And let me add the report of the 1921 Missouri legislative committee citing that if the estate became a state park it would draw 100,000 visitors a year. And here's a favorable report on the estate in a Missouri Department of Agriculture paper."

Sid breathed a relieved sigh and leaned back in his chair. Reed with his name listing had held their attention.

"How," the senator asked, "did this valuation prepared for the condemnation procedure arrive at the figure of three quarters to one million dollars? That's a figure most of us would not be able to arrive at. So let us go down the list."

Walne came to his feet with an objection and Judge Reeves reminded him again that it was he who had introduced the document to the jury and it was Reeves who had decided that all of it could be construed as pertinent to the question of valuation.

Sid was on his feet with the tabulated list that Robert Snyder Jr had prepared listing all the features and all the assets of Hahatonka. Sid noticed that the jurors leaned back in comfort when he took over for Reed. Admiration gave way to familiarization. The figures he read off— pausing after each one to give the jurors time to calculate from their own business knowledge the validity of them— were figures that were fathomable to them. When he finished the list he looked for skepticism in their faces and was satisfied when he found none.

Robert's analysis of the estate had been established and, Sid thought, accepted. When Robert's turn to testify came, Sid expected that he would be believable to the jury.

One could hope.

XIII

LACY BROWNING said to Martin Depew, "What you're saying is that you've got a plan to grab some rich guy, hold him for ransom and you want me to provide you a place to hold him and some people to help you do it."

Martin Depew said, "I can get some Italians through Vic Bonura. Let them do the rough stuff. Interested?"

"What's in it for me?"

"Ten percent," Depew said.

"Ten percent of what?"

"A hundred thousand dollars."

Browning, a tall man wearing bib overalls and denim shirt, a hand-operated grease gun in his hand, stood under a steel-framed rack that held a Ford sedan two feet over his head. The place Depew figured he would find Browning, a man he'd known for five or more years. A man that he knew had been involved in unlawful enterprises in the past.

Browning walked under the Ford, looked up, found a Zerk fitting and snapped the end of the flexible tubing coming out of the grease gun onto the fitting and pumped three shots into it.

He stood again facing Depew, grease gun in hand, and said, "You go flashing a hundred thousand dollars around it attracts attention. Next day everybody in town knows about it, including Tom Pendergast." After a moment, "And that means the police. Pendergast owns the police."

"What're you saying?" Depew asked.

"I'm saying choose another number. Seventy-five thousand, eighty thousand. Not a hundred thousand."

"Ten percent of a hundred thousand is more than ten percent of eighty thousand," Depew said.

"Not if you're in jail," from Browning. He found another Zerk fitting on the Ford and filled it with three pumps on the grease gun handle. "Or dead in a ditch somewhere."

"All right then, seventy-five thousand. You get seventy-five hundred and out of that you pay for a place we can keep the victim until we get the money."

"You going to kill him?"

"I don't kill people," Depew said.

"Hunh." Browning looked for and found another grease fitting. Looking at Depew again, he said, "That means you got a witness running around who can identify you."

"Not if you pour some acid in their eyes so they can't see. Or if you keep them blindfolded all the time."

Browning laughed. "Good luck with that."

"Interested or not? Just find a place we can use for a couple of days, three at the most."

"Who's the chump you're going to grab?"

"Not ready to tell you until you're in."

"If it's somebody connected to Pendergast count me out. You cross old Uncle Tom and you can kiss your ass goodbye."

"It's a woman. Richest woman in Kansas City."

"Hunh. That could be a lot of women. Old Colonel Nelson's wife or daughter down at the *Kansas City Star*. Or

Judge Truman's wife or daughter over in Independence. Or old Senator Reed's wife. Let me give you some more advice, stay away from old Senator Reed. Number one he's a Pendergast man—that's who got him into office you know—and number two that old son of a bitch will hang your ass. He's as hard as that Ford's axle."

"None of them," Depew said.

He was growing tired of this conversation. Browning wasn't the only man he knew that would do the job. He crossed his arms and said, "It's the Donnelly woman that owns the dress factory. Nell Donnelly. You in or out."

Browning smiled. "Well, well. Not a bad idea. A woman could be a bit easier to grab. I might take a flyer on that. Let me ask around. I'll get back to you."

"YOU ARE CRAY—ZEE," Ethel Depew said. "You're fixing to get us both killed or in jail. Count me out."

"You don't want any part of seventy thousand dollars?"

She rolled her eyes.

"You sound like that damn Browning," Depew said. "All right, have it your way. I'll do it without you."

"What makes you think you can get by with it?"

"Number one, we grab a woman. No fight, just grab her and take her out to Kansas, keep her in a place out there for a day, two at the most. We send a note to Donnelly, tell him he's got 24 hours to pay up or we kill her. He goes to the police, we tell him we'll kill her. He pays up—hell, you know he's got the money, they're the richest people in Kansas City—twenty-four hours later we're out of town with the money."

"What happens to Mrs. Donnelly?"

"We drop her on some farm road in Kansas. She's been blindfolded all this time, can't identify anyone—not us, that's for sure—and let her go to the police. They can't prove anything, it's out of their jurisdiction."

"Not if we grab her here in Kansas City."

"Yeah, well, that's a technicality. The only one she can identify will be the one who grabs her. I'll leave it up to him. If he wants to pour some acid in her eyes, that's his call. Me, I'm not a killer and I'm not going to maim someone. You and me, we'll be in some other state. If he wants to stick around that's his problem."

"He gets caught he can identify you."

"No, Browning will be the only one can do that. He's been outside the law before, he'll know how to handle it."

Ethel seated herself in a chair in their flimsy apartment. She looked around at the surroundings and detested the way they had to live. She merely worked part time when she could get work and Martin was a steam shovel operator who got laid off and couldn't find another job. Something had to be done, that was for sure.

"One other problem," she said and waited for him to ask what it was. When he did, she said, "I'm not sure Donnelly will pay to get her back. They don't hit it off like loving couples. Fact is, he's so damn jealous of her he might just be glad to get rid of her. He was always griping about her running the company on what he called his money. She's the smart one. Why don't you grab him, she would pay to get him back even though she's not that sympatico with him. He's a drunk and a philanderer and she knows it."

"Okay," Depew said. "We'll send a note to Donnelly and one to someone else too so that he can't ignore the note. Who else do you know we could send a note to?"

She thought about it. "She has a lot of relatives around. She was the thirteenth child or something like that. But sending it to a relative? I don't know. I think their first response would be to call the police."

"Okay, we can send a note to their lawyer. You still have those papers she sent you don't you? Seems I remember you had to sign some release or other and the lawyer's name was on it. Did you write it down somewhere?"

"I wrote all the names down just for my own records."

"Good," Depew said. "We're in business then. Let's drive over and tell Browning."

XIV
December 16, 1931

SID ROACH didn't feel so good. Indigestion maybe. Before court today he had chewed a couple of Tums and drank a fizzing glass of water with two Alka Seltzers in it. He put his journals and papers down on the counselor's table and slipped a glycerine tablet under his tongue. The one old Doc Moore had given him the last time he had a flare-up like this with the discomfort in his chest. He vowed to go see the old Doc who had moved to Eldon after the dam took over his office in Linn Creek, the first chance he got. But he couldn't miss court today, he needed to hear Robert Jr's testimony. It was crucial.

Robert Jr wore a well made suit, one that came off the rack. A suit the men in the jury might select if they had a good year in their business. He seemed relaxed, looked studious and made eye contact with the jurors. When he began to speak the jurors leaned back in their chairs completely at ease. That pleased Sid. After introducing Robert Jr to the court he had called him to the witness stand. Senator Reed was yet to show up in court. A few minutes after Robert began his testimony, Sid spotted the senator sitting in the back row in the courtroom and immediately understood why he sat there: to judge how Robert's testimony would go over with the public.

The story of Hahatonka was about to be told by the man who knew it better than anyone alive. He began with the Osage Indians, tall and regal in stature. How they hunted the area and how they came to Hahatonka to trade with other tribes that frequented the area: the Dakotas, the Delaware, the Cherokee and the Kickapoos.

The first date he quoted was 1801 when Daniel Boone and his brother Nathan trapped fur in the area for a hat factory. Then President Jefferson sent his emissary Robert Livingston to France to work a deal with Napolean for a port on the Mississippi but ended up purchasing all the land west of the Mississippi. Heads nodded in the jury. They remembered their fifth grade American History.

Jefferson sent Lewis and Clark out to make friends with the Indians, Robert Jr said, and to explore the newly acquired land searching for a route to the Pacific coast. Along the way they were to notify the tribes—including the Osage who claimed all the land from the Missouri River to the Arkansas River—that the government of the United States of America was now the owner of the land.

Robert told how, instead of meeting the Osage themselves, Lewis and Clark sent a messenger. He told how the Osage did not believe the messenger and it was not until 1825 when the government purchased the land from the Osage that the tribe moved on to the Indian Nation in Oklahoma.

A few smiles in the jury told Sid that some knew about the discovery of oil in Oklahoma over 75 years later and made some of those Osage descendants rich.

As he related the history of the area, Robert used the mock-up of the estate to show the giant chasm where the Osage camped and hunted, as did the Kickapoo. He told of the entrance to a theater-like pit he called the Colosseum where the Osage held tribal meetings and some religious groups convened. That brought a few nods in the jury.

Robert brought the jurors to the front edges of their seats when he began the tale of the counterfeiters. Sid had heard the story many times from his father and others in old Linn Creek. A story told daily in the barber shop or the repair shop. The story asked about by travelers in the Moulder hotel before the town was flooded by the new lake.

In 1830 a man named Garland came to the area and built a mill in the fast-moving waters coming out of the big spring. Garland had friends who were outside the law and they used the area as headquarters for a counterfeiting operation making American and Mexican coins and false bank bills. As Robert told about the men who operated the metal presses for the coins and the woman who forged names on the counterfeit bank notes, interest perked up in the jury. Sure, most of them had heard parts of the story, but now they were hearing the details. They listened intently.

Robert's talk went into the Slickers who punished the rustlers and outlaws in the area by tying them to a tree and "slicking," or beating them with green tree branches. A tale of the Wild West, of outlaws, lynchings, gunfights, vengeance. Even Walne's full attention honed in on this saga, as did the jurors. As he talked, Robert worked in the landscape where all this happened, the natural bridge, the caves, the hillside dwells. For a moment Sid thought Robert imagined himself there in those surroundings and he took most of the jury with him.

Robert Jr updated the history of the area, citing the first post office, the name change from "Big Spring," to "Gunter's Spring," after an early settler. A party of old men of the Osage nation later returned to the area and told that their people had referred to it as Hahatonka, "Laughing waters."

Sid, now watching Walne more than Robert Jr or the jury, could sense the man's impatience. Robert told how Governor Herbert Hadley introduced a bill to the legislature to acquire Hahatonka for a state park in 1909, but the bill failed by one vote in the state senate after passing the house. Governor Frederick Gardner in 1921 made the same recommendation. Governor Arthur Hyde named Hahatonka as his first choice for a state park in 1924.

The Texas lawyer, who had been squirming and shifting in his seat when Robert Jr began telling how Hahatonka was favored by the three Missouri governors, unable to contain himself further, came to his feet.

"I object, your honor," he said, "to these expressions of value by anyone, however impressive the names may be, or what choice they may have had for a park. It is the bills that is the best evidence. The bills by the Snyder family for the area they tried to get the state to purchase."

Judge Reeves hesitated a moment, then overruled Walne, saying the opinions of early day writers and former governors had historical value, but that he would instruct the jury to disregard what they said about the value of Hahatonka.

Robert Jr quoted an article in Carter's Monthly maga-

zine that called Hahatonka's scenery, "The most magnificent the human eye ever beheld."

He spoke of the gorgeousness of the blossoming
dogwoods, the lavender tinge of the landscape by the
redbuds and later the pink of wild roses giving way to the
blaze of turning leaves of autumn. Jurors nodded, they
had seen it all.

He told about several Civil War battles fought in the
area including one at Munday's Hollow where 62 Confed-
erates died and two Union soldiers.

Walne rose again in objection when Robert started to
quote Dr. Walter Williams, president of the University of
Missouri, about the beauty of the area.

"Dr. Williams can be here in an hour to give his own
testimony," Walne said.

"Very well," Senator Reed responded. "We will call
Dr. Williams."

Juror George W. Green, a merchant from Centertown,
sent a message to Judge Reeves that he was suffering
from a heavy cold and would like to be excused for the
day. Judge Reeves adjourned the trial an hour early saying it would be continued the next morning if juror Green
would be able to return.

The evening conference between the Snyders and
their attorneys was brief. Senator Reed told Robert that
he would continue the history of Hahatonka and finish up
his testimony with the building of the "Castle," by Robert
Sr and the other outbuildings with emphasis on the expenses involved which would tend to increase the value
of Hahatonka.

"If the sick juror returns," Reed said, "the day should be a quiet one comparatively. Their counsel will continue to harass and argue about value, but other than that the day should pass uneventfully."

None of them were prepared for what was about to happen in court the next day, December 17, 1932.

NELL DONNELLY noticed the automobile coupe blocking the driveway to the Donnelly house from the back seat of the family Lincoln. George Blair, her colored chauffeur stopped the green Lincoln convertible short of the other automobile leaving enough room for whoever it was to drive their vehicle out of the driveway.

"Who is it, George," Nell Donnelly asked, a bit impatient. The day had been a busy one at the garment factory, Nell having to meet with the company's lawyer, James Taylor, then to the factory to go over a half dozen new fabrics brought in for her approval. To make the day even more aggravating she hadn't liked a single one for any of her dress designs. Fabric and design, she often told the shift supervisors, that's the two secrets to a desirable gown. She had intended to leave for home shortly after four in the afternoon to be with her baby son, David, and husband Paul who was suffering from an unknown illness requiring a nurse to care for him as well as the nurse caring for David. But now it was turning dark and Nell was tired.

Now this.

George Blair said, "Somebody blocking the driveway,"

as he honked the horn of the Lincoln. Three men got out of the car in front of them and approached the Lincoln. The one in front carried what looked to Nell to be a pistol. He opened the door where Blair sat and said, "Put your hands behind you," and roughly shoved him forward into the steering wheel and before Blair could protest the man had his hands pulled behind him and was tying them together with a rope or twine. Blair tried to move away from him and shouted a warning to Mrs Donnelly, but he heard the other man telling Mrs Donnelly to get down on the floor.

"Who are you? What do you want?" she asked, moving toward the other side of the Lincoln, away from the dark featured man who now had his hands on her.

"On the floor," the man said roughly, and tried to force her to get down.

"No!" she shouted and grabbed his large hands and dug her nails into the back side of them.

"Damn you," the man snapped at her and pushed her forcibly toward the floor of the Lincoln.

"Miz Donnelly?" Blair said and he tried to force his way past the man in the front seat of the car who was now shifting gears preparing to move.

The man hit Blair hard with the back of his hand, told him to stay where he was and to shut his mouth. The other man had gotten into the Lincoln in the front seat and was now putting a muslin bag over the chauffeur's head. The driver eased the clutch out and the Lincoln began to creep backwards, then sped rapidly down Oak Street until they came to 55th Street.

"Whoa, whoa, dammit," the man in the back seat said. He had a hand now on Nell Donnelly's neck and was trying to put a bag over her head.

Nell screamed and with a hurtful shove the man put her on the floor. He put a hand over her mouth roughly to stop the screaming and cut her lip. "All right, now get the hell out of here."

Nell Donnelly used her hands to claw at the man who now had a knee in her back forcing her against the floor. Blair raised out of his seat in front trying to get into the back, but the man on the other side held Blair down. The driver, tired of hearing Nell scream, told the other man to hit her in the head, that he could, "Handle the nigger."

Nell felt the man hit her in the head, but not very hard. The Lincoln was now beginning to acquire a high rate of speed on the city street, making a left turn and Nell was sure they were now on Brookside Boulevard heading west. She would try and remember the direction they were going, wondering where they were taking her and George Blair.

She felt blood inside her mouth and knew her mouth had been wounded when the man forced her against the floor and held a hand over her mouth tightly. She tried to relax her body to relieve the pressure his knee applied against her.

"Where are you taking us?" she asked, her words coming out mumbled by the force against her back.

"Shut up," the driver in front yelled back. "Keep her quiet."

The man let her up off the floor and immediately she

grabbed the handle to the door and unlatched it. The man grabbed the handle and tried to close the door, but she placed a foot on the door sill so that the door wouldn't close. For a moment she thought about jumping out of the Lincoln, but knew she would be injured and maybe killed if she jumped into the heavy traffic on Brookside.

She felt the speed of the Lincoln, knowing they were still inside the city and hoped a police car might see them speeding and stop them. What would she do? Yell out? Did the men have guns? She remembered the driver was holding a gun when he approached the Lincoln and forced George Blair to the floor in front. The man's weight against her back lessened and she felt his body moving.

The man placed a blindfold over her eyes and she fought against him, "Got my Irish up," she would say later, thinking about it. They rode for fifteen or twenty minutes before stopping the Lincoln and she and Blair were forced out of the Lincoln and both were placed in the back seat of an older car. She thought they were probably on a dirt road under her feet.

What that meant to Nell was they were traveling west, toward Kansas. Away from Kansas City. Away from protection from the police. Away from her home, her business, her family. Would she ever see any of them again? Would she ever see her baby son again?

Worry replaced anger and tears took over.

Nell didn't fight against them, feeling that by now there was no use to do so. The men treated them better and the driver, who had spoken so firmly before, now spoke with a softer voice, but not saying much. She asked again where they were taking her and her chauffeur, but got no answer.

One man, the one who had injured her shoving her body and face against the floor of the Lincoln, was short and somewhat unkempt with a week or so growth of beard. He wore a hat resembling one often worn by ranchers she had seen in the city, a hat with a deep crease in the crown. The man pushing George Blair was heavier. She had trouble seeing his face.

The third man was dressed better than the other two. His dark hair was parted in the middle with waves on each side of his head. He looked less grim than the others, but she thought his eyes looked more apprehensive—perhaps even fearful.

When the car stopped after what seemed to Nell about an hour, they were ordered to get out and were led up one step and she realized they were inside. The house was a small frame house with a porch in front. Looking under the blindfold she had noticed the porch swing and the stone pillars at each corner. The stone in the pillars were stacked according to size, smaller stones on top, larger ones at the base. Distinctive, she would remember that.

She asked to remove her blindfold to fasten her watch band so that it wouldn't fall off. When they did, she saw the time on her watch as 7:15.

"Where are we?" Nell asked. "What are we doing here?"

The driver said, "You've been kidnapped. We hate to do this, but it's our job."

"Why are you kidnapping a woman?" Nell asked. "Turn us loose, please."

"We'll let you go after we've gotten some money from you," the driver—who Nell decided by now must be the leader of the three men—said. "We'll need seventy-five thousand dollars, then we'll let you go."

"I don't have that much money," Nell said. "I can't give you that much."

"You'll have to contact someone who can give us that much," the leader said. She couldn't see him or the other men as the house they were in was completely in the dark. "You can write to someone who can give us the money. Write to your secretary."

"I don't have a secretary," Nell said. "She was married in June."

"Write to your husband, then."

"He can't get that much money. He's been ill."

"Well, you've got to write to someone who can get the money before we can let you go. We'll leave the sack off your head if you promise not to look at us. If you can identify us we can't let you go, we'll have to . . ."

She began to cry again, she knew what the man meant. "I promise," she said. "I won't look."

The man behind her turned on a light that must have been a flashlight in his hand. "There's some paper on the table there and a pencil. Write something to your husband."

"I don't know what to write," she said, trying her best to stifle the tears.

The man said, "Write what I tell you to write. Your life depends on it."

XV

JAMES TAYLOR thumbed quickly through the daily mail on his desk—a usual chore each morning at nine o'clock when the mail arrived— and he opened an envelope holding a handwritten note in ink. The writing looked familiar, but the words were alarming. Quickly his eyes went to the bottom of the note, Nell Donnelly, and something clicked in his memory. A telephone call his wife told him about when he had returned home the evening before. Something he dismissed at the time, but now tried to recall. The call said to tell Mr. Taylor that if he went to the Country Club Plaza he could get Mrs. Donnelly's car. That had made no sense to him and he was sure that it was a mistaken or prank call.

Now, reading the note in his hand he realized what had been his mistake:

"Dear Mr. Taylor. I have been kidnapped and I suppose you might as well try to raise what they want. Nell Donnelly."

Taylor stood, alarmed by the note. He read on:

"Do not mark money or take no. of any.

James E. Taylor: I hereby give you power to draw money requested against my husband's account. The amount is $75,000. I sign my name in full. Nell Donnelly of Donnelly Garment Company."

Within a minute Taylor was on the phone to the Donnelly residence. The person answering the phone said Mr. Donnelly was ill and could not come to the phone.

When he asked about Mrs. Donnelly the woman told him she had not returned home the evening before and that no one had seen her since leaving the garment factory.

"Tell Mr. Donnelly I must see him right away. I'll be there in a few minutes."

He placed a long distance call to the hotel in Jefferson City where Senator Jim Reed was staying during the Snyder trial against Union Electric. "Get a message to Senator Reed immediately," Taylor told the clerk at the hotel. "He's in court at the federal court building. Tell him that Nell Donnelly was kidnapped in Kansas City yesterday and that he needs to return here as soon as possible."

SHORTLY AFTER court resumed a messenger from the hotel brought a note to Senator Reed, sitting at the table listening to Robert Jr who still occupied the witness chair. Reed scanned the note quickly then rose immediately and asked the judge for permission to approach the bench. Walne was right behind Reed as the Senator spoke quietly to the judge. Whatever the senator had read in the note, Sid had not been informed about. Judge Reeves listened to Walne objecting for a moment as Reed returned to the table and told Sid that he had to leave for an emergency and that Sid should be prepared to take over the trial.

When Sid rose to ask more from the Senator, Reed was already walking quickly to where the other Snyders sat. He spoke to Kenneth Snyder and the two of them left the courtroom. Judge Albert Reeves banged the gavel once and announced that court was adjourned until to-morrow.

LeRoy Snyder and Fred, Robert's son who was there to cover the story for the *Kansas City Star*, came forward to meet Sid.

"What's going on?" Sid asked. "Why is court being adjourned?"

"Big story," Fred said. "I've got to go call the newspaper about what's happening in Kansas City."

"What is it?" Sid asked.

"Kidnapping," Fred said. "There's been a kidnapping at the Donnelly house in Kansas City."

"Who was kidnapped?" Sid asked. A crowd had gathered around them, excitement reigned in the courtroom. Walne and his compatriots were gathered around their table, Judge Reeves was gathering up his papers, having dismissed the jury for the day.

"I don't know who it was," Fred said. "It could have been the baby. The Donnellys adopted a baby who's only three or four months old."

Sid had a bad feeling about the news. Maybe the senator could take charge and maybe they could rescue whoever had been kidnapped from the Donnelly house and return them without harm.

The other possibility that came to mind—and how it would affect the trial—he didn't even want to think about.

KANSAS CITY Police Chief Lewis Siegfried stroked his clean-shaven, rounded face, looked down at his slightly protruding stomach, looked at his desk clock now registering eleven-fifteen and gave thought to one more doughnut and another cup of coffee before lunch. He got no further than the thought when Chief Detective B. H. Thurman thrust his face through the opened office door, looking and waiting for acknowledgement.

When Siegfried nodded, Thurman said, "I got a call from Clyde Waers over at the *Star*. Said he had information that Nell Donnelly has been kidnapped."

"Nell Donnelly? The woman owns the garment factory?"

"He didn't say so, but I guess that's who he was asking about. Got another call at the desk from someone—deskman thought it was the federal court clerk in Jefferson City—asking if it was true that a Mrs Nell Donnelly was kidnapped."

"Hell," Chief Siegfried said, on his feet now, moving around his desk, "Get on it. Call the Donnelly house. Where did the *Star* get their information?"

"Seems Senator Reed is in court at Jefferson City and someone in Kansas City called him about it. He's on his way here."

"Get the Donnelly house on the phone. Let me speak to someone there. Mr. Donnelly, anyone . . . "

Thurman was gone, not shutting the door, and within a minute he called to Chief Siegfried, "Mr. Donnelly on the phone," and the chief had the desk phone in his hand, "Mr. Donnelly? This is Police Chief Lewis Siegfried. I have received information that your wife may have been kidnapped. Anything to that? Is she home now?"

A long pause, then Paul Donnelly shakily said, "That is the information, I mean . . . I received . . . I was warned you were not to be notified."

"I guess it's too late for that," Siegfried said, "The newspapers know about it. I'm on my way to your house. Don't do anything until we get there."

"They warned that if we didn't pay them the $75,000 or if the police were involved they would kill the chauffeur and blind Nell. I don't know what to do."

"We'll handle it," Siegfried said. "That's our job."

"I'M POLICE CHIEF SIEGFRIED," the chief told the woman answering the door. "I'm here to see Mr. Donnelly."

He pushed past her, Thurman behind him and the woman shrank back from them, bumping into another woman standing behind her.

"Wait," she said, trying to hold the door, to prevent either man from entering. "I'll tell Mr. Donnelly . . ."

"Where are they?" Siegfried asked, pushing the door from her grasp. "This is urgent. Mrs. Donnelly is gone is she not?"

"Mr. Donnelly is upstairs," the woman said. "He's with

Mr. Taylor, his lawyer. I'll tell him you're here . . ."

"I'll tell him myself," Siegfried said. He was already climbing the stairs. "Question the women," he called back to Thurman.

At the top of the stairs he called for Donnelly and two men appeared in an open doorway. "I'm Police Chief Siegfried," he said to them. He looked at the man in front of him. "Mr. Donnelly?"

"James Taylor," the man said. He gestured toward the man behind him. "This is Mr. Donnelly. I'm the attorney for the Donnelly Garment Company. Have you apprehended anyone who can tell us where Mrs. Donnelly is?"

Siegfried addressed Donnelly dressed in a blue robe: "Have you received any calls or notes from anyone claiming to have Mrs. Donnelly in their possession?"

"Well . . .I, that is we have . . ."

Taylor interrupted, "I received a telephone call last evening and a note in the mail this morning." He handed the note to Siegfried. As the chief read, Taylor said, "Mr. Donnelly received a note in today's mail. It is more in detail."

Siegfried scanned the note Taylor had handed him. The line of the note that mortified him read, "If this letter is given or reported to any police authorities it will be the last of me."

"Is this Mrs. Donnelly's hand writing?" the chief asked Donnelly.

Paul Donnelly's head nodded affirmatively. "What's going to happen to us? There's the baby . . ." he motioned his hand toward an adjacent doorway.

Siegfried ignored Donnelly, read the remainder of the note from Taylor and asked the lawyer, "What about the telephone call."

Taylor told him about the call, about Mrs. Donnelly's Lincoln at the Country Club Plaza and how he thought it had been a mistaken call.

"We'll check it out," Siegfried said. Turning to Donnelly, he asked, "Who have you checked with where Mrs. Donnelly might have gone?"

"Well, everywhere," Donnelly said. "We've called relatives, supervisors at the factory . . ."

"Let me see the note that came to the house," Siegfried said. Taylor handed him a slim, one-column paper a foot or more in length.

> Dear Paul,
> These men say
> they want 75,000
> Use your own
> judgement They
> kidnapped my
> chauffeur Wed night
> If you do not pay
> as directed 75,000 in
> each 25,000 in $50
> bills 25,000 in 20's
> 25,000 in 10's If he
> or they does not do
> as directed we shall
> take him same as
> take you if reported

to police or any
authorities we shall
blind you and kill
nigger you should
take your car 291035
tomorrow at 1 o'clock
and stand in it in
front of Mercer Hotel
for 15 minutes that
is showing that you
are ready to pay
If not stand it
at same place
at 9 30 am
Thur Fri morning
If not ready by
then it will cost
you 25,000 more
Then showing when
you are ready to
stand there at that
land point any one
of those times for
15 minutes, Then go
home and you will
receive further
instructions. Rememb
if this is reported to
police you will not
see me again

He read through it and when Chief Thurman came up the stairs, Siegfried handed the note to him. "Check it out," he directed. To Taylor he said, "What are you doing about the money?"

"Senator Reed is on his way from Jefferson City," Taylor said. "He'll take charge. What can we do to keep the kidnappers from harming Mrs. Donnelly before we can comply with their demands in the note? The newspapers are all over town with the story in them."

"I can't stop the newspapers," Siegfried said. To Thurman, still reading the long strip of a note, "Get men out in the street. Round up the informers, get down in the bottoms where all the scum is that might be involved in this."

Donnelly said, stuttering his words, "Will you leave someone here? To guard us. They said in the note, 'They will get you the same as they got me.'"

Siegfried looked scathingly at Donnelly. "Find Mrs. Donnelly. That's the number one goal here."

SENATOR JIM REED handed the notes back to Chief Siegfried. "What's been done so far?"

"We're on the street," the chief said. "We recovered Mrs. Donnelly's Lincoln at the Plaza where they said in the telephone call last night it would be. We recovered those items there that you see from the automobile. Mr. Donnelly has identified them as belonging to Mrs. Donnelly. Everything but the strip of rope that was found in the back seat. The hat is hers as are the gloves and um–

brella. Two books of checks were there. One had a stain on it, might be blood. We're checking that out."

"What have you told the press?" Reed asked.

"Nothing. They're hungry. I don't know how they came by the news of the kidnapping."

"My fault," Reed said. "I had to tell the judge, get an adjournment. Press was there."

"What will you tell them?" Siegfried asked.

"I'm going to tell them what I've told you. I'll tell them that the kidnappers can have the money in any form they want under any circumstances they desire. Then I'm going to add that if one hair of Mrs. Donnelly's head is harmed then I will personally spend the rest of my life and all of Mrs. Donnelly's fortune to bring them to justice and see that they receive full punishment for what they have done."

"I have a dozen patrols out searching the city," Siegfried said. "The Jackson County Sheriff's office has sent patrols into the countryside checking woods and side roads. We'll be covering the Mercer Hotel tomorrow when Mr. Donnelly is supposed to go there.

"You haven't uncovered anything yet?" Reed asked.

Before the chief could answer Thurman was at the door again. "Getting a bunch of calls, Chief. We're screening them. There's a crazy one on the phone now I thought you might want to listen to."

"Who is it?" the Chief asked.

Thurman shrugged. "Says her name is Madam Peri. She's a," long pause, raised eyebrows, "Says she's a clairvoyant."

"Damn," Chief Siegfried exclaimed.

Senator Reed said, "Talk to her."

Chief Siegfried shrugged, picked up the phone, said, "This is Chief Siegfried. You have information about the missing woman and her chauffeur?"

A woman's high, somewhat shrill voice said, "I saw them Chief. I saw Mrs. Donnelly and the Negro. They were walking down a slope somewhere."

"Where? Where were you? Where did you see them?"

"It was very clear, them walking down a slope. I couldn't identify the exact location, but if you want to find them start looking on some slopes."

"So you didn't actually see Mrs. Donnelly and her chauffeur. This was just a vision or something like that?"

"Yes, very real, Chief. I've had these before and they're very accurate. Look for them on a slope."

Chief Siegfried hung up the telephone. "Crazy woman saw a vision. Mrs. Donnelly and the Negro walking down a slope somewhere."

"Check it out," Reed said. "Lots of slopes in Kansas City. Check them out."

Chief Siegfried looked at the senator to see if he was serious. Satisfied, he called Thurman into the office.

"Tell the men on the street to start checking for people on a slope. And find that damn Madam Peri and bring her in here. I want to talk with the chauffeur's wife. Bring her in, too."

Thurman, looking slightly confused, left the office. Later in the evening he returned with Madam Peri, who, after questioning, knew nothing useful other than her, "Visions".

George Blair's wife Savannah was ushered into the chief's office. Thurman handed the Chief a note with $75,000 written on it.

"Found it in her purse," he said.

"How did you get this?" Thurman asked Mrs. Blair.

"I called the Donnelly home Thursday morning when George didn't return," she said. "They wouldn't tell me anything out there although I called a half dozen times. Then, this afternoon, I went to the grocery store and a man there told me what happened. I wrote the figures down then."

"Check it out," the Chief told Thurman.

Within the hour the Chief was told Mrs. Blair's story checked out. She was escorted home.

"I guess that means the chauffeur wasn't involved," Siegfried told Reed. "You have any other suggestions?"

"Not right now," Reed said. "But I will after I talk with the man in charge of the city."

"YOU'RE NOT DEALING with men of good character," Tom Pendergast said around a long cigar. "Men like that don't last long in Kansas City."

Jim Reed removed his own cigar from his mouth, pointed it at Pendergast and said, "Tom, we both know a lot of men in this town who would choke a chicken for two bits. My question to you is, are you or are you not going to help find Mrs. Nell Donnelly before something bad happens to her."

"I know quite a few men who wouldn't pass a legal examination, Senator. But they are men of character. If they aren't they're invited to leave town."

"How about Lazia? He's knows every man in town who turns a dishonest dollar. I have a hunch he might know the men who did this. Or at least, know of them."

John Lazia was the North Side crime boss. At least, that's how all of Kansas City regarded him and he took no exception to it. The question was always who had more power in the city, Pendergast or Lazia.

"Go ask him then," Pendergast said, replanting the cigar between his teeth. "Lazia and I have a working agreement, but he doesn't do me any favors outside of that."

"Everyone in Kansas City does favors for you, Tom. Don't forget who appointed you commissioner."

Pendergast clearly didn't want to hear from the Senator that it was he who had placed Pendergast in charge of city affairs. He took the cigar out again, expelled a small cloud of blue smoke and said off-handedly, "Like you don't forget who backed you for Senator." A pause, then, "And who's going to back you at the convention next year for President."

Reed created his own lapse of time. He removed his cigar, studied the ashes on the end of it, walked over to Pendergast's desk and tapped the cigar against a glass bowl that held a deposit of residue including more ashes.

He reinserted the cigar into his mouth and puffed nosily on it developing a cloud of his own.

"Important thing, Tom: Nell Donnelly. Nothing comes before that. I want her back, undamaged. If that doesn't happen, nobody owes nobody nothing."

Pendergast threw his lit cigar at the door after Senator James Reed closed it on his way out. He lifted the phone and in a commanding voice said, "Get me John Lazia."

JOHN LAZIA WAS KNOWN AS A DANDY. His clothes were the best a tailor could put together with the richest fabric one could find in New York. He wore rimless glasses, felt hat better than any formed in America, a shirt whiter than a complete absence of color and a tie of the very finest Italian silk. He wore shoes that blindingly glistened. He regarded Senator James Reed with a bemused smile.

"Senator," he began, "I don't know anyone in Kansas City stupid enough to kidnap someone as prominent in society as Mrs. Donnelly. Who would want to be known as a woman snatcher?"

Reed said, "I need your help to find her before it's too late."

"It certainly isn't anyone I know or ever heard of, Senator," Lazia said. He fitted a long cigarette into a gold plated holder and put it between his teeth, looking like Franklin Delano Roosevelt doing it. Reed thought it probably Lazia's intention, knowing the senator would be opposing Roosevelt for the Democratic nomination for President next year. He chose to overlook the slight.

"You know every man or woman in town who would do something like this. If you don't know them, the men you know knows them. Talk to your contacts, find out who grabbed Mrs. Donnelly and her chauffeur. That's all I'm asking."

"If the Kansas City cops can't find her, I probably couldn't find her either," Lazia said. He lit the cigarette and from the corner of his mouth blew a thin stream of liquid-looking smoke. Again, like Roosevelt might do it.

"Am I hearing a no?" The senator's voice had a bark to it.

"Senator, I'd be glad to do what I could, but I just don't know what low-life may have sneaked into town under my nose and did such a dumb thing. Kidnapping a woman, and a prominent one at that, is not something anyone in my circle of acquaintances would do."

Senator James Reed, around his well chewed cigar said, "You have until tomorrow noon to find her. You have the contacts, you could do it. You're the only one in the city who could. Siegfried will never find her, he doesn't have the contacts you do. So, here's my offer to you. Hit the streets in Kansas City, find Nell Donnelly. If you can't or won't do that, I will take a half-hour's time on national radio and I will tell the world what I know about John Lazia."

Slowly, deliberately, Lazia removed the gold-plated holder and the cigarette of the finest Turkish tobacco, stood and looked across the desk at Reed and said in a low voice, "That could be dangerous, Senator."

Reed stared him down. Lazia, who had diminished many men before him, had bested even the cruelest and most dangerous on the streets, broke the stare and turned aside before facing the senator again.

"John," Reed said, "remember, I was the prosecuting attorney here before I was mayor or senator. If I don't know something, it didn't happen. If you're not busy looking for someone tomorrow at noon, turn on your radio."

THE VOICE ON THE RADIO told of the kidnapping. Nell Donnelly listened closely at the sound of it from the other room. The news about the kidnapping interrupted classical music that was usually playing on the radio. The man who had been in the room off and on, came and closed the door and the sound disappeared. Nell began to cry, unable to stop, her sobs became louder. One of the men came back into the dark room, listened to her for a while and told her to stop crying, that she would be released soon.

What did that mean, she wondered.

"We made a mistake," the man said, and left the room.

XVI

December 18, 1931

WHEN DAYLIGHT CAME, Nell Donnelly lay quietly on
the canvas cot. Sleep had pretty much eluded her, she
felt no need for sleep.

After she and George Blair had been shoved inside
the small house and she had been forced to write the
ransom notes, they were pulled and pushed into a small
room with a sofa folded out and a small cot beside it.
George Blair, hands still bound behind his back, was led
to the folded out sofa and forced onto it and his feet tied
together.

During the darkness of the night, speculation on what
might happen to her and to George Blair had occupied her
mind. And what would happen to her barely three month
old son David. What was Paul doing? What would he do
when he received the note she had been forced to write
to him? Would he contact Jim Reed? Probably not, but she
was sure James Taylor would contact the senator. But
Reed was in Jefferson City handling the trial of the Snyder family against the electric company. Would he be able
to come back to Kansas City?

Of course he would come, he was the only hope for
her life and that of George Blair, her chauffeur.

One or two men had been in the room with her and
the Negro chauffeur at all times. She noticed now that no
one was in the room with them.

"Miz Donnelly?" George Blair struggled to sit up in
the bed formed by a fold-out sofa.

"Here, George. I'm here. I'm all right."

"What's going to happen to us?" he asked.

"Time, George, it's going to take time. We'll get out of this."

"I feel like I let you down, Miz Donnelly. I feel like, being the man, I should have done something when they jumped us in the Lincoln."

"There was nothing you could have done, George. The man had a pistol. If you had done anything more they would have killed you."

"They don't want me, they want you. You're worth money to them. I ain't worth nothing, they don't need me."

"No, they don't want to hurt either one of us. The penalty for that is hanging. All they want is money."

What she told him was troubling to her. The penalty for killing either of them or both would be the same: death by hanging. The penalty for kidnapping could very well be the same, but she didn't explain it that way to George. She didn't want him to worry about being killed. Nor did she want to consider her own fate. What she wanted to do was to examine the situation and find a solution.

"I know you said in the note how Mr. Donnelly is supposed to pay them the money," George said. "But what if he can't get the money together in time?"

"He will," she said. "He'll get money from the business. He'll call Margaurite Walters the cashier."

"You said we was in Kansas," George said. "The police in Kansas City won't come to Kansas."

Nell had thought of that. The police wouldn't help, Paul was ill and weak, there was little he could or would do except get the money together and drive the Lincoln to the Mercer Hotel as he had been instructed to do in her note to him. She was sure about that. The men who took them would get the money. What would happen after that depended on Jim Reed. The father of her son David. He would find a way to rescue her and George Blair.

"Tomorrow, George, we will be free. Both of us. Trust me, you're family."

"CHIEF SIEGFRIED?" John Lazia looked a bit out of place standing in the Kansas City Police Chief's office in his racoon-fur coat. "I'm John Lazia, but you know me, we met at that dinner for Jimmy Walker, the old New York mayor. I came to talk with you about the Nell Donnelly kidnapping."

The chief appeared nonplussed by the presence of the city's most notorious criminal in his office, but he recovered enough to say, "What about it?"

"I just wanted you to know that no one in my acquaintance would have had anything to do with grabbing and holding a woman for money. We gamble, sure, we drink a few beers some bootlegger left for some money to feed his kids, but no one I know would have been involved in this kidnapping."

"Who was involved then?" the chief asked.

"The reason I'm here is I don't think your force—as good as you say it may be—will ever find them."

The chief was put off by what Lazia had just said and was about to shoot back his feelings about it, but Lazia continued: "You see, Chief, I have a few more connections in finding those kind of people. And I know a few more inducing techniques in locating them than your men are allowed to use."

"What are you saying?"

Lazia shed his fur and draped it over one arm while using the other to gesture in an invitation to the chief to comply. What the chief thought was connected with the immaculate suit Lazia wore and how the chief knew when focusing on money he was on the wrong side of the division in the city between those who enforce the law and those who scorn it.

"What I'm saying Chief, is that I'm sending out some people I know who want the woman snatchers in the city run out of town before they too get tagged with that type of behavior. Seeing as how we both have crews out scouring the city for clues to what happened to Mrs. Donnelly—and my friends might be packing some hardware—I would like to know that we're not creating problems for you and your officers."

"What you're asking—no, make that what you're saying—is the police in this city should overlook carloads of men who defy the law who are carrying guns and going around threatening people."

"You won't be receiving any complaints from anyone my friends talk to, Chief."

"And just what will you do if you locate Mrs. Donnelly? And what will you do with the men who took her?"

"Enforcing the law is your job, Chief. All we want to do is find Mrs. Donnelly and see that she is returned home safe and sound."

"This is a most unusual alliance," the chief said. "I'm not so sure it will work out."

"I'll see that it does," Lazia said. "We'll be in touch after we find her. The rest is up to you."

The Chief watched Lazia don his fur and leave, looking back at the chief with a smile on his face.

Chief Lewis Siegfried felt exactly like he had just shook hands with the Devil.

PAUL DONNELLY paced the floor as the time approached one o'clock, the time he was supposed to drive the Lincoln to the Mercer Hotel as the kidnappers had demanded in the note Nell had been forced to write. He was ill, faint and weak. He asked Dr. Bohan who was there attending him, if he thought he should make the trip.

Dr. Bohan advised against Mr. Donnelly making the trip alone and the note said he was not to bring anyone with him. Senator Reed was asked his advice and the final decision was that Mr. Donnelly should wait until the Friday appearance in front of the hotel.

It would not be necessary—as it turned out—to keep that appointment.

THE BLACK SEDAN with two men inside stopped under the canopy of the Red Crown filling station closer to the door than to the gas pumps indicating they did not stop for gasoline. The lanky attendant in striped coveralls with the Red Crown logo over the pocket, dropped his feet off the battered desk that held the crank-handled cash register and walked to the door to see why the men in the sedan had stopped where they had.

A man in a black fedora stepped out of the sedan and greeted the attendant.

"What can I do for you?" the attendant asked. The man looked unlike your average citizen and the attendant felt a momentary surge of distrust. He had been held up at the station once with a man holding a pistol and demanding cash. This man looked as hard as the robber had, but he was more civil in appearance.

The black-hatted man said, "We're out looking for someone or some people who might have come around with an unusual request."

"What kind of request, exactly?" the attendant asked, unsure of just what it was the man wanted to know.

"Anything unusual. Something you would remember."

"Well, a woman stopped here yesterday wanting to know who was willing to pay her for whatever they needed."

"What did you tell her?"

The attendant smiled. "I asked her what kind of pay was she looking for. Then I sent her down to Vic's place."

"Where's Vic's place?"

"Couple blocks over, next to the drug store."

"What does Vic do?"

"You name it, he'll do it. He's trying to run what he calls a restaurant, but I think his menu has more than food on it."

"You know Vic?"

"Sure, he comes in now and then. Buys gas. Oil. Gets free water and air for his tires."

The man in the black hat stood looking at him, expecting something else, maybe. He was kind of unnerving to the attendant.

"Once he was looking for some twine when he came by. Couple of men in the coupe Vic was driving."

The man with the black hat held out a piece of rope six or so inches in length. "Twine like this?"

The attendant took the rope in his hand. "Yeah, that looks like what I gave him. All I had in the shop. He didn't say what he was doing with it."

"Where can I find this Vic?"

"Probably in his restaurant, like I said, couple of blocks. Beside the drug store. Piece of advice, don't eat the chicken."

"Anything else unusual?"

"Nothing other than a couple of guys in a black sedan, wearing a black hat, asking if anything unusual had happened to me."

"Something you're going to forget, right?"

The attendant couldn't hold the stare of the eyes under the black hat.

"Absolutely," he said as he turned away and went

back inside the Red Crown station. The dark sedan pulled out of the drive and headed in the direction of the drug store.

ANOTHER DARK SEDAN pulled over to the curb behind the one already parked there. The back door opened and John Lazia, now in a tan-fleeced overcoat, stepped into the street. The driver of the sedan in front also got out.

"This the place?" Lazia asked.

"What the man said. Vic Bonura. Small timer. One of the boys told me he was hustling a barrel of Kentucky mash couple of months ago. Never been around to pay tribute."

"Let's go see if he's ready to do that," Lazia said. He motioned to the other man in the front sedan and to the driver of his car. The four of them entered the small, run-down storefront with a hand-painted notice on the front window identifying the business inside.

A chunky man with an overly large stomach that stretched the soiled shirt front the man wore, approached them. He had very little hair and his skin was much darker than Lazia's overcoat.

"Gents," the man said in greeting, "Have a table. I'll send a waiter over."

"Victor Bonura?" Lazia asked.

"That's me," the chunky man said, now a bit unsure about his customers or if they were customers. No one this well dressed had been in his place of business since the tax auditor.

Lazia gestured toward a nearby table. "Have a seat,

Victor. We want to have a talk with you?"

"What about?" Bonura asked, quite sure now the men had not come for food or service.

One of the men with Lazia pulled a chair away from the table for Bonura. He hesitated, looked at Lazia and was now quite sure of his identity. He decided to be seated. Perspiration began to form on his extended forehead. Lazia sat across from him. He laid the short piece of rope the man in the other sedan had handed to him, on the table in front of Victor.

"Tell me about this, Victor," Lazia said.

"Looks like a piece of rope," Bonura said.

Lazia continued to stare across the table in a way made Bonura sure Lazia wanted further explanation.

"I don't know, a rope is a rope," he said. The gathering perspiration began to drip from the end of his overly large nose. He shrugged. "What else can I tell you?"

"Why did you need the rope?" from Lazia.

Victor, with a shaky hand, picked the piece of rope up and looked at it. He looked again at Lazia and knew he could be in a tight spot.

"Well, I . . . that is, I've seen rope like this. Used it sometime or other."

"What did you use it for?"

"This and that . . ."

"Tie someone up with?"

"Uh . . . well, yeah, maybe . . ."

"A woman?"

"Now wait, . . . I never . . . I don't do that to women. No sir, not Victor Bonura . . ."

"Where is she, Victor? Where's Nell Donnelly."

"Now, I heard about that and I didn't . . ."

Lazia picked up the short piece of rope with both hands and pressed it against his throat, a gesture Victor Bonura understood right away.

"Where is she, Victor?"

The perspiration now trickled into Victor's eyes. He wiped at them, trying to make it appear casual, then, looking away from Lazia's stare, Victor stuttered, "He came around, saying there could be some money in it for me, . . . you know, maybe a couple hundred . . ."

"Where's the woman, Victor?"

"It's a place . . . on out, quite a ways . . ."

"Draw us a map," Lazia said.

With his hand quivering, Bonura pulled a pad from his pocket, the one he used to write food orders for customers on. With a pencil—that he dropped onto the table in his nervousness—he began to draw lines for roads and ended with a circle, an X in it.

"There . . . there . . . that's the best I can do . . ."

"You're sure that's where Mrs. Donnelly is right now?"Lazia asked.

"The best I know, . . . I'm pretty sure . . ."

"You need to be real sure, Victor. It's important to your health."

Lazia left with the other three men. Victor sat at the table for a long minute, now wiping sweat from his brow with a large white handkerchief. He got up from the table and went to the drawer under the counter and removed all the bills and coins and put them into a drawstring bag he kept there. When he started out the door, he turned back to the black man in an apron who came from the kitchen.

"Lock up, Ephram," Victor told him. "We're closing down."

XVII

THE VOICES alerted her. The room was dark, she guessed the time as very early morning. She could hear George Blair's even, heavy breathing from his make-shift bed close to her canvas cot. Nell had lain awake for the night, her mind searching for a solution to her problem. Now she felt groggy, telling her she needed sleep. The voices from the front of the house where she had been forced to write the notes to her husband and her lawyer grew sharper. She heard a door close.

"George," she whispered. "George, wake up. Something's happening."

The chauffeur stirred on his temporary bed. She called him again, louder this time. He answered sleepily. The door to the room opened and a sliver of light invaded the room outlining two men standing in the doorway.

"Mrs. Donnelly?" a voice asked.

"Who is it?" she said.

"Friends," the man answered. He wore a long overcoat and a hat of the same light shade. She couldn't make out his face. "You're safe now, don't be frightened."

"Where are the other men?" she asked.

"They decided to leave. Don't worry about them."

"What . . . what are you going to do with us?" from Nell Donnelly, and George Blair asked, "What's going on. Who's there Miz Donnelly?"

"Friends," the man answered again. "You're the chauffeur?"

"George Blair," he said, struggling on the bed to sit up. Nell Donnelly was standing now, trying to see the two men more clearly.

"Are you tied?" the man asked, the one who had been speaking.

"No," Nell Donnelly said. "I'm not tied up. Are you taking us away from here? Will we be safe? I just want to know what's happening."

"We'll take you to a safe place, don't worry," the man said. She could see him turn to the other man with him. "Untie the chauffeur. You know what to do."

The man was gone, leaving Nell in unclear anticipation about what was going to become of her and George Blair. The man who had been ordered to untie Blair, led him from the room and told Nell to follow them. In the front room of the house a faint light allowed her to see the man more clearly. He was no one she had seen before. He looked at her and smiled.

"It's over," he said. "You'll be home before daylight."

"What time is it?" she asked.

"I'd say about four in the morning." He freed George Blair and the chauffeur began rubbing his wrists where the rope had bound him.

"Are we free, now?" he asked, looking first at Nell, then at the man who had removed his bindings.

The man motioned toward the door. "If you'll get in the automobile it will take you to freedom."

"Who sent you?" Nell asked the man. He didn't respond other than motioning toward the door again. She had little choice but to comply. She was more fearful now

than at any time since their abduction. Were these the
men who would blind and kill them?

George Blair followed her out the door. The early
morning outside was lighter than the darkness inside.
Two automobiles sat in front of the house, steps away
from the porch. The man in the overcoat stood by one of
the cars holding a door open. The other man had followed
them outside. He said, "They're curious about who sent
us," to the man standing beside the car.

"I guess you could say that the man responsible for us
being here used to be someone important," the man in the
overcoat said. He got in the automobile and it left the
house going down the dirt road and out of sight.

She turned to George Blair, immense relief starting to
flood through her.

"George," she said. "I think maybe it's Senator Reed
who has rescued us."

But, she wasn't sure of that.

ONE OF THE MEN chatted away, saying nothing revealing or important as the Buick drove along Kansas
Avenue. Once Nell asked where they were being taken,
but none of the men in the car answered her.

When the car stopped, Nell and George Blair were
told to get out and stand on the darkened street.

"Wait three minutes then walk until you come to a
concrete street," they were told. "Another car will be
along to pick you up in about fifteen or twenty minutes,"
one of the men told them, and the car sped away from
them, going toward Kansas City.

They were on a dirt road and Nell doubted anyone would come along there in the dark of night and if they did she was fearful who they might be. They started walking and came to a concrete street, then saw a highway sign that told them they were on Kansas Highway 32. They walked for about twenty minutes, Nell became tired and weak. They passed several open filling stations, but Nell said they should keep walking until the other car came for them.

"It's the Senator," she told Blair. "He'll be coming after us, I'm sure of that."

But no other car came along the street. Nell grew tired, the tears started again.

"Maybe we ought to stop, rest a bit," George Blair said.

"Keep going," Nell pushed out the words. "Got to keep going."

No traffic passed in either direction, it was if they were walking through Death Valley except for a dim light here and there and a fog—could have been smoke—blew across the street on occasion.

They passed a building with a light on inside, then came to a lighted cafe sort of street-front building with a sign on the widow identifying the American Restaurant which had a bench outside on the sidewalk. Nell, unable to walk any further, sat on the bench.

A man approached the restaurant and noticed the white woman sitting on the bench and a Negro man standing beside it.

He looked at them and asked, "Who are you?"

"That's Mrs. Donnelly," George Blair said. "I'm her chauffeur."

"My God," the man said.

CHIEF LEWIS SIEGFRIED sat at his desk, his head nodding as he slipped into sleep, then caught himself and snapped awake. Detective Chief Thurman sat at his own desk just outside Siegfried's office, managing to stay awake. The time was a few minutes after four in the morning of Friday, December 18. When the phone on Siegfried's desk rang he nearly jumped out of his chair. There had been so many fake calls from people who knew nothing about the kidnapping Siegfried was reluctant to answer the phone again. But he did.

"Chief Siegfried," he said into the receiver.

"Is this the chief?" a voice asked, gruff like someone trying to disguise his identity.

Chief Siegfried answer affirmatively. "Who is this?" he asked.

"This is a friend of yours, Chief. You know that woman you've been looking for?" said the gravely voice.

"Mrs. Donnelly?" The chief straightened in his chair, fully awake now. "What about her? Do you have her?"

"If you want to find her, drive out to Eighteenth Street," the voice said. "First filling station you come to that is open you'll find your woman."

"Eighteenth Street? Where on Eighteenth Street?" the chief asked.

"Right out Eighteenth Street near the Swift's packing plant. You know where the packing house is?"

"Of course, that's over in Kansas. Do you mean Eighteenth and Kansas Avenue?

"Yes, that's right. Go right out where the car tracks are torn up, to the first filling station that's open."

"Who are you? Give me your name."

"Hell, I haven't got time to talk with you all night," the voice said, "If you want the woman go where I told you to. Just keep going down that street," and the line went dead.

"Dammit," the chief muttered. He went quickly to the office door and saw Thurman standing looking at him, having heard the chief's phone ring. "Get everybody you can find," Siegfried said. "Get my car ready. Got another one of those crank calls, but this one sounded different. We can't take any chances, might have been one of them that snatched her. We'll go, see if we can pick her up."

"Donnelly?" Thurman asked. "Alive or what?"

"Get going," the chief ordered. Minutes later he was in his Buick with three detectives, William Robeen, Walter Goodhue and George Rayen, and accompanied by two reporters from the *Kansas City Star* who had been in the police station all night.

The chief took the wheel—easier than trying to explain the caller's directions—and in a very short time he had driven to where he thought the caller had intended for him to go. On the way they had passed two black Buicks going the other way. He pulled into a Red Crown station and stopped by the door to the small station office. When a lanky attendant in Red Crown coveralls came to the chief's lowered window rubbing sleep from his eyes, the chief shouted at him, "Has a woman been here?"

"Uh, what? No woman's been here since about a month ago when one wanted to know . . ."

"I mean tonight," the chief said. "This morning. Whenever."

"Nobody's been here since midnight some drunk . . ."

The Buick was gone.

The detectives regarded each other, the same question on their faces as on their minds: were they looking for a body or a live woman? They did not, however, voice their concern as the chief drove on westward into Kansas. Five, six, eight, ten blocks and the chief pulled over to the curb.

"I think we've been had," he announced. "I'd like to get hold of the bastard who made that call."

THE BUICK RETURNED over the same route with all the occupants watching the barren streets, seeing no one, nothing.

Finally, "Over there, Chief, look," from Thurman, in the front with Siegfried. The chief saw it, too. A cluster of people around the front of a small, all-night place with the sign in the window, American Restaurant. The Buick veered to the curb. A woman in a red business suit with fur trim, hatless, long bobbed, grayish hair approached, keeping a safe distance from the car.

"Are you Mrs. Donnelly?" Chief Siegfried asked through his open window. "We came for you."

Nell Donnelly became hysterical. "Who are you," she asked. "I'm not getting in the car with any more strange men."

"We're police," Siegfried said. "We came for you."

"Then show your stars," she said.

The chief showed his badge and the other men, the detectives, all showed their badges. The woman smiled and turned to the negro chauffeur still in uniform standing in the crowd behind her.

"It's the police, George. Let's go home."

PAUL DONNELLY saw the headlights of the Buick in the Donnelly driveway. Twice before he had hurried to meet a car pulling into the driveway, but neither had been the car he was looking for. Then he saw a woman when he opened the rear door and recognizing Nell he hastened to grab her and hold her to him.

"My God Nell, is it really you? Are you all right? Did they hurt you?"

"I'm fine," she said. She walked past her husband to Senator Jim Reed—who had been sitting up with Paul who couldn't sleep—and took his hand.

"Thanks, Jim. The man told me you were the one who sent him to rescue us."

"What happened to those men who took you?" Paul Donnelly asked. "Did they catch them? Are they in jail where they can't bother us again?"

"I'm tired," Nell Donnelly said. "I didn't sleep a wink, that bed was so filthy. That place was the dirtiest hole I ever saw."

Nancy Breach, Nell's Negro maid, brought her hot coffee and hurried to fix bacon and eggs as Nell had indicated she was hungry, that all she'd had to eat was milk.

"They kept asking me what I wanted and we planned these large meals—steak and all—but none of them materialized."

"Here's a stimulant for you," Senator Reed said, offering her a small glass of whiskey.

She drank a little and said, "I want to see my baby, I want to see David."

"But . . ." Paul Donnelly said.

"It'll keep, Paul," Senator Reed said.

Nell went up the stairs and her voice floated down to them.

"My baby! How are you?"

Senator Reed hurried up the stairs and when he walked into the baby's room, Nell had baby David in her arms. She turned to Reed. "He woke up, just to see his Mommy."

"And me," Reed said, laying a hand on the baby's head.

He left her and her soothing voice talking to the baby.

Downstairs Paul was pleading with Police Chief Siegfried to round up the criminals who had snatched Nell and the chauffeur. Senator Reed walked past them, motioning to the Chief to follow him to the Chief's Buick.

"I think the questions can wait until tomorrow, Chief," Reed said. "Everyone's pretty tired."

"Very well," the chief said. "Mrs. Donnelly told us enough in the car to get started looking for them."

He motioned toward the end of the driveway at the street where several automobiles sat and now several men stood in the driveway.

"Reporters," he told Reed. "They're not good at waiting. What should I tell them."

"What newspapers want to know," Reed said. "Tell them the truth."

KANSAS CITY picked up the morning *Times* newspaper off their front porch a few hours later and read:

MRS. DONNELLY IS FOUND, SAFE
THE $75,000 RANSOM IS NOT PAID
The Victim of the Kidnappers Tells of Fighting
Her Abductor When They Started to Put a Sack
Over Her Head—"It Got My Irish Up"

Chief Siegfried tossed the paper aside after reading just the headline and the quote from him, checking for accuracy. Of course, they got his words jumbled. Damn *Kansas City Star*.

He looked at the galley proof from the day's *Journal -Post* that had been sent to him:

UNDERWORLD AIDS IN KIDNAPPER SEARCH.

That'll make the citizens feel confident and secure in their police department, he said to himself. If we can't do it, let the crooks handle it.

He crumbled the galley proof and threw it toward the waste can. Of course he missed. The phone rang. He listened. The caller needed no identification: "I see you caved in," Tom Pendergast said.

"What the hell else could I do. They found her, she's home now."

"Just don't make a habit of it."

"WHAT'DYA MEAN?" Chief Siegfried said into the phone. "Who the hell was it took Mrs. Donnelly? How are we supposed to catch them?"

"You're the police," John Lazia said. "That was the original agreement, remember?"

"Yeah, but you had them, you could have hauled the bastards in here and they'd be in jail now."

"And Tom Pendergast would have appointed John La-zia Chief of Police?"

The line went dead.

ROBERT SNYDER JR finished his toiletries and returned to the room in the hotel where he had been staying since the beginning of the trial. His wife, Mary, was sitting up in the bed. She had arrived the night before and he had been overjoyed at seeing her. He walked to the bed and kissed her gently.

"Having breakfast with us?" He asked.

"Give me a chance to get dressed," she said. "Will court resume this morning?"

"Afraid so. Senator Reed may be gone for today and maybe we won't have court tomorrow as it's Saturday. I guess that will be up to the judge and if the other side doesn't object."

"I wish it was over," Mary Snyder said. "It's taking such a toll on you."

"I'll manage," he said.

"This Mister Egan, the one who's head of the electric company, I thought he was supposed to be a friend."

"He's a very ambitious man. A number of people besides us tried to stop the dam from being built. He has influence in the state."

"And Senator Reed, he's very expensive isn't he? He needs money, I've read in the newspaper, to run for President."

"I don't imagine we will realize any profit out of the trial, even if we win. I'm hoping we will get at least a half million. I could settle for that."

"Maybe we should think more about starting a hotel in the castle," Mary said. "It's such a beautiful place. People would love to be able to stay there."

"The castle is what I'm going to be talking about today if court is resumed. I'm looking forward to it. Come to court and listen to me."

"I'll be there. And if you make it sound as great as it is, more people will want to visit there. That is, if we decide to make it into a hotel."

"We're not there yet," he said. He went to the door, turned back to her and said, "The castle is ours. We'll spend next summer there."

She stood looking after him, worrying about him. She knew he had lost ten or twenty pounds since the trial began. If it lasted much longer she wouldn't have a husband left and that concern tightened her breast and sent a shudder through her body.

XVIII

SID ROACH worried again about the supposed indigestion. He had limited his breakfast to hot porridge, some cream and a half-spoon of sugar. Nothing there to cause indigestion if his memory of what his mother fed him at a younger age was accurate. The malady wasn't enough to prevent him from handling the trial until Senator Reed returns, just a bit uncomfortable.

According to the morning *Kansas City Times* that had arrived a few minutes ago in the courtroom, Mrs. Nell Donnelly was home safe now, having been released by the kidnappers. That would require some explanation from Senator Reed when he returned to Jefferson City.

Robert Snyder Jr was scheduled to continue his testimony today. He would be talking about his father building the giant house—castle to natives living in the area. Sid would get a rest during the morning, but Walne and the electric company would begin their cross examination that afternoon. Perhaps Reed would be back by then.

Robert Jr was quite effusive about the details of building the castle on the hill at Hahatonka. He described his father, Robert Snyder Sr, and how he had amassed a fortune by lowering the gas prices in Kansas City so that everyone, not just the rich, could enhance their lives. Jury members nodded in approval.

Robert told how his father wanted a place to relax from his high pressure position in the city. He hired Kansas City master architect Adrian Van Brunt to design a mansion on the order of the magnificent European-style buildings he had seen in magazines. Robert Jr showed a scale model of the building and described how most of the materials used in the building came from the estate. He told about the twenty stone masons who came from Scotland to lay the native stone in just the right manner to be both structural and artistic. He described the miniature railroad used to haul the quarried stone. The interior details of the three floors, the fireplaces and the outside and inside arches were shown in drawings.

At first, Sid feared Robert Jr was making the castle sound like a rich man's extravagance that jury members would perhaps resent, but Sid caught on that Robert Jr was building a case for the true value of the property.

Robert Jr told of the higher than average wages his father insisted on paying to the hundreds of locals hired to do the construction. Again, jury members showed approval. He told of the thousands of dollars spent to upgrade the roads to and from the estate and to support the local Hahatonka school nine months out of the year while other local schools closed after six months for lack of tax revenue to support them.

He showed drawings of greenhouses that had been planned before his father's death and he had scale models of the eighty foot water tower and the stables that could hold a hundred horses.

Robert Jr closed by describing the wealth of beauty and wonder in the Ozarks, particularly in Hahatonka.

"The sojourner is won over by nature, by hills draped in masses of contrasting colors, at a gorgeousness which comes as a surprise to the unsuspecting visitor. At one time it is the season of the dogwoods, at another the redbud gives its color to the countryside, and later still the tinge of pink wild roses. In autumn the turning leaves present a color that is the despair of every artist who attempts to perpetuate it."

When he finished telling about the buildings, no member of the jury could think of the place as being worth a paltry one hundred and forty-four thousand dollars.

Sid asked Robert Jr on the stand about the testimony of Stone and Webster's vice president before the State Public Service Commission before they had begun the dam. A. L. Snyder—no relation to Robert Jr's family—had testified under oath during that session that he did not know backwater would reach Hahatonka.

Walne objected to the introduction of the testimony as that particular Mr. Snyder himself was not on the stand. Judge Albert Reeves said he would reserve his ruling, but that if the testimony was properly introduced, he would accept it. Walne noted his objection.

Sid had some chicken soup for lunch as he discussed with Robert Jr what to expect from the other side that afternoon.

"You did a good job this morning," Sid told Robert. "You made the estate sound like a million dollar property. What they will do this afternoon is make it appear to be worth even more because of the lake. Your job is to say it is worth more than you're saying and the lake had diminished that value.

"We have this man Dwight Ford scheduled to testify about the mud flats created by the rising and falling of

Lake Taneycomo in the southern part of the state. If Walne takes too long on the cross with you, Ford will testify tomorrow."

Robert Jr smiled. "I'll tell Mr. Walne to shut up."

LeRoy Snyder said, "I don't think Mr. Walne knows how to do that."

WALTER H. WALNE, splendidly dressed and groomed, approached Robert Jr, large portfolio in hand.

"Mr. Snyder," he began, "I'm preparing to show you some photographs of the estate and I would like for you to identify them for me as for location and feature . . . ."

Sid Roach was on his feet: "Objection, your honor, that would be direct testimony, not cross examination on Mr. Snyder's testimony."

"Mr. Snyder testified about the estate and the condition of it. These true photographs will show the jury exactly where he stood when he described the setting . . ."

"Objection, your honor," Sid, raising his voice, approached the bench. "Mr. Snyder has done an excellent job of showing the jury exactly where he stood when describing the estate. We don't need Mr. Walne's help."

Judge Reeves reached across the bench. "I'll look at the photographs," he said.

Walne walked up to the bench slowly. "Very well, your honor. These are nothing more than true to life photographs we commissioned a professional photographer to assemble."

He handed the portfolio to the judge who examined the contents, one by one. The photographs were large, exceeding a foot and a half in width. Some of them gleamed in the light as the judge flipped through them, showing colors, bright blues and greens with red and yellow highlights.

Sid was at the bench, "Your honor, I want to examine those photographs for accuracy . . ."

Judge Reeves handed the portfolio back to Walne. "Let the counselor examine them," (to Sid), "without comment, then show them to the witness. As the photographs are intended to be a cross examination of Mr. Snyder's testimony, only he can speak to their authenticity."

"The jury needs to view these photographs, your honor," Walne said.

"Let's see what the witness says about their accuracy and applicability to his testimony," Judge Reeves said.

Walne took the photographs out of the portfolio, displaying them wholly as he walked past the jury in a round-about route to the witness chair.

Sid: "Your honor . . ."

"Show them to the witness, counselor," Judge Reeves said in a mild admonishment to Walne.

Robert Jr took the photographs, perusing them individually, stacking them from front to behind.

The print Robert Jr held atop the stack was a beautifully tinted rendition of the estate with the mansion atop the 300 foot stone cliff with a sparkling blue-water lake below.

"These prints are unfair and insidious," Robert Jr said. "They are an artist's conception of the estate. They have been tinted with brush and paint. They are false as they do not represent the true present condition of Hahatonka as backwater from the Lake of the Ozarks now affect it. Where is the muddy brown of the true color of the lake instead of the falsely painted beautiful blue as it was before the lake waters? Where are the hundreds of tree stumps of the magnificent hundred year old oak and walnut and sycamore trees cut by the electric company? Where is the burning of the picturesque grain mill sitting on the rushing blue water of the spring?"

"Your honor, these are true renditions of the estate . . ."Walne said, spreading his arms in a manner of appealing his point to the judge.

"Objection," Sid almost shouted. "The witness has testified to the falseness of these artistic paintings. If counselor wishes to present them to the jury as to what the estate would look like if the dirty river waters from the lake had not overtaken the icy blue water shown in his paintings, then we will accept them."

"Let the jury decide," Walne said. "If we could take the jury onsite, they could determine for themselves the true nature of the photographs."

"I would agree," Sid said, "only if we could also take the jury onsite to see the beauty of the estate before the dirty lake waters invaded the natural, tranquil and awesome magnificence of the area."

Sid surprised even himself in spouting forth the describing words he had even been unaware resided in his repertoire.

"Let's move on," the judge said.

"All right," Walne said. He returned the portfolio to his table, the tinted photograph boldly displayed outside the folder plainly visible to the jury. Sid walked forward so that he was directly in the path between Walne and the jury blocking their view of the falsely enhanced photograph.

Walne had a different folder in his hands now. He pulled out a sheet with figures on it and asked Robert Jr questions concerning the cost of the buildings his father had planned and built. Robert replied that he had those figures, but not with him. Walne continued to concentrate on the money Robert Sr had committed to upgrading the estate with buildings, fences, walls and courtyards. and with the water system built from the water tower to the mansion. Robert Jr's answer to each inquiry was the same: he had the figures and could supply them to the court.

When Judge Reeves finally adjourned the court for the day, Sid breathed a sigh of relief. The indigestion had flared up again following the confrontational exchange with Walne. Robert Jr's calmly given answers to Walne's fire-filled cross examination—except for the livid response to the falsely-tinted photographs—helped calm even Sid's gastronomical condition. Court would resume tomorrow—Saturday—the judge said. Sid told Robert Jr later that he would let Dwight Ford, a Kansas City insurance agent for Massachusetts Insurance, testify about the effect the rising and falling of the water level of Lake Taneycomo had on Ford's property on that lakefront in Southern Missouri.

Robert Jr appeared relieved that he would not face Walne's grilling the next day. In fact, when he returned to his hotel room, he collapsed on the bed and Mary, deeply concerned about her husband, swathed his forehead with cool, wet cloths and brought hot and cold drinks and a room service meal to him. She sat by him until bedtime, then helped him prepare for a needed night of rest.

She got little worry-free rest herself. She was determined she would have their son Fred drive them to the mansion at Hahatonka where Robert Jr could have a day of relaxation with his beloved collection of books and manuscripts.

She prayed again for an end to the trial.

XIX

December 19, 1931

SENATOR JAMES REED sat across from Nell Donnelly, an unlit well-chewed cigar in his left hand. Chief Lewis Siegfried occupied a chair at the end of the table in the senator's office and Detective Chief Thurman sat near the police chief while he took notes on Nell Donnelly's answers to the chief's questions.

"I remember the man who tried to put a bag over my head in the backseat of the Lincoln," she said. "I would recognize him again. I've given you the best description of him that I can think of at the moment. If I remember more, I'll tell you."

"You've done good," Chief Siegfried said. "Now, tell us about the other man, the one who forced you to write the ransom notes."

She began her description, slowly, reaching into her memory for every small detail she could recall about the man who had forced the pencil in her hand, the paper before her, the hand-held battery-powered beam of light he shone on the paper. She described his voice, his words, his, what she called, natural intelligence and how his accent showed some formal education, yet sounding remarkably scheming and threatening at the same time.

She described the two other men she saw in the house and in the street the night they got out of the coupe blocking her driveway and came to the Lincoln, pistol in hand.

"Ah, the house," she said when the chief had moved on to ask her to fully describe the inside and outside of the house where she was held.

"Let's say it was a three-room prairie shack," she said. She told them how the pillars supporting the front porch seemed to be poorly placed extending outside the bulk of the porch and how the stone of the pillars was haphazardly set in place by someone who was untrained in the skill. She described two "ramshackle," outbuildings off to the left of the front of the house and she placed a porch swing at one end, then told about the condition of the entry door, suitably matched to the decrepit, rundown interior of the house.

"Pictures of religious subjects lined the walls of the bedroom," she told the officers. "One was of St. Cecilia, I recognized that one. A lamp—kerosene, I'm sure—sat on an old dresser, muddy overshoes were on the floor and dust and dirt was everywhere."

"Any windows in the room?" asked the chief.

"Two," she said, "covered with shabby shades, one with a hole in it that I could see through."

"See anything of value to us?" from the chief.

"Two dogs playing in the yard, another house, oh, maybe a hundred yards away. Much like the one we were in."

"Tell us anything else you might recall, anything that would help us identify the house if we're able to find it." The chief was anxious to hear more details, but Detective Thurman was having a difficult time keeping up in his note taking. He rapidly sharpened his pencil, then broke the lead again, searched for another pencil and Reed produced a handful of sharpened pencils from a drawer under the table top.

Nell Donnelly began describing the dining room, or area, where she had been forced to write the notes. She described more religious pictures on the walls, the non-descript carpets on the soil-covered floor with a pattern she was unable to adequately describe—though fabric and cloth expert that she was—but she did describe in detail how the rugs had a worn pattern on them from the doors swinging across them. The table was described in detail—Detective Thurman writing furiously—as a round, wooden affair with claw spider-like feet supporting a round, central supporting post. A number of rocking chairs occupied the room, all on peculiar-looking rockers and oaken backs. A radio she described as "cheap," sat on a smaller table.

Detective Chief Thurman, having gone through four broken-lead pencils, relaxed when Mrs Donnelly said that was all she could remember about the house. Ten times more, Thurman thought, than even he could have delegated to memory.

"Did you happen to bring anything with you from the house?" Chief Siegfried asked.

"No, I didn't pick up anything. I was a little bit too intimidated to do that," she said.

Neither chief could imagine in their mind Mrs Nell Donnelly being intimidated. Senator Reed said, "You had a scarf around your neck when you came into the house. It didn't look like it matched the suit you wore. Did the people where you were dropped off give that to you for warmth?"

"Oh, the towel," she said, excitement in her voice. "I forgot. Yes, they gave me this towel in the house when I complained about my neck getting cold. I wrapped it around my throat and forgot about it. I left it in my bedroom at home. I could call the nurse to bring it over, she has an automobile."

"Call her," Chief Siegfried said. "I'll send one of my officers for it."

"It was just a cheap towel," she said. "Nothing distinctive about it."

"You never know," the chief said. "The newspapers are having a grand time criticizing the police. We could use a break."

"I think there were some names or numbers in one corner of the towel," Nell Donnelly said.

The chief straightened in his chair and some of the furrows in his brow disappeared. Thurman grabbed another pencil and wrote it all down.

"I think we might have something there," Chief Siegfried said.

DWIGHT FORD said from the witness stand that the fluctuation of the water level at his lake property on Lake Tanyecomo on the White River in Southern Missouri kept the value of the property below what it would have been with a constant water level.

"That'll happen at Hahatonka," he said. "It already

has. I would place the value of the estate, prior to the influx of water from the river taking over the mill pond and the trout glen on the other side of the island, at a million six hundred thousand dollars."

Sid asked Ford to go into more detail about the rising and falling water level at Ford's lake property. Ford told about the erosion of the banks, the filthy deposits left on his shores after the water receded and how the shores were unusable for weeks afterward with mud blanketing a large portion of his property making access to the water from the shore difficult and messy.

Walne delayed his cross examination of Ford until court resumed on Monday. Both Sid and Robert Jr quickly fled the courtroom. Fred Snyder waited outside by the curb to drive his parents to Hahatonka. He didn't mind doing that, knowing that his father had refused to drive an automobile after Robert Sr was killed in one.

Any reason to go to Hahatonka was welcomed.

ETHEL Depew asked, "What went wrong? How did the police find out so quickly?"

"Wasn't the police," Martin Depew said. "It was John Lazia. I recognized him."

"Lazia? He's the crime boss in Kansas City isn't he? Why was he involved?"

"Who knows. The newspaper this morning says that senator, Reed his name is, got Lazia looking for Mrs. Donnelly. Reed and Pendergast are two peas in a pod.

Anyway, Lazia told us to get out of town. Good advice. Get packed."

"Where are we going?"

"What difference does it make? We can't sit around here waiting for the cops or maybe Reed will send Lazia after us again."

"I can't pack that fast. I don't see the hurry. How do you know it was Lazia you talked to. Maybe just some guy acting big shot."

"I know Lazia, Christ, his picture's been in the papers a hundred times. He likes the publicity. He liked telling me to get out of town. With two guys standing there, hands on their pistols. He says go, we're going."

"I have to know where we're going. I'm not just going anywhere."

"I'm thinking Canada, maybe. Get out of the country so the KC cops can't send out any bulletins on us."

"I'm not going to Canada. We can go to Pennsylvania or to my brother's place in New York. No one's going to trace us there."

"Your brothers don't like me and I don't like them."

"It's a place to start. We can decide then where to go. Did you get any of the ransom money?"

"Hell no. We send the notes and before the old man can deliver the money Lazia shows up."

"You shouldn't have taken the woman. I told you that. You should have taken Paul. She wouldn't dither around like he did. She would have paid before the senator got involved."

"Thing is, the man was sick, never got out of the house. We couldn't break into the house. So we grabbed her."

She folded a heavy sweater and put it in a canvas bag.

"Take all your warm clothes," he said. "We're going to Canada. We'll catch a bus to St. Louis and make connections there."

He left the room and she took the heavy sweater out of the canvas bag and hung it back into the closet.

"Like hell we are," she said. "I'm going to Pennsylvania."

XX
December 20, 1931

A GLOWING FIRE IN THE FIREPLACE, glistening snow in the winter sun outside and a bald eagle soaring above the lake below the tall cliff soothed Robert Jr's countenance on this Sunday morning at Hahatonka. Putting thoughts of the trial aside, he starting writing again, bringing different memories to mind—memories less comforting than the scene outside.

Mary came into the room and sat across from him.

"I won't stay long," she said. "I'll give you some quiet and privacy so that you can continue your bibliography, but I want you to relax a bit, also. Get the trial off your mind."

"Actually, I enjoyed the last couple of days, the subject matter, anyway. Talking about how father planned the estate, the mansion, the outbuildings. He was almost on the stand with me, his ideas and dreams rushing out, but coming through my mouth. I remember those days, how excited he was about building this grand house."

"Sad, too," Mary said. "I can hear that in your voice. I know how you loved him. And missed him."

"He was a great man. How different life for all of us would have been if he had lived to complete the place."

"You did well," Mary said. "The house has been complete for nearly ten years. We've had some good days here. The boys have enjoyed it. All of us have."

"I'm writing that now," he said. "There is comfort in remembering it all. I just finished the part about Carey. That was difficult, but necessary."

Carey, the younger brother who had fallen into hard times. Just how Carey had become involved with men who pulled off some robberies in Kansas City, Robert Jr had never been able to reconcile. Carey had been a troubled young man, difficult to reach unlike Kenneth and Le-Roy.

"The Oregon part of his story?" Mary asked. "The robbery there and how Carey was involved? You wrote that?"

"Yes."

She touched his arm, smoothingly, rubbed there. "Did you have to? You're sure it was his body they discovered, that the robbers killed him? Maybe it would have been better to leave that part out. That was so painful for all of us, it needn't be exposed to everyone."

"I want everything in the bibliography. I want future generations to know about us—the sunshine, the darkness. Carey was part of the family."

"Be sure to include the part about your father sending you to Independence, Kansas where the oil wells were. And the charming young lady you met there."

He smiled. At last, he was smiling. "Mary Amelia Bowen. You think I should mention her? How about the first time we met? Or how about the first time we . . ."

"Not everything!" she exclaimed, joining his smile. "Some things we keep just between the two of us."

Fred came into the room. "What's going on in here? What are you two being so secretive about?"

She laughed. "None of your business." She rose from the table. "Come on you two. Let's take a walk. Let's go down to the natural bridge and walk through the Colosseum. It should be pretty in the snow."

"Good idea," Robert Jr said. "I'll grab a jacket."

CHIEF SIEGFRIED ASKED Detective Chief Thurman, "Anything on the kidnappers?"

"Nothing. We've been looking all over Wyandotte County, Johnson County. All those little towns out there. You know how many gravel and dirt roads there are in Kansas?"

"Mrs. Donnelly said it was about an hour's drive from the Country Club Plaza. She was pretty sure about all the details."

"We're still looking, but this could take awhile."

"Dammit," Chief Siegfried banged his fist on his desk. "The *Kansas City Star* is having a field day criticizing us. Look at this, a damn piece in the Hutchinson newspaper. And it's Republican. Saying how the police are being run by the crooks in this town, Lazia and his crowd."

"Everybody in Kansas is a Republican," Thurman observed. He refrained from revealing his private thoughts about relinquishing the job of the police department to the criminals.

"What about the towel Mrs. Donnelly gave us?

"Goodhue and Rayen are checking on it. Goodhue thinks he may have found a laundry in Bonner Springs that put names, not numbers, on their laundry."

"Stay on it," Siegfried said. "Get the damn newspapers off our ass."

Then added, "And Tom Pendergast."

THE TRAIL downhill to the oval-shaped opening beneath layered rocks shaped and formed as no sculptor could ever duplicate provided a slickened approach and Mary slid, screamed lightly and slipped into Robert's arms. They laughed and he kissed her softly.

"Just like old times," he said.

"I love this place," she said. "I hope the lake waters don't get this far and destroy the beauty here."

"We're supposed to forget about the lake waters for today, remember?" he chided. "Look how the snow streaks itself on the rocks, outlining every detail. I wish the jury could see this. Mr. Borglum couldn't create this spot with his air drills and sandblasting."

They walked into the opening beneath the rock formation and took a seat on one of the dolomite rocks that formed a circle on the ground.

"So this is where the Osage had their Pow Wows," Mary said. "All the chiefs sitting around in a circle under the natural bridge. Shows they knew and appreciated this place the same as we do."

"They didn't have books," he said, "they carried their history up here," pointing to his head.

"Wouldn't it have been wonderful if they had books? If we could read their history like we read our history?"

"One of the Osage chiefs visited here when Colonel Scott—the man who sold Hahatonka to father—owned the place. The chief convinced the Colonel that the Osage called it Hahatonka and that it meant Laughing Waters. Of course, Mr. Lodge who was the postmaster here in the 1880's lay claim to naming it Hahatonka also."

"So much for our books," she said. "Too bad the Osage didn't write it all on the walls down here."

"There is some scribbling on the ceiling," Robert said. "Maybe it says Hahatonka in Osage."

She looked up. "Yeah, I think I can make it out." They both laughed.

"It's been a long time since I heard you laugh like you have today," she said. "See, you can forget the trial for one day."

"What trial?" he asked, laughing.

BOODLING IS WHAT IT WAS CALLED, so that's how Robert Jr wrote it. His father had told him about it, telling him it was a lesson on how not to do business.

"I thought I had to do it," his father had said. "I paid off the commissioners, it was the only way to get a franchise in St. Louis at that time. I paid $50,000 to a councilman named Fred Uthoff to pass the ordinance and get the franchise for Central Traction street railroad company. I was convicted, but later overturned. Don't learn the hard way."

One paragraph, that's all Robert Jr was going to include in his bibliography that would be negative about his
father. Pages and pages he could write—and would—a-
bout the good Robert Snyder Sr had accomplished for
Kansas City and for his family. Before his father entered
into the gas wars of the city, people were paying a dollar
sixty cents per unit for gas into their homes. After his
father brought natural gas from the wells in southern
Kansas and Oklahoma the price dropped to twenty-five
cents.

He included the lawsuit in Kansas against the Texas
cattleman who Robert Sr said had shorted him on the cattle and land he was to furnish according to a contract between the two. The Kansas jury sided with the Texan and
a $161,000 judgement had been awarded the cattleman.
Juries can't be trusted to do the right thing, Robert Sr had
told his son. His thoughts quite naturally went to the jury
in Jefferson City and he pushed the thought from his
mind. Again.

When the day ended, he had to admit he had gained
some pleasure and relaxation in penning more information about the Snyder family. When he retired that night,
Mary turned over and looked at him.

He smiled, just for her.

XXI
December 21, 1931

SENATOR JAMES REED was back in the courtroom following his rapid departure the day after Nell Donnelly was kidnapped. Almost immediately he clashed with Union Electric attorney Walter Walne.

Dwight Ford was called to the witness stand for cross examination by Walne about the value that Ford—a Kansas City insurance agent—had, the Friday before, placed on the Camden County estate the Snyders owned.

Ford said that Hahatonka was valued at one point six million dollars prior to the invasion of muddy Niangua River water spoiling the habitat of planted trout in the cold, clear water of the trout glen below the castle Snyders had built on a 300 foot cliff overlooking the clear water of the small lake and the spring that gushed forth millions of gallons of fifty degree, clear water a day.

"That's fair market value," Ford said when Walne asked where the figure came from.

"And how much more is the entire estate worth now that it is accessible by boat to thousands of expected tourists?" Walne asked.

"Why, as a country estate its entire value has been destroyed," Ford responded. "I wouldn't place its value over a hundred thousand dollars now."

Ford went on to explain—from his personal experience—how the rising and falling river water would leave the area around the trout glen a, "muddy mess."

When Walne pushed against Ford's evaluation of the estate, Reed rose from his seat like a bobbing fishing cork in the water voicing objection after objection to Walne's insinuations. Sid Roach, as he normally did, kept his attention on the jurors and noted exasperation on their expressions over the wrangling between Walne and Reed. He thought, from his observations, that Reed's comments were more favorable to the twelve men.

Carl Crocker, Camdenton, Missouri attorney and part of the electric company's team of counselors, recalled Robert Jr to the stand for further cross examination that he had begun the Saturday before. Crocker went through each expense the Snyders had incurred in building the mansion, the garage and the water tower. Robert Jr had all the figures and read them off to Crocker from the records he had with him. Reed objected to each question from Crocker saying the figures could be included in the court record for the jury to examine, but Union Electric's attorneys quite plainly, wanted the figures read aloud for the jurors to hear. Exactly what point they were trying to make, Sid Roach was unsure of.

When court was adjourned for the day, Sid, standing close to the exit door the jurors used, overheard one of them say to another, "All this trial is becoming is one big argument between the lawyers."

KANSAS CITY POLICE LIEUTENANT Walter Goodhue asked Wyandotte County, Kansas, Sheriff Al Becker if he was sure about the information they had just received from a former restaurant owner in Bonner Springs. Goodhue, sparse of hair and firm of jaw, had been delegated by Kansas Chief Siegfried to head up the search for the laundry that might have handled the towel Nell Donnelly brought home with her from her imprisonment.

"I know him," the sheriff said. "Emil Buinger."

"And the laundry here in Bonner Springs?" Goodhue asked. "They identified the towel from the mark as belonging to this man Buinger?"

"I know my people here," Becker said, growing exasperated with Goodhue's questions. "Emil Buinger said it was his towel, that it was part of the furnished house he leased to this man Paul Scheidt who works for some dairy. Go ask Scheidt, the man told us. He can explain the towel. Do you want to find the house or not?"

"Of course we do," Goodhue said. "I just don't want to go off on some wild goose chase and waste time. The chief wants to find the house and the men who took Mrs. Donnelly."

"I'll lead the way," Sheriff Becker said. "You and your men can follow me."

Goodhue got in his automobile along with detectives Robert Cole and Harry Reid and followed the sheriff's automobile. He led them out of Bonner Springs to the north and a few miles later he drove onto a narrow dirt road bordered on each side with tall weeds.

Goodhue began to doubt they were going to find a house along such a rough and plainly seldom used roadway. The sheriff stopped his car, got out and came back to the detectives' auto.

"It's just up ahead. We might not want to just drive up to it since we don't know anything about this Paul Scheidt who is supposed to be there. If he was in on the kidnapping he won't be receptive to visitors."

"So what? We walk in?" Goodhue asked.

"I think it would be a good idea to pull our cars off the road and behind that growth of brush over there. That way, if Scheidt or his cohorts come along they won't know we're here."

Goodhue agreed with the sheriff. They moved the automobiles behind the thick growth of weeds and brush until they were well hidden from the roadway.

The three Kansas City policemen departed from their car, all of them searching through the wild growth around them, none of them seeing a building of any kind.

"Now what?" Goodhue asked of the sheriff.

Sheriff Becker understood that he would have to lead the way toward where—according to the directions they had been given by the property owner—the house stood that might be the one Nell Donnelly and her chauffeur had been held captive in.

They followed the Kansas sheriff for about a hundred yards, stealthily, until Becker stopped and pointed through the weeds.

"Is that the house?" he asked.

Goodhue looked at the shack of a house, especially at the stone pillars that stood outside the boundaries of the porch they supported and compared the place to the description Mrs. Donnelly had given them.

"That's it," he said. "Sure looks like the house she described. And the woman had a remarkable memory of the place."

"We need to get across that open space between us and the house quickly," Sheriff Becker said. He waited, the detectives waited. "Okay," he said and took off running toward the house. The three followed him, all of them nervous about who might be inside watching them.

They gained entrance to the porch without incident. Goodhue walked to one of the windows, looked inside—difficult to see anything for the dirt on the glass—pushed up on the window and it opened. He carefully peered through the opening, saw nothing, turned and said, "I'm going through. Cover me."

He was soon inside and opened the door for the others. With guns drawn, they searched the three rooms finding no one inside. Goodhue looked at the furnishings, the worn rugs, the round oaken table, the cheap radio. Kansas City newspapers were lying on the floor, the story blaring from the front pages about the kidnapping of Nelly Don.

In the bedroom he saw the canvas cot and the sofa made into a bed, the religious pictures on the wall.

"Yeah," he told Sheriff Becker and the other detectives, "this is the place all right. Exactly as she described it."

"What next?" the sheriff asked.

"I guess we wait for this guy Scheidt to come home," Goodhue told him.

"He's gone," Becker said. "If he was involved he's not going to be sticking around here waiting to be arrested."

Detectives Reid and Cole agreed with the sheriff. "Leave one of us here, just in case he does return," one of them suggested. "The rest of us could go to this dairy where he worked and see what we can find out."

"I don't know," Goodhue said. "Lets wait around here for an hour or so. If he does come back, we'll have one of them. He'll lead us to the others. This is the only lead we have. If we don't find this Scheidt we're back to starting over."

"Question is, where's the best place to find him, here or where he works?" Becker said. "I know the dairy, they're honest people. We can trust whatever information they give is."

"Okay, let's make it a half hour," Goodhue said. "Then we'll move on."

They searched the two tumbledown outbuildings outside the small house. In one of the shacks they found two dogs slinking in one corner. They were mongrels with some hound in them plus just about every other breed in Kansas. They tucked their tails and laid their long ears down, eyes searching for a friendly motion by one of the detectives. Kirk, the taller of the two who stood in the doorway, spoke to the dogs and they came forward. They followed the detectives back into the yard and started running in circles coming closer to Detective Kirk with each turn.

"Look what I found," he said to Goodhue. Too bad they can't tell us where this guy Scheidt is."

Kirk and Cole encouraged the dogs in their racing through the yard, clapping their hands and calling out to them.

Sheriff Becker said, "I think I see a dust cloud down the road. Car coming."

"Let's get inside," Goodhue said to the dog fondlers. Through the windows, the four of them watched the dirt road. An older car led a rolling boil of dust into the yard and a man got out, looked around and called out, "Paul, you here?"

"Not our man," the sheriff said quietly. "You want me to handle this?"

"You know him?" Goodhue asked.

"No, but I'll find out who he is." Becker walked to the door, waited until the man saw him, then said, "Who you looking for?"

"Why, Paul Scheidt. He lives here." The man wore an inquiring look on his face. "I take it you're looking for him, too."

"What's your name?" the sheriff asked. The man told him Thad Kennedy without hesitation. By this time he had observed the badge Becker wore on his shirtfront with his jacket open to show it. He saw the holstered revolver, also. He looked tentative and waited for Becker to tell him why he was here. Becker walked onto the porch and the three Kansas City detectives followed him outside. The man was really perplexed now.

"You a friend of Scheidt's?" from Sheriff Becker.

"Well, yeah. I've known him for some time. At the dairy."

"When was the last time you were at the house here?"

"A couple of weeks ago, I guess. What's this all about?"

"When's the last time you saw this Scheidt?"

"I don't rightly recall. Last week, I believe it was. At the dairy."

Goodhue stepped in front of Becker. "Your friend is mixed up in a crime committed here. If you know what crime I'm talking about, speak up. If you were in on it with him, we'll find out about it so it would benefit you to tell us what you know."

Kennedy looked truly stunned. "I know nothing about any crime," he said. "I can't imagine Paul Scheidt being mixed up in anything criminal. He's a decent, law abiding man."

"The woman who was kidnapped in Kansas City was held here. Four or five men were involved." Goodhue waited for the man to respond. He did not.

"I'm sure you've heard about the kidnapping," Goodhue said.

"You mean that woman who owned the dress factory? Nelly Don?"

"You know about her? Ever see her?"

"No, no, hell no. She couldn't have been here. I mean, he's not the kidnapping kind. You'd have to be crazy to do something like that. Paul's not a crazy man."

"How did you know about it?" Sheriff Becker asked.

"I read the papers. It's been all over the front pages. Hard to miss seeing it. Hell, everybody knows about it."

"Were you supposed to meet him here today?" Good-hue asked.

"No, I just dropped by. I've done it before. I wait around, he shows up after he gets off at the dairy."

Becker looked at the two dogs standing close to Kennedy, looking at him, friendly-like.

"Dogs seem to know you," Becker said.

"Oh, yeah, we're acquainted." Kennedy rubbed the head of the nearest dog.

"Come inside," Goodhue said. "Stay out of sight. Scheidt shows up, don't try to warn him that we're here."

"Well, I thought I would get on down the road. I own a place across the river in Johnson County and I need to get down there."

"That'll have to wait," Goodhue said. "Come inside."

They waited another half hour or so, Kirk and Cole amusing themselves with the two dogs, Sheriff Becker showing impatience as he continued questioning Scheidt's visitor. When another dust cloud appeared on the horizon, moving along the dirt road in the direction of the house, everyone went back inside where they watched out the window again at an approaching automobile.

The car parked beside the one the visitor had driven to the house. A square-jawed man with a small mouth looked at the other car, then came toward the house in no hurry. Sheriff Al Becker stepped out the door.

"Paul Scheidt?" Becker asked the man.

"Yes." The man stopped before stepping onto the porch. He looked the sheriff over and Becker pulled his coat aside showing the badge on his shirt and his holstered pistol.

"You the law?" the man wanted to know.

"Sheriff Becker. You live here?"

Scheidt didn't answer right away. Goodhue and the other two detectives stepped out onto the porch and lined up beside the sheriff.

"What is this?" the man asked. "What's the law doing here on my property."

"I'll be asking the questions," Sheriff Becker said. "This is Detective Goodhue of the Kansas City Missouri Police Department and Detectives Kirk and Cole. They'll be having some questions for you, too."

"I haven't been to Kansas City for a month or more. What's this about?"

"Were you here at your house last Wednesday night or Thursday?" Goodhue asked him.

"Yes, of course. I live here."

"Who else was here?"

"Nobody. I didn't have anyone here."

"Was a woman here in the house?"

"A woman? No, of course not. Is that what this is about? You think I had some woman here doing things to her?"

"No, we think you were holding a woman here for ransom. Seventy-five thousand dollars ransom."

Scheidt laughed a short, "Hah," then looked at Sheriff Becker and said, "Sheriff, you've got the wrong place. The wrong man. Nothing happened here last week nor did anything like that ever happen here."

"This house is the same house Nell Donnelly described as the house where she was held against her will and her husband asked to pay a ransom of $75,000," Sheriff Becker said. "It doesn't look good for you Mr. Scheidt."

"That's preposterous," Scheidt said. "I'm not going to stand here and be accused of something like that that I never had anything to do with. I'm going to have to ask you to leave my property unless you have some kind of proof of your outlandish claims. You came to the wrong house. There are houses all over this part of Kansas just like this one. Same man built this house probably built a hundred others just like it."

"If we have to prove it to you, Mr. Scheidt, that would mean you are lying to officers of the law on a legal investigation," Goodhue told him. "That wouldn't go so well for you in court."

"And if you're out here harassing me at the wrong house, that won't look so good for the Kansas City Police Department," Scheidt snapped back at him. "I've been reading in the newspapers about how you people, paid by the taxpayers, are allowing the criminals in your town to call all the shots and do your work for you."

Goodhue turned to Sheriff Becker. "I've had enough lying from this man. I'm going in to call the chief and have him bring out someone who can identify the place. Will you see that this man will be here when we get back? Shouldn't take more than an hour?"

"He'll be here," the sheriff said. "We'll have a nice visit."

PAUL SCHEIDT continued to strenuously deny any participation in the Donnelly kidnapping. Detectives Kirk and Cole, tired of the attention of the dogs, walked around the place until the December cold drove them back inside. Scheidt visited with his friend who had come calling and Sheriff Becker tried to stoke a fire in the one stove inside the house. Detective Kirk said, "Car coming," and all of them watched the approaching police car driven by Detective Goodhue followed by Chief Siegfried's Buick.

Goodhue led the way inside and everyone there showed surprise at the person following the chief. Nell Donnelly. She was dressed stylishly with her own silk scarf around her neck under her black, belted coat. Sheriff Becker walked out to meet them and Detective Goodhue made the introductions.

Nell Donnelly looked the house over carefully, attention paid closely to the two stone pillars holding up the corners of the porch.

"This is the place," she said. "I remember those two outbuildings over there. Inside the door you'll see the table I described, round, oaken, a central post with four claw feet at the bottom. You'll find the cheap radio if someone hasn't moved it. There will be a rug on the floor with a pattern worn in it by the door."

Chief Siegfried said, "Let's go see," and led the group inside. She looked around, Scheidt and his visitor standing nearby, but she paid scant attention to them.

"In there," she pointed toward the door into the bedroom with the sofa made into a bed and a canvas cot where she had been held for almost 36 hours, and she described what they would find in the room. "More religious pictures on the wall in there, similar to the ones hanging here," pointing them out.

They advanced to the bedroom where they found the articles exactly as she had described them. They returned to the front room of the house. Nell Donnelly walked over to the table she had described in exact detail. "This is where they made me write the notes."

Chief Siegfried pointed to Scheidt and his friend. "Do you recognize these men?"

She looked at them patiently as they shuffled their feet and Scheidt looked at the floor.

"I don't recognize them, but in the dark I did not get a good look at all the men in here that night. They could have been here."

Chief Siegfried said to the men, "Which one of you is Scheidt who has been lying to my officers and Wyandotte County Sheriff Becker?"

Scheidt's visitor stepped away from him, leaving the resident of the now identified house of incarceration standing nervously by himself.

"Okay," Paul Scheidt said. "I admit this is the house where the woman was kept for a day and two nights. But I'm not the one who did that.

"Lacy Browning brought this man to me several months ago and he offered me a thousand dollars to use my house to hold someone in," Scheidt said, his voice nervous, his words stammered and halting as he breathed deeply trying to keep himself under control.

"Who was the man?" Chief Siegfried wanted to know.

"He said his name was Depew. Martin Depew. He said he knew how I could make some easy money, a thousand dollars, just by letting them use my house. I wouldn't have to do anything. I told him I was interested."

"Why did he want to use your house?" from the Chief.

"He didn't give me any details that first time. He came back several times, telling me more each time. By then I was committed—I mean, who wouldn't be? I don't have to do anything, just let them use my house for a couple of days for a thousand dollars."

The chief waited for him to continue. Scheidt nervously shifted his body, glanced over at Nell Donnelly who stood, arms crossed, staring intently at him.

"Finally he told me what they wanted the house for," Scheidt continued. He looked at his friend who had distanced himself from Scheidt. "They were going to bring this man out here he said, just to keep him until somebody paid them to bring the man home. Nobody was going to be hurt, Depew said. But he didn't say who the man was or when they would use the house. So, yeah, I agreed. Didn't see any liability for me. A thousand bucks."

"What else did you agree to do?"

"Nothing. Nothing at all. That was why I agreed to do it. Use the house, pay me a thousand bucks. Deal over with."

"You realize that makes you an accomplice to the kidnapping of Mrs. Donnelly and her chauffeur?"

"I don't see how," Scheidt said, spreading his hands.

Looking at Mrs. Donnelly he said, "I wouldn't have agreed to anything like that, to a woman? No way."

The chief stared him down, keeping quiet, waiting for Scheidt to tell him more, more than he intended to. The others, the detectives, Sheriff Becker, Scheidt's friend who now appeared to be a former friend, all watching him, Mrs. Donnelly with her intent stare. He blurted out, "Look, I came home that night, Wednesday it was, I think the sixteenth, here was these two greaseballs, dagos, Italians—I knew they were from their accents. I found out they had two people in the other room—I didn't know who it was, there was only supposed to be one person, a man."

He shuffled around some more, unable to meet their eyes any longer. "The next morning, I went out, got a paper and found out who was in my house. I showed it to the two Italians and they got nervous as hell, saying they didn't know who they had, that they hadn't had any part in grabbing them. One of them wanted me to take him to a telephone so we drove over to the dairy where I work sometimes and he made a call."

"Who did he call?" the chief asked.

"I don't know. He had this slip of paper, he dialed a number, asked how many potatoes do you want and how many eggs, then he hung up and tore the paper to shreds and threw it away."

"Where do we find this Martin Depew?"

"I don't know. I don't know anything else about him. Lacy Browning brought him to me, didn't tell me anything except I could trust him and I could make some money."

"Did he tell you how you would be under arrest and go to trial for being an accessory to a kidnapping?" Chief Siegfried asked.

"But I didn't do anything," Scheidt protested. "I rented out my house, that's all. You can't go to jail for that."

"You'll need a lawyer," Sheriff Becker said. "You and this guy Lacy Browning. Take us to him."

HOLLIDAY, KANSAS, a wide spot on an out of the way rural road in Johnson County, across the Kansas River was a half hour drive from Scheidt's home. Wyandotte County Sheriff Al Becker returned to his office in Bonner Springs and the caravan to Lacy Browning's was reduced to Chief Siegfried's Buick and the Kansas City patrol car carrying the detectives. Nell Donnelly sat in the front of the Chief's Buick—declining an offer to return her to the city, saying she wanted to meet the man who planned her kidnapping. Scheidt, in the rear of the Buick with one of the detectives, continued to plead his innocence until Chief Siegfried, sensing Mrs. Donnelly was becoming annoyed with his whining, told Scheidt to keep it quiet.

Browning lived on a few acres with a house not unlike Scheidt's leading Chief Siegfried to wonder why they hadn't used Browning's house instead of bringing another man into the kidnapping.

Browning was a tall, taciturn man who seemed a bit aggravated at the confrontation of Scheidt and the police.

Browning's wife asked, "Who are you? What do you want with my husband?"

"I'm the chief of the Kansas City police department," Siegfried told her. "We're here to arrest Lacy Browning for the kidnapping of Mrs. Nell Donnelly."

"That's crazy," she said. She turned to her husband and asked, "Who are these men? What kind of joke are they playing on us?"

Siegfried showed his badge. Browning's wife looked at it, looked at her husband and immediately began crying hysterically, shouting at her husband, "What have you done? What are you mixed up in?"

Chief Siegfried told Browning that he was under arrest for suspicion of aiding and abetting in the major crime of kidnapping. Browning immediately started confessing to being a part of the scheme, blaming it all on the man Martin Depew.

He said a bunch of professionals at doing this sort of thing was coming from New York City to do the actual kidnapping. Looking at Mrs. Donnelly, Browning swore that Depew didn't tell him that they would be taking a woman prisoner.

"Hell—beg pardon, M'am—I wasn't going to be a party to anything like that. He said it was going to be Mr. Donnelly and that Mrs. Donnelly would pay the ransom the next day and it would be over with."

"Why did you bring Scheidt into it?" the chief wanted to know.

"I got kids at home, couldn't use my place. Depew made it sound so easy, all I had to do was find a place to keep him—Mr. Donnelly, that is—and I got seventy-five hundred dollars. It sounded so easy. That was going to be the money to send my kids to college. Give them an education like I wanted them to have."

"How much money did this Depew give you?" asked Chief Siegfried.

"Nothing, yet. He said I would get the money the day after the ransom was paid which was supposed to be Saturday or yesterday."

"So where does this Depew live and how were you supposed to contact him?"

"He worked for the Marion Steam Shovel Company in Holliday. I knew him from a job we were on."

"Let's go find him," the chief said.

"Wait," Browning protested. "We didn't do any actual crime, me and Paul Scheidt here. You're not taking us into jail, are you? I've got a family here."

"Tell them goodbye," the chief said.

XXII

WALTER WALNE began his questioning of Robert Snyder Jr with an inquiry about the thirty acre Lakeside Resort that operated across the trout glen lake below the castle. The land where Union Electric had sent men in to cut trees and burn them.

"Let's understand this for the jury," Walne said, approaching the railing fronting the jury box. "This place you call Hahatonka was actually a summer resort. We want to introduce into the court records some newspaper advertisements from the 1920's and some as late as last year, 1930, promoting Hahatonka as a resort. Tell us about this, about the facilities offered to the public."

"Lakeside Resort with the summer cottages, camping facilities and a dining hall was leased to individuals who operated and maintained it," Robert Jr said. "Our family continued to own the property so that we would have some control over how it was operated. We had no income from it other than the lease money."

"The advertisements said this resort was located at Hahatonka," Walne said.

"I believe the ad says the Lakeside Resort in Hahatonka," Robert replied. "The name of the post office since 1895 has been Hahatonka. Prior to that it was Gunter Springs."

"But people came there expecting to have access to everything in this resort that is called Hahatonka, did they not?"

"I believe the ad was specific about the facilities available," Robert Jr said.

"Now," Walne said, "you testified that three Missouri governors favored Hahatonka as a state park, but were never able to get legislative approval to purchase it, is that not correct?"

Robert Jr glanced at the court clerk and the stenographer who was recording the trial proceedings. "I remember so testifying," he said. "I think the record would confirm that."

"So the state and you—the Snyder family—came to an agreement on what the price of the estate would be if they were to get legislative approval," Walne said, referring to a paper he held.

Senator Reed, on his feet, "Objection, your honor. Whatever price was discussed as far back as 1909 is immaterial to the price today and to the price before the dam waters invaded the estate and ruined the value."

"The Snyder family is here today claiming an outlandish amount of damage to an estate whose value they have testified to. This is just one more price they have put on the estate and should be shown to the jury to consider," Walne said. He turned towards the jury box wanting them to see him in a competent light that would put the senator in a position of trying to deny information to them.

"Conditions at the estate have changed," Senator Reed said. "A price agreed upon years ago has no bearing on the value today."

"But, your honor, the witness testified that three governors favored purchasing the property for a state park.

Governor Hadley in 1909 when the vote to acquire the estate failed in the state senate by one vote. Governor Frederick Gardner in his second biennial message on January 6, 1921, recommended the purchase of Hahatonka for a state park. A value was discussed and apparently agreed upon by the Snyders. A special committee of the state legislature appointed to visit and report on Hahatonka unanimously recommended that the state purchase the property. A value was discussed in the legislature. In 1924 Governor Arthur Hyde named Hahatonka as his first choice for a state park. Now, is the jury supposed to believe all these recommendations were made without a price tag being applied?"

"Of course a price was discussed," Senator Reed said. "Listen to the years when they were discussed. They are no longer material to the value we must apply, have to apply, today."

"The bills are the best evidence," Walne said. "The Snyder estate was offered several times to the state for a park for substantially less than they have come here to seek for only a part of the estate that was condemned and for an alleged loss of scenic beauty to the rest of the estate."

Judge Reeves held a hand in the air and both counsels turned silent and regarded the judge.

"I'm going to sustain the objection to introducing those earlier day values," he said. "I will instruct the jury to wholly disregard what early day writers and others have said about Hahatonka except for the historic value contained in them."

Robert Snyder Jr was dismissed from the witness stand and Colonel Robert G. Scott, 87 years old, was called to the stand. Colonel Scott said Hahatonka was, "A rather wild looking place when I first saw it in 1894, but I could see these natural beauties."

The colonel, a retired Union army officer and veteran of the Civil War, a guard at the White House when President Lincoln was in office and a civil engineer, purchased Hahatonka and lived there for fourteen years. He wrote an article for *Carter's Monthly* magazine in which he called Hahatonka's beauty, "The most magnificent the human eye ever beheld."

He said he had been in nearly every state in the union, but had never seen anything, "That you could begin to compare with Hahatonka in beauty," calling it the, "Outstanding place to see things that there is in the United States."

Colonel Scott who owned property near Hahatonka, sold the estate lands to Robert Snyder Sr in 1905.

CHIEF SIEGFRIED and a contingent of detectives—with *Kansas City Star* reporter Clyde Waers trailing them—drove to the Marion Steam Shovel Company and talked with Depew's supervisor. After going through the records he gave the police an address on Campbell Street in Kansas City where Depew resided. The caravan sped there quickly.

The chief, sensitive now about the press coverage his department was receiving because of the Lazia agreement, allowed Waers to accompany them when they entered and searched Depew's room. Several letters were recovered and Waers found a telephone number scribbled on a scrap of paper which he called immediately after leaving the room. The man at the other end of the call said he had a picture of the Depews.

When Baers gave the picture of Depew to the police, they began sending copies to police all over the country. After going through the mess of papers and debris the Depews had left scattered about their rented room, the police discovered that Mrs. Depew had relatives in Bloomsburg, Pennsylvania and immediately contacted the sheriff there.

Chief Siegfried showed the picture of the Depews to Nell and Paul Donnelly.

"That's him," Nell Donnelly said.

Paul Donnelly looked at the picture and nodded his head. "Yes, I remember her. The nurse, last year." He handed the picture back to the chief. "So that's how they picked who to kidnap. She was in on it with her husband."

"Looks that way," Chief Siegfried said.

"He's the one who made me write the ransom notes," Nell Donnelly said. "I'm quite sure of that. Show the picture to George, (George Blair, the chauffeur) he can identify the man."

One of the detectives called George Blair into the room and the chief showed the picture of the Depews to him.

"That's the man. Looks like the nurse who was here in the house last year."

He looked at Paul Donnelly for confirmation and got it.

"All right, then," Chief Siegfried said. "I've contacted the sheriff in Bloomsburg, Pennsylvania. I think we've got them."

He gave the *Star* reporters a satisfied, boastful look.

The noose was closing on Marshall—or Martin—and Ethel Depew.

XXIII
December 23, 1931

MARTIN Depew spread the large map of the entire country on the bench inside the St. Louis bus station. What a lousy ride that had been. Some damn drunk causing a ruckus on the bus and had to be told to shut up or Depew would, "Whip his ass."

What an asshole.

They had been traveling for a day and a half, sleeping inside the station on the bench, waiting for the bus to Chicago.

"See," he said, "we'll be just that far," (holding thumb and forefinger apart several inches) "from Canada. We could be there in one day after we get to your brother's."

"Or, we could stay at my brother's house in Brocton, New York," Ethel Depew said. "We're broke, not enough money to rent a hotel room, buy food and gasoline. We'll stay in Brocton."

Martin Depew traced the highway to Brocton, noticed how close it was to the Canadian border, then slowly folded the map. He looked off toward the eastern horizon as if gauging the distance, then to the North, toward Canada. "All right," he said. "We'll try it your way. Maybe your brother can fix me up with a part time job, get us some money to get the hell out of this country."

It became quite apparent the rest of the day that Martin did not want to be engaged in conversation with Ethel so she maintained her silence. Martin had always been a difficult person to talk with, anyway. Not talking about his

past life or places he had been or things he had done. She
had time to cogitate his latest scheme at making big
money, the kidnapping. She wondered what Nell Donnelly
and her husband were dong now, if they were busy trying
to determine who was responsible. Had she recognized
Martin? Would she be able to tie him to the time when
Ethel had worked for the Donnellys?

Paul Donnelly had been a weak person compared to
Nell. Nell ran the garment company and ran the household. Martin had made a serious mistake in kidnapping
Nell instead of Paul. According to the one account Ethel
had read in the Kansas City newspaper before fleeing
town, the Donnelly's neighbor, Senator James Reed, had
become involved and had coerced the Pendergast machine into finding Nell Donnelly. She doubted if the Senator and the hoodlum, Lazia, would have been involved if it
had been Paul that Martin had taken instead of Nell.

Oh, well, a few days with her brother in New York
where no one would be looking for them and they could
regroup, find new jobs and live without having to look
over their shoulder. They had just enough money for
tickets to Brocton—so Martin said, but what about that
roll of bank notes he had in his small valise?

The bus trip to Chicago had been tedious. Martin got
into an argument with the driver over smoking cigarettes
and another man Martin had talked with argued with the
driver, also. They were short of money—so Martin said—
and the transfer to buses headed for Buffalo was getting
monotonous. When would they ever get to her brother's
house?

When finally they did arrive there, Ethel's brother was aghast when he opened his front door in Brocton and recognized them.

"What are you doing here?" he said. "Don't you know your name is in all the headlines? You are fugitives, they are looking for you in the Donnelly kidnapping case in Kansas City. You can't be coming here."

Both the Depews were surprised. "They can't be looking for us here, in New York," Ethel said.

"They're looking for you everywhere," the brother said. "You can't stay here. Sooner or later they'll come here looking for you."

"I told you we should have gone to Canada," Martin said. To Ethel's brother he said, "If you could loan us a few dollars or drive us over into Canada we'll be out of your way."

"I don't know . . ."

"We're not going to Canada," Ethel said. "We don't know anyone there, we aren't citizens there, no papers, nothing. Drive us to Bloomsburg in Pennsylvania where mother is. We're out of money. At relations there we can lay low until it cools off about the kidnapping. They won't be looking for us there."

"What if they pull us over on the way to Pennsylvania?" the brother asked. "I'll be in trouble same as the two of you."

"You don't want us to stay here, do you?" Ethel asked.

The brother was nervous, his eyes shifted around as if he was looking for a solution to the trouble where his sister and her husband had placed him.

Martin took several dollar bills from his pocket and offered them to Ethel. "Here, take this money and find your way to this town in Pennsylvania. I'm headed for Canada."

"And they catch you on the way or at the border and they will tie you back to me," the brother said. "I'll take you to Pennsylvania and then I'm out of it. Get in my car."

"Don't leave me alone, Martin," Ethel said. "I agreed to be with you on this kidnapping scheme and I don't want to be the one held responsible for it. If you leave me now I'll be the one that goes to jail for it if they catch us. They won't be looking for us in the little town of Blooms-burg."

Reluctantly, Martin stuck the money back in his pocket. "All right," he said. "We'll try it your way."

They drove across the state line into Pennsylvania and stopped at the town of Blossburg for gasoline. Martin saw a sign on the front of the bus station with a schedule of time and money for a ticket to New York City. He counted the money in his pocket and got out of the brother's automobile and walked toward the bus station.

Ethel Depew watched her husband walking away. "Let's go on to Bloomsburg," she told her brother.

SENATOR JAMES REED pulled the half-chewed cigar from his mouth and said to Tom Pendergast, "I can count on your support at the Democratic convention next year in Chicago?"

Pendergast wore a partial smile. He worked at clipping and licking his own cigar to ready it for lighting.

"First vote, I told you. Favorite Son. I'll swing my delegates toward you. After that I have to take a look at Roosevelt. He's got most of the South and this part of the country."

"Sure," Reed said, "hell, he's promising a job for everyone. Hoover's promising a chicken in every pot and two cars in every garage. There's a middle path for the country, we don't have to go into debt putting food in everyone's mouth when they can just go out and plant a garden."

"Roosevelt's talking about public works, bridges, roads and buildings. That's a whole lot of concrete," Pendergast said, puffing on his now burning cigar. "Ready Mix Concrete."

"Pendergast Ready Mix Concrete, you mean," Reed said. "There's not enough money in the whole country to do what he says he's going to do."

"Maybe," Pendergast said. "I'll stick with you until he needs my votes. If I can put him over the top, to the 770 votes he needs for the nomination, then he'll be in debt to us. Be good for Kansas City if we could get some of those public works."

Reed contemplated Pendergast's words. Through a cloud of blue cigar smoke he said, "Well, Garner and Al Smith will be after votes, too. Don't give in to them."

"Have you been campaigning in the other states? Iowa, Illinois, Nebraska. Kansas even? Give us more votes to swing over."

"There aren't many Democratic votes in those states," Reed said. "I've been getting around, sending out some letters. I contacted some people down in Oklahoma, but they say Old Alfalfa Bill Murray is trying to lock up the votes down there."

"That's the governor who's been declaring martial law every time someone goes against him," Pendergast said, finding it amusing. "He's the one tried to start a state for the Indians, but he's dead set against the coloreds. Built the bridge across the river to Texas and Texas wouldn't let anyone cross it."

"Alfalfa Bill won't get very many votes at the convention," Reed predicted. "Those votes will end up going to Roosevelt."

"The women are against you," Pendergast said. He pointed his cigar at Reed. "You voted against them for the right to vote. You went against the Children's Bureau, saying the old maids in there ought to be taught how to get a husband and have kids of their own. Didn't go over too well with the women delegates and there are quite a few of them now from the other states."

"So you're thinking Roosevelt's going to win this thing," Reed said. He studied his words, flicked ashes off the end of his cigar, puffed and blew more blue smoke.

"He's crippled, you know. Infantile Paralysis they call it. Could have affected his brain, who knows. Stick with me for two votes. If Roosevelt hasn't won it by then, offer your votes for some favors here in Kansas City. I don't want anything from him, I'm against his policies, they'll run the country into a debt we'll never get out of."

Pendergast's smile grew. He reached into a bottom drawer of his desk and pulled out a bottle that had a Canadian whiskey label on it. "He's going to repeal this Prohibition thing, you know. Might as well get a head start, want a drink?"

Reed regarded the bottle for a moment. "As long as it's sociable and private."

Pendergast retrieved two glasses from another desk drawer, poured two inches of the bottle's content into each glass, pushed one across the desk which Reed picked up, looked at Pendergast and both said in unison, "Cheers," and drained the glasses.

"How you doing with those rich boys' trial down in Jeff?" Pendergast asked after getting his cigar glowing again.

"It's going well. Sid Roach is helping. The Snyder boy—oldest one—is pretty convincing. Judge Reeves has been more favorable to us than to the electric company. Surprising, I guess, since he wasn't any friend of yours."

"An honest judge," Pendergast said, still grinning. "Be careful of an honest judge. You've had your share of famous trials, you should know that. Lost the one where Henry Ford wrote against the Jews. And that one where you tried Jesse James' son. You did get the woman off who shot her husband for playing the wrong cards in a Bridge game."

"Trials are a roll of the dice," Reed said. "You just have to have a feel of the dice before you throw them. I feel pretty good about this one."

"You're going to have a lot of practice," Pendergast said. "I hear the cops are hauling in all the kidnappers of that woman who runs the garment factory. You'll be representing the mother of your child, I reckon."

Reed didn't like the remark, too close to home. He rose, took the cigar from his mouth and said, "First two votes, Tom, that's all you owe me."

"You owe me the chance to pour some more Pendergast Ready Mix Concrete," Pendergast said, picking up some papers off his desk by way of dismissal.

XXIV
December 24, 1931

COLUMBIA COUNTY, PENNSYLVANIA Sheriff Arthur Rabb drove up to the house with the address on it he had written down from the information given him in the telegram from the Chief of Police in Kansas City, Missouri. He checked his notes again, disembarked from his automobile and walked to the door of the house and knocked on it.

When a woman answered the door, he asked for Ethel Depew.

"I don't know anyone by that name," the woman said.

"Will I have to get a warrant?" the sheriff asked. "If I do, everyone in this house will go to jail."

A woman in her thirties, attractive, slim, lithe with brown hair parted down the center stepped in front of the other woman to face the sheriff.

"I'm Ethel Depew," she said. "What can I do for you?"

"I'll need you to come down to the courthouse with me," Sheriff Rabb said. "I have a warrant for your arrest in connection with a kidnapping in Kansas City, Missouri."

"I know nothing about any kidnapping," Ethel Depew said. "I only learned about my husband's involvement when he forced me to leave Kansas City in a hurry."

"You can explain all that to the detectives from Kansas City. I'll have to hold you until they get here."

"But, there's no need," Ethel Depew pleaded. "I had to hitchhike here after he forced me out of his car in Buffalo. He gave me two dollars and said I could catch a ride down here to my relatives."

"Do you want to get some stuff—clothing, personal articles to take with you?" Sheriff Rabb asked, a bit impatient.

"But, I didn't do anything," she protested. "Martin said he cheated some Italians in a card game and had to leave town in a hurry. I didn't know he was part of the kidnapping until we got to Buffalo and he told me about it. He wanted me to go to Canada with him, but I refused."

"We have to be going, Mrs. Depew. You can tell your story to the Kansas City detectives, I can't help you."

"But, see, if I was guilty, I would be in Canada now with my husband. If I could make you understand . . ."

"Ma'm, we need to go, NOW." Sheriff Rabb stepped into the house forcing both women to back away from him. Ethel Depew started crying and the other woman hugged her. "NOW," Sheriff Rabb said again.

Ethel Depew stepped away from the other woman who still held her arms. "I'll straighten this out Mother," Ethel Depew said, "I'll talk with Mrs. Donnelly, she'll tell them I had nothing to do with this."

The woman watched the sheriff's car go down the street toward the courthouse, Ethel Depew, in the auto with the sheriff. Under arrest. And she had come here, to this house, for help.

"I can't believe Ethel was involved in a kidnapping," she said. But there was no one there to hear her.

————————————————

THE CHILL of the late evening caused Nell Donnelly to hover under her heavy coat and snuggle behind the colorful, stylish scarf around her neck. Her cold, kid-gloved hands held the leash as her German Shepherd attended to his necessities. Senator Reed came up behind her silently holding his own dog leash and the two animals greeted each other as Nell leaned her body into the Senator.

"How's David?" he asked. "You hang up a stocking for him?"

"He's a bit young for that this year," she replied. "Next Christmas maybe we can both hang his stocking. Together."

He made a grunting sound deep in his throat. "Maybe," he said.

"When this is all over, I'm filing for divorce," Nell said. "When they've caught all the kidnappers and sent them to prison and the whole thing drops off the front pages of the newspapers, then I'm going to file."

"I can't do that now," he said. "Not as long as Lura is alive."

"I understand. You certainly can't do it if you're a candidate for President of the United States. What does it look like as far as the convention goes?"

Reed scuffed a shoe through the thin layer of leftover snow and yanked on his shepherd's leash. "Looks like Roosevelt is going to win it. Tom can't wait to throw his votes that way, but he says he'll support me through the first couple of votes. Favorite Son, that sort of thing. But not if the Roosevelt camp offers him a deal."

"Are you doing any campaigning?"

"I'm tied up in that Snyder trial down at the capitol. I'll go down to Springfield for the Jackson Day Dinner, try and raise some money and some backing. But we know who controls the votes in this state."

"Hoover can't win again," Nell said. "I'd probably vote Democratic next year if you were running."

He smiled and gave her arm a squeeze. "Maybe I could tell that at the convention, that I've got one Republican vote if they'll nominate me."

They were silent for several moments. "Come over tomorrow," she said. "Anytime. Have a drink with us, say hello to David. Bring Lura if she's able."

"She won't be," he said. "I'll bring a gift. Play Santa to our son."

They separated the German Shepherds. "Next year," he said. "Things will be different."

"Yes," she said, "and better."

XXV
December 29, 1931

JUDGE ALBERT REEVES, anxious to get the fifth week of trial underway, banged his gavel sharply and awarded the floor to Union Electric chief counsel Walter Walne who told the court he had a few more questions for Colonel R.G. Scott, former owner of Hahatonka. Scott had given direct testimony about his opinion of the value of the estate before the Christmas break.

The 87-year-old ex-Union Civil War soldier repeated his claim that the estate was the outstanding gem in the United States for natural beauty.

Walne's sole objective was seemingly meant to impress on the jury that, regardless of the Colonel's praise for the estate, he did sell it to Robert Snyder Sr for $28,000, not the $1,654,000 the old man now claimed it to be worth.

Reed had four witnesses lined up for testimony on this first day of court following the Christmas holidays. He called Dr. Walter Williams, president of the University of Missouri to the stand. Dr. Williams said he had lived in Missouri all his life and had travelled extensively throughout the world. He visited Hahatonka for the first time forty years earlier and, in his opinion, it had, "The most glorious array of natural beauties in a small area of any place I have ever seen. It is the only place of its kind in Missouri and was most appropriately chosen for a capitol mural decoration."

His reference was to the mural W.H. Wurepel of Washington University Art Department had painted and now hung in the State capitol building in Jefferson City.

"How long has Hahatonka been regarded as the beauty spot of Missouri?" Reed asked.

"I can hardly remember when it was not," Dr. Williams replied.

"And you and I are not very young anymore, Doctor," Reed commented.

"Speak for yourself, Senator," Williams said and for, perhaps the first time since the trial started, laughter filled the courtroom.

Williams said he had written 200 letters to lawyers, doctors, engineers and citizens of all walks of life in Missouri several years before, asking them to list the seven most beautiful spots in the state and that with the exception of "two or three," all had listed Hahatonka first. He said he wanted the information for a magazine article he planned to write. Walne objected several times during this testimony, saying this testimony had no bearing on the trial, but the judge overruled.

Williams said about the trout glen that existed before lake waters overran it that, "There is no way to put such beauty into words, it was one of the half-dozen or so most beautiful places I had seen in the world."

Reed, in a lengthy hypothetical question about the damage to Hahatonka by the invasion of lake waters, about the cutting of thousands of trees by the electric company, burning of the mill and destroying the dam that kept river waters out of the waters gushing forth from the spring, drew this comment from Williams:

"It would destroy a large part of the beauty. How seriously, of course, could not be said without actual observation."

Edgar Shook of Kansas City, former chief counsel for the state highway department, started the questioning of Dr. Williams, asking if he had seen Hahatonka since Bagnell Dam was built.

"Only at a distance," Dr. Williams said.

Shook handed several photographs to Williams of the area taken since dam construction.

"I would say there is still beauty there," Dr. Williams said, "but the old beauty has been destroyed."

Dr. John Pickard, professor of history of art at the University of Missouri, told the court why the mural by Wurepel was exhibited in the capitol building. "It was a spot we picked to represent the beautiful scenery of Missouri."

Pickard had been president of a capitol decoration committee.

Frank H. Decou, former state game and fish commissioner, said the reputation of Hahatonka as a beauty spot ranked second to none. It's potential as a fish hatchery was diminished for trout, which once were plentiful in Hahatonka Lake, he said, before the Lake of the Ozarks entered it.

"Trout have to have cold, clear water to live," he said.

Frank Bushman, Kansas City insurance executive, testified that before the lake filled the Niangua River and overflowed into Hahatonka Lake, a fair value of the estate would have been $1,379,850. Now, he said, it was not worth more than $179,260. Bushman said he had wide experience in development of country estates in Michigan. Before the hydro-electric project, he said, Hahatonka was, "The most perfect site I have ever seen for a country estate." He called the large trees—6000 of them cut and destroyed according to the Snyders' testimony—priceless and estimated their value before cutting at $100 each.

After an exhausting day for both counsels, Walne repeated his request to Judge Reeves for the jury to make the journey to Hahatonka to view the estate.

"I would be more inclined to permit the jury to see the property if they could view the estate under all the varying conditions which will result from the fluctuations of the lake instead of only at one specific time," the judge said as he adjourned the session.

CHIEF LEWIS SIEGFRIED, seated behind his desk, regarded the staff of detectives he had called into his office.

"Where do we stand on this kidnapping case?" he asked Chief Detective Thurman.

"We have the woman," Thurman said. "Can't find her husband, Depew. Detective Cole has a lot of new information about him, though. Under different names. Seems he changes his name every time he gets married. Case of bigamy along with the kidnapping."

"What about the rest of them?" Chief Siegfried asked.

"Scheidt, Browning and didn't they lead you to a couple more involved?"

"Yeah, a man named Charles Mele. Claims he's innocent, but Mrs. Donnelly identified him in a lineup. He's thick with Vic Bonura that ran a restaurant over in Kansas. Vic skipped town so we're looking for him.

"Mrs. Donnelly says Mele's the one tried to stuff her head in a bag and forced her to lie on the floor of her Lincoln. Pretty good case against that one."

"The woman, the Depew woman? Prosecutor feel like he's got a case against her?" Siegfried asked.

"She's lied so much it's hard to get her to tell the same story twice," Thurman said. "She's on her way back here, Mrs. Frances Trowbridge will escort her under guard as soon as the extradition papers are signed. They're on your desk, there."

"So what's she telling now?" the Chief asked.

"Well, she lied about the hitchhiking she said she did from Buffalo to Pennsylvania. They checked with her brother in Brocton, New York, and he admitted taking her to Pennsylvania. So now she's saying that Depew was telling her they had to leave Kansas City and get a job somewhere else. She wasn't willing to do that, according to her, so he lied to her and said he'd cheated some Italians in a card game and they were after him. So she agreed to go to her brother's house in Brocton and the brother started with them in his car for Pennsylvania, only when they got to Blossburg, Pennsylvania, Depew left her without telling where he was going. That's when she says her brother told her they were wanted all over the country for the kidnapping. She says that's the first she knew of it."

"She never reads the papers here, huh?" the chief said. "She must have been the only person in Kansas City didn't know about it. So Depew's got other names? What's the story on that?"

"Seems his real name is Deputy. He's got a string of different first names, too. Marshall, Martin, William. Our men talked to his other wife when he was William Martin. We've tracked him to New York City," Thurman said. "I think it's only a matter of time before we run him to ground."

Chief Siegfried leaned back in his chair, relaxing for the first time since Nell Donnelly was kidnapped. "Good," he said. "Maybe the damn papers will get off my ass now."

XXVI
December 30.-31. 1931

SENATOR JIM REED presented two witnesses to the court, then told Judge Albert Reeves that, "I think we are through," and Sid Roach saw every one of the 12 men in the jury relax in their seats. The strain of the trial, now in its fifth week, showed in their faces

But, Reed continued, "Though, unlikely, I will leave the way clear for further testimony until morning."

Sid, however, did not relax. The indigestion—or whatever the hell it was—had returned, but he had no choice other than ignoring the discomfort. He had to begin preparing for his portion of the closing statement Senator Reed had assigned to him.

E.L. Williams, a hydraulic engineer, said from the witness chair that he had discussed with Robert Snyder Sr the possibility of using the Hahatonka spring to generate enough electricity to furnish the demands of the estate with an additional $16,000 worth of power that could be sold. Electrical Engineer W.J. Squires of Kansas City verified Williams' statement, saying that it would have been possible to sell or utilize all the power the spring was capable of producing.

W.L. Drummond, an expert on land development projects, talked about the effect a thirty-foot draw down of the lake level would have on the property. He said it was impractical and impossible to properly landscape the shoreline in such a situation.

Senator Reed, Counselor John Wilson of Kansas City and Sid Roach took a turn at reading into court records official notations of the Smithsonian Institution and U.S. government geological reports describing caves, springs and lakes in the natural resources present in Hahatonka. Several large maps showing the condemned land in Camden and neighboring counties for the Lake of the Ozarks created by building Bagnell Dam were introduced by Reed.

Walne told Judge Reeves court that the Union Electric side of the trial would probably take ten days to two weeks to present.

Sid Roach could detect no thrill from members of the jury at the announcement.

NOT GIVING UP THE FLOOR EASILY, Senator Reed read several more reports on the scenery at Hahatonka into the record. Union Electric chief counselor Walter Walne also read some official State reports about Missouri springs. One report stated that the Hahatonka spring was the eleventh in size in the state. Reed then relinquished the floor to the other side and rested his case.

Walne began by repeating the claim he had made at the beginning of the trial, that Union Electric owed, "Not one dime to the Snyders."

He then asked and received permission from Judge Albert Reeves to recall Robert Snyder Jr to the witness stand.

Walne began the questioning of Robert Jr with inquiries into the financial condition of the Snyder family since the death of Robert Snyder Sr in an automobile accident in Kansas City in 1906. Robert Jr, from his notes, gave detailed answers to all the questions.

When the afternoon session began, Reed asked Sid Roach to assume the role as chief counselor, complaining of slight indigestion himself. Sid knew the feeling, but he agreed to assume the senator's role.

The electric company's first witness was Edward Rudolph of Eldon, Missouri. He said his title was Hydraulic Engineer and that he was employed by Stone and Webster, builders of Bagnell Dam. His job, Rudolph said, was studying the flow of the Osage River before the dam was constructed on the river. When construction started, he was transferred from an office at the company headquarters in Boston, Massachusetts to the dam site.

"It would be fair then to call yourself an expert on the water conditions in the Osage River, would it not?" Walter Walne asked.

"That was my job," Rudolph said.

"Tells us then what you have found out about the water levels in the river and what effect those levels have on the Osage River Dam and on the levels of the lake created by the dam," Walne said.

Rudolph produced charts he had made on the water flow in the Osage River and with rainfall in the river basin.

"What information have you gathered on abnormal conditions of rainfall on water levels in the Osage River?" Walne asked.

Rudolph showed charts he had made concerning extreme flood conditions in Kansas in 1928 and how those conditions affected the Osage.

Judge Albert Reeves adjourned court for the day at this point, telling the jury and instructing Edward Rudolph and both counsels to return the next day, New Year's Day, for a half-day of testimony.

Sid Roach gathered his notes to give to the senator. Depending on whose indigestion was the worse, Sid preferred the senator take a shot at Rudolph's testimony, but thinking he would have to prepare himself to cross examine the engineer just in case.

Happy New Year, Sid thought sarcastically.

1932

Nell Donnelly   Paul Scheidt   Lacy Browning

Martin Depew—Marshall Deputy   Ethel Depew

Charles Mele   Walter Werner

XXVII

JUDGE ALBERT REEVES tapped the federal court into session at nine o'clock, January 1, 1932, for what he promised would be only a half-day's session. The desire to finish the five-week trial was evident in the judge's attitude.

Senator Reed was still indisposed and told Sid Roach he would wait until Monday to return to court to cross examine Edward Rudolph. Sid was relieved in his mind at that knowledge, though his own indigestion had not eased overnight.

Walne, chest thrust forward, walked directly to the front railing of the jury box. "You will recall that the witness, Edward Rudolph, is an engineer whose sole responsibility was to record the water levels of the Osage River, before and after construction of that mighty dam built by his company, Stone and Webster, the country's premier builder of dams and hydro-electric projects. We could find no one who has more knowledge or recorded information about those water levels than Mister Rudolph."

Walne turned to his witness.

"Now, Mister Rudolph, tell the jury and the court what affect are we talking about on the shoreline of the lake with these different water levels in the Osage River?"

Rudolph produced charts on the spillway capacity of Bagnell Dam, the backwater influence on Hahatonka Lake and on Hahatonka Spring, explaining each chart as it was presented to the court.

"What affect would these rising and lowering water levels have on the shoreline of Hahatonka Lake? Would we expect acres and acres of mud flats?" Walne asked, strutting to the front of the jury.

"No," Rudolph said, "there would be sand and gravel beaches on that shoreline, not mud flats."

Sid Roach noted how Walne was using Rudolph's testimony to contradict their own claims of shoreline destruction and ugliness.

"If the owners of Hahatonka Lake were genuinely concerned about river water invading the lake and allowing it to become part of the public waterway of the lake created by the dam, is there an easy and inexpensive way of preventing that?" Walne asked.

"Oh, yes, quite easily," Rudolph said. "A boom could be constructed without much expense or effort to keep boats out of Hahatonka Lake."

"And how would such a boom be constructed?" Walne wanted Rudolph to tell the jury.

"Why, by lashing logs together, end to end," Rudolph said.

Judge Reeves adjourned the short session of court at this point.

Rudolph had testified in direct conflict with testimony Senator Reed had extracted from witnesses he had placed on the stand.

What a way to start a new year, Sid Roach thought.

"WHAT'S YOUR ESTIMATE of how it's going?" LeRoy Snyder asked Robert Jr.

The three Snyder brothers and their families were gathered in the Governors Hotel in Jefferson City for New Year's

Day, deciding not to make the trek to Hahatonka, weather conditions being unsettled.

"I have confidence in the jury," Robert said. "I don't think they like the electric company's lawyer. He's abrasive and condescending. He's made some damaging points, however. The engineer, Rudolph, tried to make us look foolish by not constructing what he called a 'boom' across the lake. We've already found out how impossible that would be with the rising and falling of the Niangua River."

"The Senator missed all of that testimony," Kenneth Snyder said to his brothers and their families. "I hope he's able to contradict it."

"The senator has many projects going," LeRoy said. "The kidnapping of the rich dress manufacturing woman, running for President. He says he has to go to Jackson Day in Springfield next Saturday. I hope he has enough time in between all those other projects for our case."

"Plus he's been sick a couple of days," Lillian Ethel, Le-Roy's wife said. "Is he being paid by the day?"

"He gives us a bill," Robert said.

"Everyone needs some time off," Robert's wife, Mary, said. "Robert, you're spending too much time on this. Why don't we put the trial aside for the rest of New Year's Day and just talk about us. Mary Louise, tell us about your and Kenneth's daughters."

"Wait," Kenneth Snyder said, laying a hand on his wife's arm. "One more comment about the senator. I drove him to Kansas City the day after Nell Donnelly was kidnapped, after he was unsuccessful in renting an airplane to fly him there. Let me tell you, the man is a walking history book about what's going on in Missouri and the country. He is by far the most knowledgeable man I know . . . well, with the exception of you, Bob, with all your collection of books about the area and the state. What the two of you don't know isn't worth knowing. We have to trust him and have faith in him. If he should get the nomination for President—which he won't because Roosevelt has it sewed up—I would vote for President Reed."

Robert Jr's wife Mary held two hands in the air. "Court's adjourned," she said. "Let's find a good restaurant and have dinner."

Slowly and reluctantly the others rose and made preparations with coats, gloves and scarfs to follow Mary Bowen Snyder.

She saw to her husband's winter wraps, pulled the collar of his coat up around his face, looked him in the eyes.

And worried.

SENATOR JAMES A. REED stormed to the front of the courtroom, stood facing the witness Edward Rudolph and said, "Tell me, Mister Rudolph, who decides the water level of the Lake of the Ozarks that was created in 1930 by the building of this huge, thirty-five million dollar dam on the Osage River."

"The engineers in charge of the dam," Rudolph answered.

"Engineers like you," Reed said.

"Yes."

"And you report to whom?"

"My supervisor is . . ."

"No, no, I'm not looking for names. I'm looking for titles. And companies. You report to the electric company? To Union Electric?"

"I report to Stone and Webster who built the dam . . ."

"Will Stone and Webster decide the level of the water in the lake, say, next year? Or ten years from now?"

"No, of course not. The electric company, Union Electric Company will decide the water level . . ."

"And they have the final say so about the water level?"

"Yes, that will be based on the information we provide to them, the charts, the information they paid us to assemble . . ."

"And the decision about the water level in the lake will be decided solely on the information you have gathered about one summer in Kansas? The rainfall there? You have charts and information about the water level if an abnormal amount of rain should fall in Missouri? On the Lake of the Ozarks?"

"No, but it can be extrapolated . . ."

"And the decision on the lake level, on when to open the spillways and how much to open them will always be based on mathematical charts of rainfall? Never on what the cost might be to the generation of electricity? On whether to shut off the generators because of a low water level in the lake?"

"Well, I suppose that would enter into it," Rudolph said.

"And that decision would be made by Union Electric?" now facing the jurors.

"Yes."

"And not by the North American Company? Union Electric is a subsidiary of the North American Edison Company that is in turn a subsidiary of the North American Company, is it not?"

"That is my understanding," Rudolph said.

"So your charts and flood information in Kansas would not be the only basis for deciding the water level in the lake?"

"The operation of the dam would be pretty much the same

no matter who makes the decisions," Rudolph said. "That's because decision will be made based on the economic facts at the time."

"But you don't know that for sure, do you?" Reed said, turning from the jury to confront Rudolph again. "The decision on electrical generation and when to curtail it because of the water levels in the lake would have to go through three levels of management, would it not? And that would be the major question before those levels of management, would it not? Whether to shut down the generation of electricity they are being paid for and not decided on what a thirty-foot draw down would do to Hahatonka or any other shoreline of the lake?"

"Shuttting down the generators would be practical only on rare occasions," Rudolph said.

"Who would consider what is practical?" Reed asked. "What level of management would decide that? The fact is, we're talking about draw downs that could destroy beautiful, irreplaceable scenery. And we're talking about a huge, multi-layered corporation with assets of over $600,000,000 that would make decisions based on the economic effect on that corporation, not on rarities of the weather.

"I have no more questions with this witness."

UNION ELECTRIC CHIEF COUNSEL Walter Walne had his witnesses scheduled for the next several days. R. G. Strand-berg, another Stone and Webster engineer took the stand to repeat essentially the same material that Edward Rudolph had.

Reed declined to cross examine Strandberg.

Next Walne called two former members of the Camden County Board of Equalization, Robert T. Brown and Robert Jacobs told the court that Robert Snyder Jr had appeared before the board in an effort to have the valuation of Hahatonka reduced from $60,000 to $40,000 for tax purposes.

Senator Reed on cross examination asked both the men if they remembered everyone who appeared before the board. Both said they did not, but they did remember Robert appearing before them.

Walne asked the next witness he placed before the jury, Cecil Jackson, a guide in the Hahatonka area to describe the roads and the caves in Hahatonka.

Jeff R. Montgomery, attorney in the corporation department of the Secretary of State's office read the last several year's annual report of the Snyder Estate.

The jurors all showed great relief when Judge Reeves adjourned court for the day.

JAMES R. PAGE, Jackson County prosecuting attorney, laid the paper in front of Circuit Court Judge Thomas Seehorn.

"That's what we have right now," Page said. "We need to get these people into court as soon as possible while the public still remembers how Mrs. Donnelly—Kansas City's best known and best liked woman—was brutally snatched from in front of her home and held captive for two days for ransom."

The judge read the list:

Paul Scheidt, dairyman, Bonner Springs, Kansas, 29, rented house where Mrs. Donnelly and chauffeur, George Blair, were held captive. IN CUSTODY

William Lacy Browning, 42, farmer, planned the abduction with Martin and Ethel Depew. IN CUSTODY

Charles Mele, Italian-born, gambler, assaulted Mrs. Donnelly in back seat of her automobile. IN CUSTODY

Ethel Depew, wife of Martin Depew. Former nurse for Paul Donnelly, December, 1930, helped plan kidnapping with Browning and Depew. Kansas City Detective Robert Cole arrested her in Pennsylvania—returned to Kansas City. by Mrs. Frances Trowbridge, Kansas City Police woman IN CUSTODY

Martin Depew, (Marshall Depew, Martin Deputy, William Martin), Kansas City detectives in New York City following clues and reports, leader of kidnappers, identified by Mrs. Donnelly from photographs, NOT IN CUSTODY

Judge Seehorn said, "What are you suggesting?"

"Take them to the Grand Jury, get indictments. We could go with this guy Scheidt. How soon can we schedule a trial for him if he's indicted? He's not going to confess. We've threatened him with the death penalty, but he's sticking to his claim of innocence. I think the others will confess if we trade a confession for life instead of death penalty."

"What about the woman?" the judge asked.

"She's sticking with the not guilty plea. We don't have confirmation from Mrs. Donnelly on her as Mrs. Donnelly never saw her after being kidnapped. The man Browning claims he can put her in on the planning, but he'll be a confessed kidnapper if he appears in court. The jury will know that."

"The Italian? Mele?"

"Had nothing to do with it, he says. No confession. Hard case." Page told him.

"We'll have to try him?"

"Yeah, be a big mistake for him. He's the one tried to stuff Mrs. Donnelly's head in a bag. She can identify him. He was smart he'd take the plea."

"You have a deposition from Mrs. Donnelly and the Negro chauffeur?" the judge wanted to know.

"Not yet. We will have those within a week or so."

"Here's what I will do," Judge Seehorn said. "Depending on the Grand Jury's indictments, I'll set aside some dates for court action against Scheidt and this Mele next month. I'll wait until you've decided about the woman after the depositions and after the three confessions and sentences. The other man with all the names? Depew? You may never see him again."

"Police Chief Siegfried feels confident about finding him. If they do, and if he doesn't confess, he'll hang."

"The chief should be feeling pretty good about all this," Judge Seehorn said. "His department took loads of criticism over getting Lazia involved."

Page smiled. "Chief Siegfried says it was blown out of proportion and the newspapers got it all wrong. Might say he's in kind of a denial."

Judge Seehorn nodded his head. "I don't blame him."

NELL DONNELLY led her dog gingerly along the icy-crusted pathway between the Donnelly home and the Reed home. Senator Reed joined her leading his dog, Jeff. His cigar lifted heavy blue smoke into the frosty air.

"I received a subpoena for you," he told her. "You've been called before the Jackson County Grand Jury on January 5."

"This is in relation to what exactly?" she asked.

"They want you to testify in connection with the kidnapping. I got a subpoena and so did your chauffeur, George Blair. Jim Taylor and Police Chief Lewis Siegfried both got called."

"What do I tell them?"

"Just answer their questions. Page, the prosecutor will do the interview. He's no friend of mine—we clashed during the Bennett trial—but he's fair. I think they want to indict the guy who rented his house to the gang. And the other one they arrested, Browning. I'm sure Page will try and convince the grand jury that the wife, Ethel Depew, should be tried. I hear that her attorney, George Charno, has offered to have her testify before the Grand Jury, but Page said she wouldn't be called. He thinks he has enough evidence to hold her."

"Where is she now?"

"She's being held while they're trying to provide bond of $20,000 that Judge Southern set when he granted a writ of habeas corpus."

"It's getting complicated," Nell said, then reached down to help her German Shepherd shake some ice off its foot. "I don't know anything about this Ethel Depew. I can't tell them anything."

"Just answer their questions, that's all you can do."

"If the grand jury indicts them does that mean they'll be tried in court?"

"Page has asked Justice Dougherty to continue preliminary hearings for the three of them. They'll decide about the trials after the Grand Jury has completed their investigation."

She was silent.

"How's David?" Reed asked. "How's my little partner?"

"Come over tonight, we'll have a drink and you can see how he's growing. Paul has taken back to bed, medicine, a nurse and a shot to warm him up. He'll be asleep."

SID ROACH found himself in charge of the Snyder case the next day when Senator Reed returned to Kansas City for health reasons and to prepare for his speech at the Jackson Day Banquet in Springfield on Saturday.

The next witness for Union Electric, George Mann, said he had lived in the Hahatonka area for 40 years. Carl Crocker, the Camdenton attorney with the electric company's counsel, asked Mann about the caves at Hahatonka.

"Holes in the ground," Mann said.

"Did you see any beauty in the caves? Any particular one?" Crocker asked.

"I didn't see any beauty in them," Mann said.

"How about Bridal Cave? Did people enjoy that?"

"There was no road up there," Mann said. "People had to walk a couple of miles to get there."

Sid remembered their side had presented evidence that a road to Bridal Cave existed.

"You worked for a woman, Mary George, who leased an area on the shore of the Hahatonka lake, did you not?" Crocker asked.

"Yeah. I rented boats to people who stayed there. Twenty-five, fifty cents a day. People went out on the little lake to fish. Fishing wasn't very good. Once in a while some-one caught a Rainbow."

"Were people who came to the camp restricted to just the camp area?"

"Nah, people went wherever they wanted to. Walked all over the place," Mann said.

"What kind of valuation would you place on Hahatonka?" Crocker asked.

"Except for the central part where the lake and the castle are I'd say it was worth about five dollars an acre," Mann said. "I wouldn't know how to put a value on the central part of it.

To start the cross examination, Sid asked Mann what his duty was when he worked for Mrs. Mary George at the camp she rented from the Snyder Estate.

"Different things," Mann said.

"You rented boats?" Sid asked.

"For a while," Mann said.

"What year or years was that?"

"It was about 1923. Maybe a couple of years after that."

"And have you ever been paid to place a value on property?" from Sid.

"No"

"No more questions," Sid said, turning away from the witness.

XXVIII

SENATOR REED received a hearty welcome from the Andrew Jackson Day rally on January 8, 1932, in Springfield. For two hours the former senator blasted the Republicans, especially President Herbert Hoover.

"I can't even describe how opposed I am to the policies of our President," he declared and received a loud round of applause.

"And how about old Artie Hyde, our secretary of agriculture? Artie doesn't know enough about agriculture to tell the difference between a bull calf and a heifer."

More cheers.

"I am greatly disappointed in the destruction of this country's sixth largest industry. I'm talking about the brewing and bottling of alcoholic beverages," Reed announced. The crowd especially liked his take on the question of Prohibition. "What the residents of our state want in that regard should be decided by the people of our state, not the federal government. Police power should be returned to the states instead of federal officers snooping in our ice boxes."

More cheers.

As long as he criticized Hoover and Agriculture Secretary Arthur Hyde and denounced the national policy of Prohibition, the crowd cheered enthusiastically.

"That so-called League of Nations is a worthless tribunal," he said, and the attitude of the large crowd changed completely. The senator had obviously struck a tender spot in the hearts of the crowd. Undeterred, he continued to rail against the world court.

It became plain to the more than 2500 men and women in attendance that Reed was announcing his candidacy for President when he told them, "I am now speaking for James A. Reed."

A man wearing a tag that said he was from St. Louis reminded him after the speech that Roosevelt support had the backing of several leaders who thought that, "It's time Missouri Democrats rallied around a winner."

Most who talked with him, though, assured him that they owed, "Jim Reed a complimentary vote and would vote for him as long as it is politically expedient to do so." They would not desert him, they said, unless it was shown he could not achieve the nomination.

Delegates from Kansas City expressed disappointment to Reed following his speech that the city had lost its bid to hold the Democratic convention there in June. Chicago had outbid the city, $200,000 to $150,000 to hold the convention.

"Jim Reed as candidate for President will get along just as well in Chicago as he would at home," proclaimed a Kansas City banker named Kemper who Reed recognized when he approached the senator and shook his hand. "You have a way with you of getting what you want."

The man said that Kansas City delegates would concentrate their efforts on nominating Reed as its Favorite Son.

A man Reed did not know said, "He's right about that," indicating the banker who was moving on through the crowd. "I see you met the leader of the Kansas City delegation."

Reed looked toward the crowd of people and saw Tom Pendergast looking back at him.

"Yes," Reed said, "I know the Kansas City delegation leader."

THE WEEK PASSED QUICKLY for Sid Roach and the jury. Senator Reed had returned and had engaged the artist from Washington University in St. Louis, W. H. Wurepel, who had painted the mural that hung in the state capitol building. He called Hahatonka, "Exquisite before and more magnificent now," after the incursion of lake waters and cutting of trees in the area. He said the cutting of the trees on Hahatonka, "Increased the grandeur."

After viewing photographs handed him by Walter Walne showing the stumps left on Hahatonka by the electric company's tree cutters, Wurepel said the scenes were, "More beautiful," than scenes of the same places before the trees were cut, adding, "If they mar the beauty for some persons, those persons are small-minded. I don't see the stumps."

"What a man gets out of a scene depends on what?" Walter Walne asked.

"Himself," Wurepel said.

"What is beauty?" Walne asked.

"Beauty is a thing that is in you," Wurepel told the court. "It's absolutely a spiritual thought. I think every one of us has a sense of beauty. It largely depends on our attitude. Beauty is around us everywhere if we can see it, feel it."

On cross examination, Reed showed the witness a photograph of the picnic grounds by Hahatonka lake covered with debris washed in by invading lake waters.

"The picture is perfectly ugly," Wurepel said, "But I didn't see that condition in the area."

"Tell me, Professor, what makes those pictures of stumps and debris more nobler than pictures of the beautiful trees that stood there before the hundred or so tree cutters chopped them down," Reed wanted to know.

"Well," the artist said, "I could give you a three-hour lecture on that."

Reed snapped, "You could give me a thirty-hour lecture and I wouldn't understand any of it."

Testimony of a dozen witnesses for Union Electric Light and Power Company took up the next week, the eighth week of trial. How alert, how inquisitive were the members of the jury after nearly forty days listening to witnesses and the two lead attorneys battle each other over minor points of law the jurors didn't fully understand?

Sid Roach wondered about that because at times his own attention began to wander. He straightened in his chair and fingered the handful of sharpened pencils and the few pens he kept handy.

Rex Allaman of Forsyth, Missouri, president of the Ozarks Boosters' League and secretary of the Ozarks Playground Association valued Hahatonka at $75,000 before Bagnell was constructed and $100,000 after.

Kansas City Real Estate man and operator of a resort in Arkansas, Walter Eaton, testified that the Snyders' property in Camden County had been worth between $75,000 and $100,000 before parts of it were inundated by Lake of the Ozarks water. Now, he said, the property value had increased between 20 and 25 percent.

Senator Reed asked the witness frequently about the injury to the estate's value by lowering the water level of the lake and exposing mud flats.

"That would be injurious to the beauty of the estate and depreciate its value," Eaton admitted.

Reed objected to Walne's introduction of taxes for the Snyder estate for several years on the grounds they were immaterial to the, "Question at hand."

W.L. Nelson, former clerk of the Camden County Court, testified that Robert Snyder Jr had appeared before the board of equalization asking to have the assessed value of the estate reduced after it was increased from, "$30,000 or $40,000 to $60,000," in, "1922 or 1923."

"Is it unusual for persons to ask to have their assessed valuations on their property reduced?" Reed asked Nelson.

"No," the former clerk admitted.

William Buchholz, Kansas City attorney, testified that Robert and LeRoy Snyder had asked him to introduce them to Governor Caulfield of Missouri. Reed asked one question of him, had he looked at the material they carried into the governor's office. He said he had. Later.

Two engineers, John Bargenbrook and N. W. Fendley testified about maps and measurements they had made of caves in the area.

The pace of the eight-week trial had slowed. Confrontations between Union Electric's chief counsel, Walter Walne of Houston, Texas, and the Snyder family's lead attorney, former U. S. Senator James Reed, were less frequent.

That would change with the introduction of three witnesses for the electric company.

XXIX

JOHN T. WOODRUFF, Springfield attorney, banker and businessman, gave the court an evaluation of Hahatonka lower than the million and a half dollars the Snyders were claiming. When Reed's turn to cross examine came, he asked if Woodruff had offered to testify for the Snyders. Woodruff said he had not.

"As I recall, Senator, it was you who invited me to your hotel room to have a drink with you," Woodruff said.

"Let's review this incident," Reed said. "I admit to taking a drink of whisky once in a while and if it's good whisky, I might invite a gentleman to share it with me. On this particular occasion we're discussing, I don't recall offering an invitation to you. You're sure about that?"

"It's possible I may have come to your hotel room without an invitation," Woodruff said.

"And is it possible you made the offer to testify for the Snyder Estate instead of the offer being made to you?" Reed asked.

"My memory is pretty clear on that."

"In that case," Reed said, "Let me dismiss this witness and call for rebuttal from John Wilson who is a member of our counsel."

After Wilson was sworn in and took the place of Woodruff , Reed said, "Tell the court about your experience with Mr. Woodruff who preceded you on the stand."

"Mr. Woodruff approached me with an offer to testify for the Snyder Estate in the Hahatonka trial for $500 and a contingent fee."

"Mr. Woodruff approached you, without an invitation, to testify for the Snyder Estate for financial considerations?" Reed asked.

"Yes, sir, he approached me without invitation."

"But you declined Mr. Woodruff's offer?" Reed asked.

"I considered it for a few weeks before declining it," Wilson told Reed and the court.

"And this William T. Woodruff is the same William T. Woodruff who joined two gamblers in the game of chance on where the new county seat would be located after the previous county seat of Linn Creek was flooded?"

"The same."

"And those three gentlemen waited until the Missouri Department of Transportation located the intersection of two major highways in Camden County and they purchased the farm land there and established the present county seat of that county on their land."

"Mr. Woodruff was part of the trio who established the city of Camdenton and sold lots there for the new county seat," Wilson said.

"Dismissed," Reed said and turned to Walter Walne who made a few notes and called his next witness.

Former U. S. Congressman William Willett, Jr, a real estate broker and attorney from New York, said in answer to Walne's question about the worth of Hahatonka that he considered it to be approximately $100,000 before the creation of the Lake of the Ozarks, but had been enhanced by about 25 percent by the building of Bagnell Dam.

"Were you a member of Congress?" Reed asked.

"My last term in Congress was 1911," Willett said.

"Other than routine service in Congress, anything else you want to tell the court?"

"No."

"Is it not a fact that you have been convicted of a felony and you served time in Sing Sing prison in New York?" Reed asked.

The courtroom became silent, then a slight hum from the crowd that packed the room, anticipating an end to the contentious trial. Jurors leaned forward in their seats and Sid Roach scribbled rapidly on his papers.

Willett tried to appear unrattled, but he shuffled briefly in his seat.

"That is true," he admitted. "I served a short part of a sentence in state prison before I was fully pardoned by the governor of the State of New York."

"I need nothing else from this witness," Reed said by way of dismissing the witness.

The hoped for dramatic introduction of the next witness by Walter Walne had somewhat diminished by the admission of the previous witness's record of prison. Despite that, the courtroom's observors and the jurors became more attentive when Union Electric president, Louis Egan was introduced to the court.

Egan sat in the witness chair imperiously, not even looking at the former friend Robert Snyder Jr he had threatened to keep in court for seven years if the Snyders did not accept his offer of $28,000 for the 150 acres of Hahatonka that had been taken for expansion of the Lake of the Ozarks.

He answered Walne's questions about his position, about the company, about the dam and how he was unaware when he made the offer for condemnation that the water would invade the Hahatonka property.

Reed would not let that pass. On cross-examination he asked Egan just when he did become aware of the expected lake level.

"It would have been after June, 1929," Egan replied. "I was present at a session of the Missouri Public Service Commission that year when A. L. Snyder, an engineer for Stone and Webster, said that the water would not invade Hahatonka."

"And you believed him?" Reed shot back.

"Yes, that was my belief at that time." Egan said.

"Well, then, tell me, Mr. President, why was it that your company attorneys for Union Electric Light and Power Company of St. Louis, Missouri, placed notices in the area newspapers about the construction that was proposed at the time, warning area residents about the water levels of the lake?"

"As a precaution," Egan said.

"And why was it that the Snyder family, in 1924, knew that the lake waters would flood their beautiful estate when they had nothing to do with the construction, yet you, the president of the company paying for the building of the dam, did not know what the final water level of the lake you created would be?"

"I heard the testimony in the Public Service Commission," Egan said, "and had no reason to think otherwise."

"Your company, the Union Electric Light and Power Company of St. Louis, Missouri, is a subsidiary of what national corporation?" Reed asked.

"Union Electric Light and Power Company is a subsidiary of the North American Edison Company."

"And the North American Edison Company is a subsidiary of the North American Company, correct?" Reed asked.

"That is correct."

"Now, counting the Union Electric Light and Power Company as one subsidiary of those two corporations, how many other subsidiaries are there?"

Egan said, "I don't know the exact number."

"Is it more than ten?" Reed asked.

"I think so, yes."

"Is it more than twenty?"

"As I testified, I'm not sure of the exact number," was Egan's answer.

"Well, let's just say there are more than ten subsidiaries, maybe twenty, maybe more. And each of those subsidiaries could ask for electrical power that is generated at the Bagnell Dam to be distributed to them, is that correct?"

"If they are on our distribution network they could ask and would probably become a customer."

"And if they were not on your distribution network, you could put them on could you not?" Reed asked.

"If it was economically feasible we could."

"If you at Union Electric Light and Power Company were ordered by the North American Edison Company who in turn was ordered by the North American Company to add a subsidiary to your network you would do so, would you not?"

"That is a hypothetical question," Egan said.

"Bagnell Dam could end up being an electrical generating and distribution facility for any number of North American Company subsidiaries is the correct answer to any question." Reed said, and dismissed the witness.

Dr. Arthur W. Nelson, Democratic nominee for governor of Missouri in 1924 told the court that in his opinion the Lake of the Ozarks had enhanced the value of Hahatonka.

Reed asked him what he thought a thirty-foot draw down of the lake level would do to the beauty of Hahatonka in summer or in winter.

"An excessive draw down would detract from its beauty," he said. "More so in summer than winter."

Walne rose to tell the court and Judge Albert Reeves that the counsel for Union Electric rested.

Reed brought his rebuttal witnesses to the stand, one by one. Oscar Jones who had worked on the Snyder Estate for 25 years and Floyd Roofener, a Hahatonka employee, testified that the water on the new lake at Hahatonka was frequently chocolate brown and the draw down of the lake level exposed slime and debris on the lake shore.

Frank Decou, former chief warden for the game and fish department, described eight of the most outstanding springs in Missouri and said the Hahatonka spring before inundation was more beautiful and more magnificent than all the others in the state.

Wes Einfrey, presiding judge of the Camden County court in 1924, said that Robert Snyder Jr did not appear before the board of equalization or the board of tax appeals that year. John McCrory, presiding judge in 1923, said that Snyder did not appear that year.

Two witnesses who were with the Knights of Columbus in 1919 when they visited Hahatonka with a view of purchasing the property took the stand. W. V. O'Donnell, St. Louis insurance agent, said that Robert Snyder Jr expressed no interest in selling Hahatonka, but that he would submit a bid of $500,000 to the family if the organization wanted to make it.

Scott Myers, a member of the Knights of Columbus committee, testified for Union Electric that Robert Snyder made a firm offer to sell the property for $500,000.

Both sides now rested their cases. Groundwork for the final arguments would begin the next week, January 26, 1932.

That's when the real fireworks between two of the leading attorneys in the country would begin.

XXX

JUDGE ALBERT REEVES noticed two differences in the courtroom that he had not observed before this day: the courtroom was overly packed with people and Snyder family attorney Sid Roach had an unhealthy pallor to his face.

The judge called one of the bailiffs to the podium before gaveling the court into session. With people standing two and three deep around the inside walls, he feared the atmosphere would be oppressive inside for the participants and the jury. "Give us some air," he instructed the bailiff.

"It's quite chilly outside, your honor," the bailiff protested slightly.

"Better that than having no air inside to breathe," Judge Reeves said. The bailiff talked with two other officers serving the court on that day and they began going around the court-room opening the windows. Those standing near the windows raised their coat collars and buttoned their coats against the invading January air.

On his other matter of concern, the judge beckoned Sid Roach forward. The Union Electric Counselors, Carl Crocker and Edgar Shook, rose from their seats, curious and expectant. Whatever the judge was going to tell Sid Roach, surely he would have to tell them, also. What they heard was the judge asking Sid Roach if he was ill or in discomfort.

"Only from the cold air," Sid Roach said, partly in jest.

Reeves opened the session and gave the floor to Roach to begin the Snyder's final argument.

Sid Roach began: "You have heard men of intelligence, of sophistication and sound judgment tell you of the beauty that has been spoiled and diminished by the influx of outside waters never meant to be on this exceptional spot on earth. This special place called Hahatonka. This land of Laughing Waters as the first residents of Nature's best work called it.

"These are not men with any purpose or reason to appear here and express their wonder of this place except to bemoan the destruction that has invaded it and to tell you the extent of its former beauty and of its demise as a perfect gentleman's estate.

"These are men of experience, men who have seen the mighty Alps, the Mediterranean shores, the natural wonders of the world. And they have made that comparison to you, those wonders that ranked with the ones in Hahatonka."

Roach spoke with elegance, with passion, emphasizing his points with gestures and facial expressions. Judge Reeves noticed the pallor had disappeared, replaced by a redness that bordered on alarming. But Roach went on listing one by one the points Senator Reed had spent days pointing out to the jury. He named names, Gutzon Borglum, sculptor of a mighty feature of former Presidents' likenesses on a mountain in South Dakota. Walter Williams, esteemed president of the University of Missouri. Four former governors of the state. Person after person who had appeared before the jury telling of the beauty of Hahatonka.

Roach excoriated those who thought so little of the prime estate as to say the dirty, filthy, muddy waters of the nearby river that were forced onto that lovely land had actually improved this remarkable phenomenon of Nature.

"If we were to average the value of Hahatonka that has been expressed by the eight witnesses we have brought forward, we would arrive at a value of $1,358,000 and that would be the fair market value of Hahatonka before this inundation occurred."

When he rested, Roach looked completely exhausted. The judge called a short recess, thinking that might save Roach from collapsing.

Mary Bowen Snyder looked with concern at Lillian Ethel and Mary Louise Snyder who had accompanied her to observe the final days of the trial. They acknowledged her apprehensiveness and all three glanced along the bench where they sat, toward the family of Sid Roach. They too showed concern about their relative's obvious discomfort.

Senator Reed spoke briefly with Roach. The two of them rose and left the courtroom. Roach's family left their seats on the bench and followed out the door. Reed had said something to the judge before leaving about getting his overcoat and the judge said thirty minutes would be allowed.

"I'm worried about Sid," Lillian Ethel Snyder said to the other Snyder women when they put their heads together. Mary Bowen looked at her husband, Robert Snyder Jr, hunched forward in his seat behind the counselors' table.

"Yes," she said. "Him too."

"HARD TIMES and farm problems are over," said Carl Crocker, Camdenton attorney on the Union Electric team of counselors, as he raised both arms in a "Hallelujah," type of gesture.

"Why do I say that?" he asked the jurors, facing them, sarcasm spreading across his features. "Why, we've just been informed that the world famous Gutzon Borglum, praised by the counselor for the Snyder family as being intelligent, sophisticated, knowledgeable, one who has travelled the world, has pronounced that farmland in the Ozark hills is worth $250 an acre based on the value he claims for the rock-strewn cliffs at this place called Laughing Waters.

"Who's laughing about that?

"What we're here for is an honest inquiry into the facts. We have been reminded over and over of the prejudice of the other side against Union Electric Light and Power Company, but no decision should be made based on small-minded prejudice."

Using a map of the Snyder land in Camden County showing the acres taken to make way for the Lake of the Ozarks, Crocker said that, "Based on the one and one-half million dollar demand made by the Snyder family, Union Electric is being asked to pay $9,362.12 an acre for the property condemned."

Senator Reed, who had suffered some illness over the past few days, sat now quietly hunkered inside his overcoat protecting him from the chill in the room.

Edgar Shook, not as amusing as Crocker, read off a list of offers the Snyders had entertained for the estate.

He then went into the details of the law of eminent domain under which Union Electric had acquired much of the land now covered by the lake of the Ozarks.

Groundwork for the two major figures in the courtroom had been completed. Anticipation was rampant amongst the people packing the courtroom for the next day.

But not for Sid Roach.

"HEART ATTACK," Mary Bowen Snyder told her husband when he returned to the hotel after court had been adjourned. "Sid looked so awful when he left. It has been such a terrible strain on him, this trial. I wish it was over."

"Almost," Robert Jr said, sipping the hot tea she had prepared for him.

"This is taking such a toll on all of you," she said, laying a hand on his shoulder. "It isn't worth it. Sid's family all looked so worried. They took him to St. Mary's Hospital where his condition was pronounced as dangerous."

"Sid hasn't looked good for the last week or two," Robert said. "Sure hope he pulls through and recovers."

"I don't want you to fall into that same category, Robert," she said. "Please don't worry so about what happens inside the courtroom. Don't let it affect your life."

"I just need some rest," he said. "Another week should do it. Then we can relax, maybe go down to Hahatonka, weather permitting, build a fire, read a good book. Hold some pretty woman's hand."

He took her hand in his, felt the warmth there and clasped it tighter.

What she felt was an icy palm and frigid fingers. More worry.

XXXI

"ANYONE MAKING ANY DEMONSTRATION whatsoever will be brought before the court immediately by the bailiffs," Judge Albert Reeves said, opening the jam-packed courtroom on the morning of January 27, 1932.

People from all walks of life filled the seats and stacked the walls of the courtroom and the halls leading into it. The audience consisted of, not just locals, but business people, attorneys, medical professionals and merely the curious from as far away as Chicago, St. Louis and Kansas City.

The stage was set for a showdown between the two legal giants: Walter Walne of Houston, Texas, lead counsel for the Union Electric Light and Power Company of St. Louis and the esteemed three time Senator from Missouri, James Reed of Kansas City.

Walne, dressed every bit the part of a well-to-do Texas lawyer, stepped in front of the jury, chest forward, eyes staring at each member, shirt white enough to reflect their images, and wasted no time nor no small words of greeting to the jury.

"The only issue for you to decide is the fair market value of Hahatonka on December 16, 1930, before it was touched and its value afterward," he began. "For 21 years a diligent effort has been made by the owners to sell this property. Four times an attempt has been made to sell to the State of Missouri for a park, but always the effort has failed although the greatest sum ever asked was $300,000. Four times the state legislature refused to buy the property, the last time it was defeated 26 to 6 because the state senate could not agree on a price that was just one-fifth of what is now sought.

"A large number of other attempts to sell the Snyders' estate failed. They never asked for more than $500,000 until condemnation proceedings started by Union Electric to build the Bagnell Dam hydro-electric project on the Osage River."

Walne grasped both lapels of his expensively-tailored jacket and leaned even further toward the jury. "All this sales talk brought into this courtroom in an effort to obtain one and one-half million dollars for this property is the same that has been used for more than twenty years in an effort to market this estate."

He glanced toward Senator Reed who's face showed clearly his opinion of the lead counselor's words.

"Don't interpret the Senator's sneers and innuendo as testimony," he said, strutting back to front the jurors. "Decide this case on its merits. We don't make the beauty of Hahatonka an issue. It doesn't hurt our case to admit this spot was a beautiful gem in the Ozarks before condemnation proceedings were started. We have proved it is a beautiful place now."

Standing now in front of the Snyders' counselors' table, Walne said, "The Snyder family received bad legal advice when it attempted to show the waters of the Lake of the Ozarks introduced on their property were navigable and for that reason open to the public. Pictures were brought in here to show hundreds of fishermen lining the banks of the lake there to prove an invasion of privacy on theory those waters were public. I know Senator Reed will get up here and tell you men that he doesn't care what all the courts in the land have decided on this question; that he knows what the law is. I have a great deal of respect for his ability, but I am not willing to admit that he knows more law than the courts in the land."

The Texan took a break to pour and drink a tall glass of water. The chill of the January air that came through the open courtroom windows had soon been warmed by the body heat of the hundreds packed inside. Walne showed no effect from heat nor cold. His suit remained unwrinkled. His demeanor remained unchanged from the first moment he spoke (except for a the slightest of smiles when he frequently referred to the Senator's "Sneers and innuendoes.") to now.

Returning to front the jury, Walne digressed from taking the other side to task and started going through a litany of witnesses for each side, making abbreviated references to each and to what they testified. On the Snyder family's witnesses he concentrated on the sculptor, Gutzon Borglum who said Hahatonka had been worth one and one-half million dollars before the Lake of the Ozarks had been created and was now worthless.

"He cared nothing for the market value," Walne said, discussing Borglum, "but fixed the value on beauty alone. Most of their witnesses have not seen the property since change was made by creating the lake, but their champion beauty expert, Mr. Borglum, never saw the property *before* the change was made. You can ignore his testimony."

Walne then switched his scorn to the two engineers, E. L. Williams and E. E. Howard who testified for the Snyders about the ability to create electricity from the flow of the Hahatonka spring. He belittled their qualifications and called Williams' testimony, "Simply ridiculous."

"The Lake of the Ozarks is a paradise for fishermen from throughout the Mississippi valley," he told the jury. "Thousands will visit the region where only a few visited it before.

The benefits of the lake compensate the Snyder estate for land condemned for it."

With closed fist, Walne hammered the railing to the jury box. "We don't owe the Snyders one slick dime."

Another break. Another long drink of cool water. Then to the witnesses the electric company had brought to the stand.

He went into detail listing the positions of trust John T. Woodruff, who testified for Union Electric, held. Snyder attorney John Wilson testified that Mr. Woodruff had offered to testify for them for $500 and a contingent fee. Wilson said he had considered the offer for weeks before declining.

Walne said, "They have failed to prove their charge. I'm going to defend Mr. Wilson. I know he is an honest man and he would have repudiated such an offer instantly. Mr. Wilson's only fault is a bad memory. Lawsuits are settled on facts, not by insulting questions and innuendo."

Walne defended another one of their witnesses, ex-New York Congressman William Willett Jr, who, under cross examination from Senator Reed, admitted he had been convicted of a felony and had served time in Sing Sing Prison in New York.

Walne read off a list of prominent clients of Willett's since his release from prison and commended him for reforming and living a life of usefulness.

Using a pointer and a map prepared by power company engineers, Walne ended by discussing the question of "Drawdown," of the lake waters, saying they would not be disturbed as frequently and as violently as had been charged by the Snyder attorneys.

He sat down with a flourish.

The crowd broke into a clammer of many hushed remarks

and discussions. The bailiffs pleaded with them to, "Be quiet." Judge Reeves gaveled the court to a noontime break, then looked at his watch: three hours. That's how long Senator James Reed would get for his final closing remarks.

"HE WAS VERY GOOD," Robert Snyder's wife, Mary said at the table where members of the Snyder family had gathered for the noontime meal while court was adjourned. "I hope the senator is as good or better."

Kenneth Snyder raised a fork and said, "Here's to Senator Reed. He'll not just do better, he'll knock it out of the park, to use a baseball term. I rode to Kansas City with him. The man is worldly, knowledgable. He's spoken on the floor of the United States Senate numerous times . . ."

"Against women's right to vote," Kenneth's wife Lillian Ethel said with a touch of sarcasm. "Telling the old maids to go get a husband and have their own children instead of work- ing for the Childrens' League."

"Well, yeah," Kenneth smiled. "Not that he always said something everyone agreed with, but would you like to switch and have him speaking for them and Walne speaking for us?"

"No," Lillian Ethel admitted.

"The man was close to being nominated for President," LeRoy Snyder said, coming to Reed's defense.

"Except for two words," Kenneth said. "Tammany Hall."

"Or two more," from LeRoy. "Al Smith."

"Two more," Mary Louise, his wife said. "Herbert Hoo- ver."

"I've still got my money on Senator Reed," Kenneth said.

"Our money, you mean," LeRoy said, grinning and laying a hand on Kenneth's arm."

"OUR money." Kenneth said, correcting himself and smiling around the table, letting his glance linger a bit longer on Robert.

Fred Snyder, son of Robert and Mary, covering the trial today for the *Kansas City Star* and *Times*, said, "I sneaked a look at what our competitor from the *Journal-Post* wrote for a headline about Walne's speech. I caught the word BRILLIANT."

"Figures," Kenneth said. "Editorializing in the headlines, that's their style."

Mary Bowen Snyder looked at her husband. "What do you think about Mr. Walne's closing argument, Robert?"

Robert studied his plate a moment. "It was good," he finally told them. "I trust the Senator. And I trust the jury. They were impressed at his delivery and with some of the points he made. Especially the one about the Lake of the Ozarks becoming an attraction for fishermen and tourists. I think that's what everyone wants, the people on the street, members of the jury. But I still believe they will give us more than the electric company is willing to give us. Maybe not a million, but a lot more than Louis Egan is willing to come up with."

"A half-million?" LeRoy asked.

"Close," Robert said.

"They'll appeal," Kenneth said.

"Oh, God, will this ever end?" Mary Bowen Snyder said.

XXXII

"I WANT TO SHOW YOU what Hahatonka looked like after the great national corporation you heard from this morning, flooded the shores of what was a clean, cold, blue spring-water lake,"Senator Jim Reed told the jury. He instructed the film projector operator to begin displaying film of a shoreline strewn with debris, mud and slime.

"There's what was left exposed after the flood waters," he told the jury following the showing of the motion pictures.

"This Lake of the Ozarks is the great benefactor of bull-frogs. You heard from the expert lawyer of this great organization embracing many companies that spread over the nation like a spider's web. This company, acting under the federal power act which, thank God, I voted against, has destroyed the greatest scenic spot in Missouri, perhaps in the world. It is not a public enterprise, but a private enterprise, operated for profit. Now gentlemen, I denounce the whole defense as a sham and a fraud."

He paused for effect, then began again in a lower, earnest tone. "Hahatonka was a gem set in the mountains, shaped and fashioned by Almighty God.

"But everything is gone now. The beauty is gone. The privacy is gone. The only thing that is left for the Snyders is compensation."

Changing tones again, speaking now directly facing the jury, Reed said, "Let's review all those alleged offers of the Snyder Estate to sell Hahatonka. Some of those offers were made nearly a lifetime ago when the Snyder family was under heavy financial obligations. Some of them were made even before many of the improvements were made. Those offers cannot be compared to what the real worth was before the invasion of all that dirty lake water.

"Now," he said, "lets talk about the expert witnesses they brought here to talk to you. One, a cheap promoter named John Woodruff. He said that I invited him to my room in Springfield to have a drink of whiskey. On cross examination he admitted he might have come to my room without an invitation. I said frankly to the jury that I take a drink of whiskey once in a while and if it's good whiskey I'll invite a gentleman to share it with me. I believe they still do that in Texas, even in dry counties.

"The other witness they thought so highly of would not be legally allowed to sit on a jury such as yours because he is a convicted felon.

"Now they can hire a smiling and fat and sleek and good looking man to front for them—with one share of stock."

Union Electric President Louis Egan smiled at the remark and snickers broke out in the crowded room prompting bailiffs to caution onlookers to silence.

Reed's three hours expired at five o'clock. He appeared exhausted. When the senator sat, Judge Reeves asked both attorneys if they wished him to read his instructions to the jury.

"If the jury is as tired as I am," Senator Reed said, "I'd rather wait until tomorrow morning."

No objections came from the attorneys for the electric company.

"My instructions will take from an hour to an hour and a half," Judge Reeves said, and adjourned for the day.

XXXIII

AT 10:30 ON FEBRUARY 3, 1932, the jury sent for Judge Albert Reeves, telling him that after 28 hours of deliberation they had reached a verdict.

> We the jury find the issues for the defendant, the Snyder Estate Company, and against the Union Electric Light and Power Company, by reason of appropriation of tracts A, B, C and D and assess the award at $350,000 damages.
> H. A. Meisenbach, Foreman

The jury had spent parts of five days in arguments of the, "Toughest kind," as one juror expressed. Several members said they were glad the case was finished although, "The work has been pleasant," some said.

The tracts in their decision were identified during the trial and in the judge's instructions as:

Tract A—Hahatonka spring, upper and lower lakes, beach and picnic grounds.

Tracts B and D—heavily timbered sections upstream on the Niangua River

Tract C—Bridal Cave on a separate 40 acres, four miles from the central part of the estate.

Court officials estimated the total cost of the trial, including fees of witnesses and jurors, court costs and attorney fees would exceed $150,000. The case records took more than 6000 pages and 450 exhibits, the largest ever assembled in a United States district court trial in that division. The cost of the record alone was more than $7000.

Carl Crocker, Camdenton attorney, was the only electric company attorney in the courtroom when the verdict was read. He had no comment on the verdict except to say that Union Electric would appeal the case to a higher court.

The three Snyder brothers were in the courtroom as was Senator Reed when the jurors reported. Robert Snyder Jr spoke for the family:

"We're not exactly pleased with the amount of the verdict," he said, "but we're happy it was in our favor."

The jurors made no comment on what part the claims of destruction of beauty had on the amount awarded to the Snyders.

Judge Reeves ruled that Hahatonka Bay, the waters of the lake extending into the Snyder property on the two lakes there was private property and not navigable. He said that the expanded banks of the Osage River and other navigable rivers alone were navigable and that streams and parts of the Lake of the Ozarks not navigable before were not public waters.

The Snyders were $212,000 ahead of the $143,000 they had been awarded by three appointed commissioners in the condemnation proceedings in October, 1930. They were $1,150,000 short of what they had sought in the trial.

Reports from the jury following the decision indicated that members had favored damages ranging from $150,000 to $1,000,000. The jurors favoring the highest figure lowered their award to $750,000 and the ones favoring the lower figure negotiated until the final compromise figure was agreed upon by all the members.

Mary Bowen Snyder was happy with the verdict. "Now you can relax," she told husband Robert.

Robert looked off into the distance, thoughts running through his mind.

"Now I have to prepare for the appeal," he said.

XXXIV

JACKSON COUNTY PROSECUTOR James Page said to the two attorneys representing Paul Scheidt on Monday, February 15, that it was Judge Brown Harris who had insisted on starting the trial of Scheidt the next day, February 16, in connection with the kidnapping of Nell Donnelly on December 16. Ralph Latshaw Jr said they would ask the court for a continuance.

"We were told on Tuesday, last week, that the trial would start tomorrow. That gave us six days to prepare. We need more time than that."

James Anderson, Scheidt's other attorney, said, "We didn't get a copy of the indictment until Wednesday. And when we tried to get a deposition from one of your witnesses, Lacy Browning, you advised him he didn't have to answer our questions."

"And we can't get in touch with the victim, Mrs. Donnelly," Latshaw added. "We're not going to trial without depositions from those two witnesses."

The three turned to Judge Harris who had called them into his chamber.

Judge Harris looked at the calendar in front of him, at the attorneys, then at Page. "Here's the way it's going to be," he said. "We're going to trial tomorrow. Lacy Browning and Mrs. Donnelly will not be allowed to testify until they have given you a deposition about what they intend to say at the trial. I'm ordering a jury panel to be called immediately."

"Your honor, the wrong charge has been filed against our client," Latshaw said. "First of all, he committed no offense in the state of Missouri. If he broke any laws it was in the state of Kansas. There is a law in Missouri with a penalty of two to ten years for taking a victim of abduction across state lines. If Mr. Page thinks Mr. Scheidt did that, let him charge our client with that offense. Not the kidnapping law that has a penalty of five years to death."

"The Grand Jury set the charges," Page said. "The evidence was presented to them and they issued the indictment."

"We'll settle it in court," Judge Harris said.

NELL DONNELLY told Jim Reed that she had been asked to give a deposition to the lawyers for Paul Scheidt. "I can't identify him as one of the men who kidnapped me," she said. "I heard the name Paul mentioned, but I never saw him, or at least didn't see anyone who looked like him. They say I can't testify in court unless I give a deposition. I don't know what to do."

"Go ahead, give the deposition," Reed said. "Testify and tell the jury exactly what happened. Let them decide."

"The other man—Mele they said his name is—he's the one who was so rough with me in the Lincoln and cut my lip. I'll be glad to testify against him." She thought about it for a moment. "I don't care if they hang him or not. That's the penalty for kidnapping isn't it?"

"It is," Reed said, "and I'm all for it.

PROSECUTOR JAMES PAGE told the 12 man jury—selected from a panel by strike-offs by the defense and prosecution—that he would tell them of the plot to kidnap Nell Donnelly on December 16 of last year. He said he would present evidence of her seizure on that date, in the driveway of her home, holding her in the tonneau of her Lincoln convertible, transporting her to a country cottage and holding her and her chauffeur there for 34 hours as captives. A country cottage that the defendant, Paul Scheidt, had rented to the kidnappers for $1000 of the $75,000 ransom asked for Mrs. Donnelly's return.

"I'll read you the confession by Mr. Scheidt," Page said. "A confession that he knew the cottage was to be used to hold someone captive in.

"Those are the facts you will hear, and if you gentlemen find the facts as we have presented them, we ask you," closer now to the jurors, "to assess the highest punishment that you can impose under the law."

The highest punishment in Missouri for conviction of a charge of kidnapping was death. That was what Page was asking of the jury, death by hanging.

Nell Donnelly sat impassively in the courtroom with her friend, the wife of Robert Curdy, a neighbor. She wore brown today—hat, coat, shoes and a fur piece. Aware that she would be the first witness called, a calmness claimed her. She would do exactly what Jim Reed had advised her to do—tell the story of her abduction as no one else could do. Subdue emotion, he had told her, let the facts provide that element. Yesterday her friend had come with her when she gave a deposition to Scheidt's attorneys and telling the facts, truthfully, was like a rehearsal for her. She was ready to talk.

Called as the prosecution's first witness, she began her testimony in an informal manner, beginning with the scene in her driveway and her captivity for two nights in a dirty cottage until her eventual release.

She noticed that the jurors were following her words with intense interest.

She told of being whacked a couple of times in the head at the orders of Martin Depew, the driver. She told of tearfully writing the notes to her husband and to her lawyer, James Taylor, at the direction of Depew. She told the jurors—looking at them directly—that she had cried almost all the time she had been a captive.

Without pause or interruption by Page, she said that Depew had ordered the guards to kill her and her chauffeur if they attempted to run away.

"He said he would blind me and kill George Blair, my chauffeur, or possibly kill me if the ransom wasn't paid," she said, unable to completely keep all the emotion out of her voice. The jurors noticed that.

"They gave me a towel to wrap around my neck," she said. "The towel had the name of the owner of Scheidt's house on it. That's how the police found Mr. Scheidt."

She told of the guard who had been left with her and George Blair, who had told her they were going to be released as soon as a car came for them. The car never came.

She told how the guard had taken the ropes from the

chauffeur and that he told them they were free to go if they wanted to leave.

"Did you leave?" Page asked her.

"Where could we go?" she asked with a shrug. "We didn't know where we were. If we left the others might try to kill us."

On cross-examination, Attorney Latshaw asked, "Was the guard in charge of you the defendant, Paul Scheidt?"

"He was not," she replied.

"At any time from the time you were abducted until you were released did you see the defendant?"

"I did not."

"When was the first time you saw the defendant?"

"When I was at the farm with the officers December 21 after the place had been found," Nell answered.

The defense started their presentation with the assertion that any testimony related to what happened in Kansas did not extend the venue to the state of Missouri.

"A point of law will favor the defendant," Defense Attorney Latshaw said. "He was merely a tool in the hands of the abductors. He violated no Missouri law. He was never in Missouri plotting with the kidnappers. If any law was violated, it was a Kansas law. Any Missouri law he might have violated would not have been a capital offense law."

Lawyer Anderson then told the jury that it was the efforts of Paul Scheidt that led to the release of Mrs. Donnelly and her chauffeur.

"When he found out who was being held captive in his own house, and despite threats of death, he insisted he was having no part in the kidnapping of a woman and that the men guarding her and her chauffeur had to remove them from the premises.

"He's the one who purchased food and aspirin for the captives. He had first been approached by two mature schemers—Martin Depew and Lacy Browning. 'You want to make some money?' they asked. He was told they wanted his house to store some illegal whiskey for some government agents. He refused to enter into that scheme and several weeks later Depew came back to him with a plan to kidnap a wealthy oil man with his consent, and hold him until his wife paid the ransom, which would be used to help the oil man's brother. Depew was to get $9000 dollars and Scheidt would get $1000 for using his house."

Scheidt's attorneys called nine witnesses to the stand, all testifying that Scheidt was an industrious young bachelor who had a good reputation in the area.

When Scheidt took the stand, Ralph Latshaw asked him, "Did you know that Mrs. Donnelly and her chauffeur were really the ones to be kidnapped before you saw them in your house that night?"

"No," was Scheidt's answer.

"How many times did you tell the guards in your house to remove Mrs. Donnelly and the chauffeur?"

"At least three times."

"What did the guards say?"

"They told me to shut up or they would kill me," from Scheidt.

"Then what happened?"

"We had a heated argument. I said, 'You have to take them away,' and eventually they agreed to call a car to remove them. I no longer believed they would do that so I insisted on taking one of them to make a telephone call for a car. I took an Italian to Bonner Springs and he made a call about sacks of potatoes. I guess that was the code to send a car."

Under cross examination Page asked Scheidt, "Could you identify the two guards in your home?"

"No."

"But you say they threatened you and you were afraid to tell authorities in Bonner Springs about the unexpected captives on your place because of the threats of the guards. Why wouldn't you remember men who had so threatened you?"

"I don't."

"You rode to Bonner Springs with one guard and yet you say you couldn't identify him?"

"I can't identify him."

Page made it plain from his facial expressions and body language that he did not believe Scheidt. Latshaw shot to his feet and objected to Page's, "Grandstanding."

O'Hara, assistant prosecutor, summed up the prosecution's case with a demand for the extreme penalty for Scheidt, which under the charge against him would be death.

Latshaw spent a large part of his summation to the jury criticizing Page, declaring the tactics the prosecutor used were unethical and used to, "Seek publicity for himself for personal advancement."

Nell and her friend sat through the final arguments by the lawyers. Nell's friend asked her, "Why didn't the prosecutor call that Lacy Browning you told me about? Wouldn't he have made that man Scheidt out to be a liar?"

Nell was nodding her head in agreement. "His lawyers said

they would ask for a mistrial if he took the witness stand because he wouldn't give them a deposition."

"But when they call a witness to testify against the testimony the other side's witness gave—I think they call it a rebuttal witness or something like that—I thought they could call anyone they wanted to."

"Paul Scheidt never brought him up in his testimony so they couldn't call him as a rebuttal witness."

"You're learning a lot about trials over this awful kidnapping, aren't you?" the friend asked.

"More than I ever wanted to know about kidnapping trials," Nell confessed.

Judge Brown Harris then told the jury that if Scheidt, prior to December 16 had agreed to participate in the abduction of any person he should be found guilty of kidnapping. The jury started deliberation at seven-fifteen that evening, continued for three hours, then began again the next morning at nine.

At noon the next day the judge called the jury into court and asked foreman John Sisson, "Is the jury making progress in consideration of the evidence presented in court?"

Sisson said, "No, your honor, we have made no progress."

"Do you believe the jury could make progress if allowed more time to deliberate?"

"No, your honor, I do not," Sisson said.

The judge then addressed the jury as a whole. "Has the jury made any progress?"

A chorus of "No's," came from the jury.

"Would further deliberation bring progress?" the judge asked.

"No," from most of the jurors.

Judge Harris declared the jury discharged from their duty thus ending the trial. Reporters flocked around the jury as they left the courtroom, but only one member—refusing to identify himself—told the reporters that the first ballot taken was 7 to 5 for conviction, but during further deliberation two members changed their vote for acquittal and the final vote was 7 to 5 in favor of Scheidt.

"We were unable to believe that he was implicated in the kidnapping of Mrs. Donnelly," the juror said.

"Even though he confessed to agreeing to be part of a kidnapping of someone else?" a reporter asked.

"We did not believe he agreed to participate in the kidnapping of Nell Donnelly," the juror said.

Nell's friend, sitting in the courtroom with her, asked, "Now what?"

Nell sighed. "Try him again, I guess, until they get it right."

XXXV

PROSECUTOR JAMES PAGE said to Senator James Reed, "Let me get this straight, you want to be the prosecutor against this Charles Mele?"

"He's the one who hit Nell in the back seat of her car and split her lip making it bleed. Yes, I want the chance to put the bastard away. And I want to see him get the maximum. The noose."

"I gave him the opportunity to escape the noose, but he wouldn't take it. One of them did—pleaded guilty— and got a sentence."

"But not the young guy with the house."

"No," Page said, "We didn't have any concrete information on him. They should have convicted him, but they didn't. Next time we try him—probably be later this fall—I think we can nail him. If the guy Lacy Browning testifies I think the jury will see through all Scheidt's lies. He had about three different stories."

"What happened with Browning?" Reed asked. "Why didn't you put him on the stand?"

"I was negotiating with him. He wanted probation, then agreed to a year in jail. He was afraid if he testified he might say something that would be used against him. We never came to an agreement so we'll leave it up to the judge.."

"He should get the noose," Reed said. "Every damn one of them should get the noose."

"If I let you help in the prosecution you won't have a crying spree like you did in the Bennett trial will you?" Page asked, a huge smile on his face.

"I got the impression you enjoyed that," Senator Reed responded. "You seemed to be captivated by Mrs. Bennett."

"I have to admit she was rather attractive," Page said, still grinning. "Just wouldn't want to be her partner in a bridge game."

Now Reed grinned along with Page. "Nor I," he said.

Page thumbed through some papers before saying, "Judge Brown has that case down for February 23. Would you be ready by then?"

"I'm ready right now," Reed said. "It won't take much to convict the man who roughed up Nell Donnelly."

XXXVI

"NEXT MONTH THE DOGWOODS AND REDBUDS will be out down at Hahatonka," Mary Bowen Snyder told her husband Robert. "We'll take your books and manuscripts down and spend the entire summer there. The boys can come on weekends, Kenneth and Mary Louise want to come down over the Fourth and Leroy and Lillian are thinking about it also if he can get away. He had to take so much time off for the trial."

"I want to finish up this part of the family biography before starting on the appeal. A date hasn't been set yet, so I should have the summer to finish this." Robert looked more rested than Mary had seen him in quite some time.

"What part are you working on?" she asked.

"I have to write that part about Dad in St. Louis and the conviction there. And the lawsuit with the Texas man. If I don't write our version, two or three generations down the road people won't know the real truth in the matter."

"Don't you have something more pleasing to work on? That's going to be rather painful to put all that down on paper. After the ordeal of the trial, write something with joy and fun in it."

"I already did that," he said, smiling at her. "Remember, I wrote about how we met and how we hugged and kissed and how we finally . . ."

She slapped his arm playfully. "You'd better not put everything in there. I'll tear it up if I find it."

"I thought you would be showing it to all your friends."

"There's been enough talk about the Snyders lately," she said. "Do me one favor when we get to Hahatonka."

"Sure, name it."

"Don't take it so hard when you see all the brown water where the beautiful blue water used to be."

His expression changed to one of sadness and she wished she hadn't brought up the brown water. He said, "That's what the trial was about. The loss of all the beautiful blue water."

"TELL ME what you wrote about your father," she said.

"About my dad?" Robert Snyder Jr asked. "I thought I had already told you about it, a long time ago."

"You did, but I have forgotten the details. If you tell me about it maybe it will help you to write it. From an impartial viewpoint."

"You need Freddie to tell you, he's the nonpartisan news-man. I'm not sure I can be impartial when I talk about my fa-ther. The story in part makes him sound like a crook, but I know first hand what a good man he was, how he tried to work for the better way that business was conducted. In that time and place the good things you might try to do couldn't get done without crossing the line. Remember, my father was the man who lowered gas prices in Kansas City from a dollar sixty to twenty-five cents so that everyone, rich and poor, would be able to afford it."

"That's why I want you to tell it to me before you write it," she said.

He thought about it, shuffled the papers he had collected on the subject, then read from what he had written about the incident.

"Robert M. Snyder, in 1898, met this man, George

Kobusch, a railway car builder in St. Louis who was interested in bills that were up for a vote in the City Council in St. Louis for suburban rail lines. Mr. Snyder went to this man named Edward Butler who was active in St. Louis politics, who bragged that he had been stealing elections in St. Louis for thirty years. The bill father presented to Butler was called the Central Traction bill for rail lines and for cars on routes already served by the Suburban Railway. The Suburban Railway people were paying the members of the Municipal Council $5,000 a year to turn away all competitors."

"Bribing them, you mean," Mary said.

"Yes, of course. It was called 'boodling,' and the people engaged in it were 'Boodlers.'"

"So your father became a Boodler."

"There was no other way a business could get a contract with people who were already engaged in accepting a bribe. My father was a businessman who started honest businesses and treated people right. He was not a politician. If he had been he would have tried a different method and not succeeded. He was a man of action who used the tools that were needed to get better things accomplished. You know that from the way he brought the gas from the wells in Kansas to Kansas City."

"Your father met this man Butler who was the master boodler in St. Louis."

"Butler was being paid to watch the people who had been receiving $25,000 a year, to see that the boodlers were getting what they were paying for and they were keeping the franchise in power. He sent Frederich Uthoff to a meeting between Mr. Snyder and the seven council members being paid by Suburban to see what they would charge to consider Central Traction. Uthoff was to cause a disagreement or set a price so high that my father would refuse to pay it."

"But your father outbid the other people," from Mary.

"There was a wild scramble with the boodling going on with each member setting his own price. Money was being passed around and the money to pass the Central Traction bill won out and the bill was passed. That's when the honest politician entered the scene."

"Good for him. Who was with him?"

"The newspapers, generally. The *St. Louis Globe*, the *Post-Dispatch* and the *Republic*. And the *Kansas City Star*. Joseph Folk, the St. Louis Circuit Attorney began investigating the Suburban Railway in 1902 and ended up starting a Grand Jury investigation. The only trouble was, the Missouri statute of limitations barred prosecution after three years of the commission of a crime like this if the parties accused lived in Missouri. This protected Butler and Uthoff and all seven of the council, all of whom were getting money from Suburban and from Central Traction. So Folk investigated my father and decided he lived most of the time in New York and didn't qualify for the three year exemption from prosecution. He was arrested and indicted by the Grand Jury for bribery."

"And your father's attorney—was it a Mr. Priest?—entered a plea that your father was actually a resident of Missouri. Kansas City, Missouri."

"He did," Robert agreed. "Yes, it was Mr. Priest from Ralls County, Missouri, that defended father. The Grand Jury, however ruled against the plea in April, 1902 and father went to trial in St. Louis."

"Pleading Not Guilty."

"Correct. So Folk puts Uthoff on the stand and he says father came to his house and Uthoff told him the price to get the Central Traction bill passed was $50,000. Uthoff was admitting to asking for a bribe because it had been over three years and he was a state resident so they couldn't bring him to trial. He says father sent him a package containing $50,000 by a guy named Louis Dieckmann who was the speaker of the St. Louis House of Delegates. Uthoff returned the money and said the price had gone up to $100,000. Father refused to pay that and went back to New York. Uthoff followed him, met him at the Waldorf Astoria Hotel and demanded the money. Father gave him $5,000 for a receipt saying he had not accepted any money to pass the Central Traction bill."

"But the receipt didn't persuade the jury."

"No. Father was found guilty of bribery and sentenced to five years in the state prison."

"You have to admit it was an exciting story," Mary said.

"It was, especially the way it ended. Father never went to prison, he took it all the way to the State Supreme Court who set the verdict aside in June, 1904, saying father never lost his residency in Kansas City."

"In summation didn't Mr. Priest say that bribery was just a trifling offense of the law and the real crime was perjury—how was it he put it? 'So foul and black that it could only be atoned for in the blood of the Son and Savior?'" Mary was grinning now at how ridiculous she thought Priest's words had been.

"Yeah, well he was a bit overwrought.

"How much did your father spend boodling all these boodlers?"

Robert said, "I think the total was about $250,000. I don't know if he ever got the money back in benefits or not. Two years later in the Spring of 1906, the circuit attorney filed a new suit against father but it was *Nolle Prossed*, dismissed, when this guy Uthoff fled St Louis for Denver. The circuit attorney went to Denver and got Uthoff to agree to come back for a new trial against father. Unfortunately, my father was killed in October of that year so he never had to go to trial again in St. Louis."

"And that's how you wrote it?" Mary asked. "That sounds very fair and it doesn't make him out to be some horrible man."

Robert gathered all the papers and stacked them neatly beside his writing pad. "He was my father," he said, "and I loved him very much."

NELL DONNELLY turned her head on the pillow and looked at Senator Jim Reed who had just entered her bedroom.

"The doctor called you?" she asked. "I asked him to. I'm not feeling so good, Jim. A cold has gotten me down."

"Sorry to hear that. He said you wouldn't be able to testify at Mele's trial tomorrow."

Nell took a long moment to answer. "It's just too much, Jim. I need some time away from this, the kidnapping thing. I need rest."

"You deserve it," he told her. "I'll contact Page and Judge Brown. We'll have the trial postponed."

"Tell me about the nurse, Ethel Depew and her husband, then stop talking about kidnapping stuff for a while."

"Mrs. Depew is still in prison here in the city. They're looking for the husband in New York City now. Chief Seigfried thinks he may have left the country on a ship, but he's determined to find him. So is Page. I think they will."

"More trials, huh?"

"This time next year it will all be over and you will forget about it," Reed said.

"This is something I will never forget about."

She turned her head away and he left the room.

Eight days later kidnapping again was at the front of her mind.

LINDBERG BABY KIDNAPED screamed newspaper headlines across the country and in Europe. Late in the evening of March 1, 1932, someone had put a homemade ladder against the Lindberg house in New Jersey and went into the room of Charles Lindberg, Jr the 20 month-old son of world famous flyer and wife Anne Morrow Lindberg and took him from the house.

The news hit Nell Donnelly harder than most as she had lived through such an experience. It angered her to the point that she took pen and paper immediately and wrote her feelings about such a dastardly crime.

She discussed it with her friends, her husband, her employees at the garment factory and with the father of her own son, Senator Jim Reed.

"I want to do something," she told him. "It is such a horrible, horrible crime. A young child, 20 months old. David is almost that age. What kind of people do this? Are they like this

Depew man and this Charles Mele who took me from my home?"

"It's hard to see in the mind of people who do these things," Reed said. "What you can do is tell the court what Charles Mele did to you."

"I'm ready," she snapped. "Have they set a new trial?"

"He set it for the July session. I wanted to give you more time to rest up."

"I'm ready to do it today after reading the news. But, July will be all right. This Lindberg baby, I want to do something now. Today."

"Write something in your own words from your own experience. I'll talk with someone down at the *Kansas City Star* and the *Journal-Post*. They'll publish it," Reed said.

"I want it to go all over the world, not just here in Kansas City. I want everyone to know what a terrible, horrible crime this is."

"All right," Reed said. "I can get them to put it on one of the press releases. Associated Press, United Press, one of those."

"Okay," she said with conviction. "I'll bring it by your office."

On March 4, 1932, an editorial by Nell Quinlan Donnelly appeared in the *Kansas City Star*, the *Kansas City Journal-Post* and in newspapers all over the United States through the Associated Press in which she wrote:

"Society is challenged by the underworlds in the series of kidnapings. The audacity of the Lindberg baby kidnaping this weeks shows there is no limit to what the criminal element will do. The extreme penalty for convicted kidnapers should be death. I know wealthy women here in Kansas City who have not stirred outside their homes at night, even with chauffeurs to guard them since I was kidnaped and held for ransom. Kidnaping is the most terrifying experience. From the time my captors hit me on the head, I realized they would hurt me physically at will and would kill me without hesitation if that would serve their purpose."

XXXVII

KANSAS CITY POLICE CHIEF Lewis Seigfried on April 25, 1932, picked up the phone in his office when told Jackson County Prosecutor James Page was on the line.

"Where the hell are you?" he asked Page.

"We got your man, Chief. We got Depew, the leader of the kidnap gang."

"Last I heard from Bob Cole was that the man got on a ship for South Africa."

"Yeah, that's where they got him. Your detectives talked with one of his relatives who helped build a freighter name of City of New York. We got hold of the passenger list and studied it. One of the names, John M. Long, looked a lot like the writing of Depew. The same handwriting as Depew's signature. We sent off some cables to the towns in South Africa served by the America-South Africa Lines and found out John M. Long had deserted the ship in Durban, South Africa. All the police over there got our cables and we got an answer from the police in Johannesburg that they had arrested a man under the name of Jack Anson who matched the identification of Depew."

"You're sure it's the right man?" Chief Seigfried asked.

"Positive identification, Chief. We showed his photograph to crewmen on the City of New York freighter when it docked here yesterday. They had some personal items he left behind on the ship and we can tie those to Depew. There was a shirt made in Kansas City and other stuff we can prove was his. Had five .32 caliber bullets in his pocket, but no pistol."

"What's he say, this guy Long or Anson? He admit who he is?"

"He admitted he is Marshall Deputy or Martin Depew. They're shipping him back as a prohibited immigrant so all we need is extradiction papers from the state of New York which I will take care of before I come home."

"Good job Mister Prosecutor. That's five of them. We need the driver of the car."

"Depew knows and I think he'll tell us. My bet is he'll plead guilty if we make a deal with him, life in prison instead of hanging."

"Just as soon hang him," Chief Seigfried said.

"Save us a trial and he'll help us out with his wife, Browning, Scheidt, Mele and the driver when he tells us who it was."

"Glad you got our man," Chief Seigfried said. "When are you coming back?"

"Going to a Broadway play tonight. Be back in a couple of days. You should be here."

The chief hung up his phone and muttered, "Happy in Kansas City, thank you."

LEROY SNYDER said, "I think the estate would make a very profitable development of permanent and vacation homes. I can have a developer I know work up a plan, draw up a map and see how it looks."

Robert did not look pleased with LeRoy's suggestion. "Too early," he said. "I don't think the trial is going to be overturned. We can use the money the electric company pays us to cover our expenses on the trial. That should leave everything with Hahatonka free and clear."

"There's still the ongoing expense of keeping the place up," Kenneth said. "I love it out there and want to keep it in the family as long as possible, but can we afford it, that's the question."

"Okay, here are the options," LeRoy said. "Assuming the trial won't be overturned by the Appeals Court, we can keep it as is, sell it to the state for a park or develop it."

"And if the trial is overturned, what then?" Kenneth asked. "More expense, another trial which we may get nothing from. Another option would be leasing it out for a hotel. We have to wait until the Appeals Court rules on it. Has the hearing been set yet, Bob?"

"It will be later this year, maybe as late as December. Keep the options open until then."

LeRoy asked, "Is the senator representing us in the appeals hearing?"

Robert said, "Yes. He has already registered with the appeals court, blocking out June for the Democratic Convention and November for the national election. Sid Roach is out. He's recovering from his heart attack and won't be able to help out. Sid was very helpful to us and to the senator. He'll be missed."

"What if the senator is selected as the nominee in June? He'll be out campaigning, he won't have time for a trial," Kenneth asked.

"I don't think there is much chance of that," Robert said. "If it happens then we'll make different arrangements."

Robert was growing anxious over the discussion, wanting to end it. He rose and gathered the papers he had on the table. Outside a bright, typical June day was spreading its colors and sunshine.

"Must be pretty nice down at Hahatonka now in June," Le-Roy said, understanding his brother's anxiety.

"I'll let you know," Robert said. "I'm going there tomorrow."

JUDGE BEN TERTE behind the bench in Criminal Court in Jackson County during this June session, looked down at Martin Depew. "State your true name," he said to the prisoner.

"Well, my real name is Marshall Deputy, your honor, but here in Missouri I go by the name of Martin Depew."

"I have a signed statement here that you confess to—quoting your statement—'Hatching the plot to kidnap Mrs. Nell Donnelly.' Is that correct?"

"I did that, your honor."

"And you did that in an attempt to collect $75,000 in ransom from her husband and you held her and her chauffeur in captivity for 34 hours in a house in Bonner Springs, Kansas."

"Well, I did all that, yes. I had some help from Mister Lacy Browning who arranged for the house. I believe he has signed a confession to that effect and he will appear before you to plead guilty."

"That's another matter for the court which you need not bother yourself with. You are pleading guilty to committing the crime of kidnapping and you admit to fleeing the country to avoid capture. Is that a correct statement?"

"I did leave the country. I felt like the people I was associated with had collected the ransom and left me out high and dry to get the blame."

"You are pleading guilty of the crime of kidnapping are you not?" Judge Terte asked.

"Oh, yes sir, I admitted to that in my statement, your honor. I have entered into an agreement with the Prosecuting Attorney Mister Page to plead guilty and he has promised me he would approach you and recommend life in prison in lieu of hanging."

"But you understand that decision will be made by the bench?"

Depew smiled slightly. "I understand that your honor."

Judge Ben Terte asked, "You have been treated well since your return to this country?"

"As well as I had any right to expect, your honor. Two Kansas City detectives met me in Philadelphia after I got off the boat and escorted me back to Kansas City. Had lunch in Gettysburg on the way back. They kept pretty tight reins—or I should say shackles—on me. Since I have been here I have scarcely been used as a prisoner. I have been treated wonderfully by every officer since I was captured. I just want to get to wherever it is I'm going, your honor."

Judge Terte looked down at the papers on his bench. "I've received your confession and your plea of guilt. I've considered your crime and what you have done to both the victims of your crime. I have received the recommendation of the prosecutor that you be sentenced to life in prison and I have considered it. I therefore as presiding judge of the criminal court of Jackson County, Missouri sentence you to spend the rest of your life in the Missouri State Penitentiary."

Judge Terte tapped his mallet on the bench. "Case closed," he said. "Next case."

Senator James Reed sitting in the audience between Police Chief Lewis Siegfried and Detective Robert Cole said to Detective Cole, "Takes care of Depew. How many times did you have to beat him with your club to get the confession?"

Cole turned to look at Reed to see if he was joking or serious. Then he remembered the senator was always serious.

Chief Siegfried answered for him, "We don't do that anymore, Senator."

"Uh huh, sure," Reed said.

"We got in the cab in Philadelphia," Cole said, "and he says, 'Well, boys, I did it. I'll probably get the noose, but I'm not afraid to die.'"

"What about his wife?" Reed asked. "What did he say about her?"

"He said he married her without divorcing another wife in Downington, Pennsylvania. The present wife, Ethel Depew, is a nurse and he claimed she helped him kick a narcotics habit," Cole told him. "He gave us this guy Walter Werner, some auto mechanic he hired in Kansas City. Werner was the driver of the car who pointed a gun at the chauffeur."

"He's pleading guilty today, too," Chief Siegfried said.

"And this Lacy Browning? He's pleading guilty?" Reed asked.

"That's right. He's a minor figure and has agreed to 25 years. I think the judge is going to give life to Werner because of pulling the gun," the chief said.

The senator got up to leave. "Good. Three down, three to go. Let me know what the judge gives them. I've got to go report to Nell. I think she'll be pleased."

XXXVIII

THE DEMOCRATIC NATIONAL CONVENTION opened in Chicago (because they put up $50,000 more than Kansas City) June 27, 1932 with New York Governor Franklin Roosevelt holding the majority of votes, but Al Smith loyalists were in control of the convention. The pro-business establishment wing of the Democrats decried Roosevelt's, "Forgotten Man," appeal he had made in a national radio address earlier in the year.

"I will take off my coat and fight to the end against any candidate who persists in any demagogic appeal . . . setting class against class and rich against poor," Al Smith cried in the convention hall.

Roosevelt countered with, "Modern society, acting through its government owes the definite obligation to prevent the starvation or dire want of any of its fellow men and women who try to maintain themselves and cannot."

Midnight drew near on the third day of the convention, nominations continuing endlessly and the first ballot had not been taken. Senator Jim Reed, through tired eyes, told Tom Pendergast, sitting with the Missouri delegation, that he was going to bed.

"I'll see you at breakfast," he said. "They won't vote until noon tomorrow."

"If they do," Pendergast said, "I'll cast the Favorite Son vote for you."

"The State's got 36 delegates," Reed said. "How many can I count on?"

"Not all of them," Pendergast said, and moved on through the delegation.

Reed woke earlier than usual, dressed and went for breakfast about five o'clock. Pendergast was siting at a table with Kemper and some of the other Kansas City delegates. He waved Reed to the table.

"First vote about a half hour ago," Pendergast said. "You got 24 votes as Favorite Son. Roosevelt is a hundred votes shy. Ripe for a fall, Smith says."

"Which way is it leaning?" Reed asked.

"Too early to tell," from Pendergast. "We're not jumping on board until we're sure he's going to get it. If Mississippi jumps off his side he could be in trouble. We'll vote for him when he needs us and owes us."

Kemper was smiling. "He's got a new theme song, anyway, *'Happy Days are Here Again.'*"

A man Reed recognized, but could not remember by name, rushed up to the table and addressed Pendergast. "They're starting the second ballot, Tom. And damned if they aren't polling the delegations individually. Better get down there, they're at Illinois."

The table emptied quickly except for Reed. Pendergast looked at him and asked, "Coming Favorite Son?"

"After I eat," Reed said and watched them rush away. He knew now how fruitless it was for him to wish for the nomination. It was all a game, one he was tired of playing. He ordered eggs and bacon with dry toast on the side. And coffee. At eight o'clock he entered the convention hall and joined the Missouri delegation.

"You lost six votes, down to 18," Kemper told him. "Roosevelt is still leading. If he can hold Mississippi he will get it."

"Uh-aw," one of the delegates said. "There goes Huey Long of Louisiana over to the Mississippi delegation. I want to hear this," and he hurried off toward the Mississippi delegation on the floor.

When he returned he wore a huge grin. "Shoulda been there," he said. "Old Huey Long went right up to the governor and said, 'You break up the Unit Rule and vote for someone besides Roosevelt you sonofabitch I'll come back here and break you.'"

"Third vote coming up," Kemper said. He looked at Pendergast. "We ready to go with Roosevelt?"

"Not yet." Pendergast looked at Reed. "Get to work, get some more votes so we'll have more to bargain with."

Reed did not take kindly to the remark, but he did walk toward the Oklahoma delegation hoping to pick up some support that Alfalfa Bill Murray was losing. When the third ballot was taken, Reed picked up ten votes. He took some pleasure in that, but it was a long ways from the 770 votes needed.

The convention recessed until evening and delegates headed for the dinner tables. Midway through the meal, House Speaker John Garner from Texas came by the Missouri table. "I think it's time to break this thing up," he told them. "I'm dropping out and Texas and California are going with Roosevelt."

"Who's on the ticket as vice president," Pendergast asked, watching Garner for response.

"To be decided," Garner said. He looked at Reed. "Your name has been mentioned.

Pendergast looked across the table at Reed, tipped his glass he had spiked from a flask and said, "What about it, Favorite Son?"

"I said this four years ago and I'll say it again," Reed said. "I'll not sit in the rear seat in a hearse."

Garner nodded his head as if he understood and agreed with Reed's decision. "I'll tell them that," he said, and moved on.

"There goes your vice president," Pendergast motioned toward the retreating Garner. "Could have been you," he told Reed who stared but didn't answer. "I'm going to have to go with Roosevelt," Pendergast said. Reed was silent as the group broke up and headed for the convention. Senator James Reed was waiting for someone else. She came into the dining area, saw him and came over.

"Am I too late to congratulate you?" Nell Donnelly asked.

He smiled. "It's over. They're going with Roosevelt."

"Let's go stop them," she said and pulled on his arm.

The fourth ballot was already in progress when they made their way to the Missouri delegation under the state banner. By 8 p.m. Franklin Roosevelt got 945 votes, including the Missouri votes, more than enough for the nomination. The Roosevelt celebration began and the demonstrators lined up on the convention floor. A woman who Reed knew was from St. Louis grabbed the staff for the state banner.

"Come on," she shouted, "let's get the Missouri banner in the Roosevelt parade."

Nell Donnelly stood up. "That would be a slight to our Favorite Son, James Reed," she said. "This banner is not going to be moved."

But soon it joined the rush to the man who said he was for the little guy and the Missouri Banner marched in the Roosevelt parade.

Reed and Nell left the convention somewhat disappointed but not surprised. Looking ahead, he had a trial to get ready for. Prosecuting Attorney James Page had agreed to add Reed to his team for the trial of Charles Mele, the Italian who had beaten Nell Donnelly. They discussed it that night in the hotel room.

"He'll be sorry he ever put a hand on you," Reed said after they got into bed.

"Speaking of putting a hand on me . . ." Nell said.

XXXIX

NELL DONNELLY and Senator James Reed rode to the Jackson County Criminal Court together with Nell going into a waiting room before being called to testify and Reed going into the courtroom to assist Prosecutor James Page. Judge Ben Terte opened the trial for Charles Mele, Italian-born known gambler in Kansas City and close friend of Vic Bonura, the restaurant owner who fled town after disclosing the location of the rural house where Mrs. Donnelly was held captive.

Reed called his first witness, Mrs. Nell Donnelly. Nell had prepared for her testimony and had rehearsed it many times, for the police, for the press, for her family and friends and under oath in depositions and testimony against Paul Scheidt who had supplied the house near Bonner Springs she remembered so well.

She told her story, straightforward and with very little emotion. She told of being thrown to the floor of her Lincoln convertible, of her lip bleeding, of seeing the car driving along Brookside Blvd. the night she was kidnapped. She told of the house where she and chauffeur George Blair spent two nights imprisoned, of being forced to write notes to her husband and her lawyer and last, she told of the strangers who came into the house and drove them to freedom early in the morning on a street in Kansas City, Kansas.

The jury listened intently as if she was a friend or neighbor telling each of them individually of her ordeal. Reed was pleased with their obvious attentive attitude.

Defense attorney Joseph Lasson was also very attentive. He scratched notes, listened and showed no concern except intense interest.

"Have you seen the defendant before?" Reed asked his witness.

"Yes I have," Nell Donnelly said. "I last saw him in the house where my chauffeur, George Blair, and I were being held under guard."

"And what role did the defendant have in the house when you last saw him?"

"He was one of the guards," Nell answered. "There were always at least one or two guards in the room with us."

"You positively, under oath, swear that the defendant was one of those guards?"

"I do," Nell said with conviction. Some in the jury nodded their heads at her response.

"Let me read one of the ransom notes received by me from the kidnappers and I will show it to you to see if you have ever seen it before," Reed said. He began reading:

MR REED

MRS IS OK NO HARM HAS been done to Her SHe wiLL be HoME Sunday if THis Letter gEt in PaPer or police or Postal Authorites you wiLL NEVER SEE Ag HER Again For being so daM SMART For NotiFying PoLice For WE KNOW if you get Any one oF us it would be X death so WE CAN do THe SAME to Her if any $ our MAN ARE TaKe while we WE gETTing MONEY SHe weLL die WE MEAN wHat we say NO EXcauses FROM you or ANY oNE.

He then showed the crudely printed note to the witness. "Yes," she said. "I have seen it before. The defendant wrote that note when we were in the house in the prairie."

The court's business was done for the day, but not Nell's. That evening she confided to Reed how desperately she wanted Mele to be convicted.

"Getting through these trials is further harassment for me to relive it all over again. But . . . it's my duty. I have to contribute whatever I can to stop these terrible kidnappings."

The next morning on the stand she concluded her testimony. Defense Attorney Lasson approached her, asked permission to give a newspaper to the witness. Reed asked permission to see the newspaper and was granted that opportunity by Judge Terte. The newspaper, dated December 11, 1931, contained an article that Nell had contributed to and her name was included. Reed handed the newspaper back to Lasson who handed it to Nell Donnelly and asked her to read the article. Reed objected as did Prosecutor Page. Reed said to Judge Terte, "Let Mr. Lasson read the article to Mrs. Donnelly. Why should she have to read his newspaper? What bearing does the article have on this trial?"

"I presume it is to test her eyes," Judge Terte said. "She testified to having seen the note."

Reed sat down. Judge Terte told Nell to go ahead, read the newspaper article to Mr. Lasson and to the jury. She did that, then was excused from the stand.

Lasson took a paper from his table and told the court he was reading from a deposition given by Nell Donnelly on February 20 in the trial of Paul Scheidt. He then read the part where Nell told Scheidt's lawyer, Latshaw, that Charles Mele was the man who struck her in the back seat of her automobile on December 16.

"Now she says he was merely a guard in the house where she and the chauffeur were held. She identified one man in two different roles. I don't think she can do that. I don't think she can positively identify Charles Mele as either one of these men. Which one is he . . . "

"He's both of them," Reed said, coming to his feet. "Her deposition doesn't contradict her testimony today, it only strengthens it. He beat a woman in the back seat of her own automobile making her mouth bleed, then he stood guard in that ramshackle house where they imprisoned her without food or water and threatened to blind or kill her. He's the man. This woman runs one of the most successful businesses in Kansas City and offers employment to hundreds and treats them with honest pay and dignity. Is Mr. Lasson standing here in court and calling this woman who has gone through so much mistreatment from the defendant, a liar? Let me hear him say that here in open court without one piece of evidence to back him up."

"He can't be both . . . " Lasson tried to work in, but Reed said plainly, loudly and with authority, "He's both, your honor. Both the batterer and the cruel guard and threatening note writer. The state can bring in an expert to prove that."

Lasson surrendered the floor. Reed called George Blair who told the details of the kidnapping as he remembered them and of driving Mrs. Donnelly from her attorney's office to her garment factory, then to her home on Oak Street where they were accosted by the kidnappers.

To open the defense's case for Mele, Lasson referred to the testimony Marshall Deputy—Martin Depew—gave to the Kansas City police before his sentence for life in prison when he pleaded guilty to kidnapping Nell Donnelly. Depew told the police that Walter Werner was the driver of the car that stopped the Donnelly car and took them captives, but that Charles Mele was not the man in the back seat who struck Mrs. Donnelly.

Reed muttered loudly and clearly, "Oh, hell."

C.C. Franklin, assistant to Lasson, jumped to his feet and immediately demanded the judge reprimand Reed for yelling, 'Oh, hell.'"

Before Judge Terte could address Franklin's demand, Reed stood and said, "I don't know who this young man is or even if he is a member of the bar with any right to address the bench. What I said was, 'Oh, well,' not, 'Oh, Hell.'"

Judge Terte considered this a wise place to end testimony. "I wish this trial to end," Nell Donnelly said to Reed that evening. So did Judge Terte. He was determined to hurry the proceedings along the next day and give the trial to the jury. He ordered a night session to get testimony on the record. Walter Werner, the unemployed auto mechanic that Depew had implicated in the kidnapping as the driver and who pleaded guilty along with Depew, receiving a life sentence for their plea, avoiding the ultimate penalty of death, began a lengthy testimony as to his involvement.

"I joined in because they told me it was a stunt," he said on the stand. "Mr. Donnelly wanted some publicity for the dress factory so he had a banker and his attorney to plan the whole thing. It would be a big story in the paper, people would want to buy the Nelly Don dresses after reading about it in the paper. Otherwise, I wouldn't join in such a stupid thing as it turned out to be."

"Was the defendant, Charles Mele, in on this supposed stunt?" Lasson asked Werner.

"No, he wasn't," Werner said, straight-faced.

"Were you alone?"

"No, there were three Italians with me. Didn't know them, called each other Joe, Frank and John."

Reed laughed and Franklin jacked out of his chair, but the judge tapped his gavel before Franklin spoke. He sat back in his chair, shooting glances at Reed.

Lasson had Martin Depew scheduled to testify, but the hour was late and court was recessed until the following day.

"One more day," Nell said in exasperation on the way home to her young son who would now be asleep with the nurse watching over him. "I'll miss talking to David again to-day," she said.

"I've been watching the jury," Senator Reed said. "I think they will return a guilty decision."

Nell was silent for some time, Reed's chauffeur weaving his way through traffic to their southside homes. "I wonder," she finally said, "how I will feel if the jury condemns him to hang. My testimony sending a man to death, how will it feel?"

"Read the note again," Reed said. "The part about killing you if they don't get the money."

She said no more.

Martin Depew took the stand the next day. Word had gotten around—articles in all the newspapers implying as much—that both sides would be summing up today before the trial went to the jury. People stood around the walls inside the courtroom, twice as many as were able to be seated, and July stifling Missouri hot and humid air oozed through the open windows bringing no relief to those crowded inside the building.

Depew admitted to being part of the kidnapping gang—as he had in court earlier to avoid a sentence to hang, saying that to the best of his knowledge the gang was headed by a man named Vic Bonura who was still hiding from police.

"Who was involved in the plot?" Lasson asked.

"Well, Walter Werner has already pleaded guilty and so has Lacy Browning as well as myself," Depew said. "Vic Bonura, for sure. Some Italians came into town—I guess Bonura invited them here,—I didn't know them."

"Was Charles Mele the man who struck Mrs. Donnelly in the back seat of her car?" Lasson asked.

"To the best of my knowledge, he was not in the gang," Depew said.

Under cross examination Depew said he had made one visit to the house where the kidnapped victims were being held. "Charles Mele, I mean Charley . . . ah . . . ah . . . Scheidt, that is Paul Scheidt was there in the house. Not Charley Mele."

The standing-room-only crowd got their money's worth if they came to hear Senator Reed's flamboyant summation, calling repeatedly for the ultimate penalty for Mele. Lasson said that conviction would be a terrible injustice to an innocent man. A bit after five that evening the judge called an end to testimony and summations and told the jury to go to dinner.

At 7:17 that evening Judge Terte sent the jury into deliberation with instructions. One hour and three minutes later they returned with Charles Mele's future decided.

When the buzzer sounded, indicating the jury had a verdict. Mele sat at his counsel's table, leaning forward with one hand shading his eyes and listened as Judge Terte asked, "Have you reached a verdict, gentlemen?"

"We have, your honor," Jury Foreman Daniel Elliot said and told the judge and the court that Charles Mele was guilty of kidnapping Nell Donnelly and George Blair.

Mele showed no emotion. He looked at his attorneys and was overheard saying, "Pure political influence, nothing else. I don't know anyone connected with this case."

Mele's attorney, Joseph Lasson, told the reporters gathered around him that the verdict was, "One of the most outrageous miscarriages of justice I have ever seen."

Shortly after Judge Terte pronounced a sentence of 35 years in prison, Senator Reed and Nell Donnelly arrived in the courtroom. They thanked Foreman Elliott and each member of the jury for their decision.

"The verdict was as it should have been," Mrs. Donnelly told the members of the jury. "You made no mistake."

Elliott, when asked by the press, said only two ballots were taken in deliberation. "The first ballot was 11 to 1 for conviction. The one vote was cast by a member who believed the defendant was guilty, but felt we hadn't argued the case at great enough length. We took a second ballot and it was unanimous."

Elliott explained that the principal factor was Mrs. Donnelly's positive identification of the Mele. "There certainly was no reason to doubt the word of a woman of her reputation."

"I hope the manner in which this gang was brought to justice will serve as a deterrent to this terrible crime," Nell Donnelly said.

Home once again in late evening, she found her baby son asleep in the nurse's care.

Ten days later Nell and Senator Reed sat through another jury verdict, this time for acquittal. Paul Scheidt, five months after a mistrial the first time Prosecutor Page charged him with kidnapping Nell Donnelly, this time he went free. A disappointed Page indicated he might bring charges against Scheidt again for kidnapping George Blair. He did not.

Only Ethel Depew, former nurse to Paul Donnelly, awaited her day in court for the kidnapping.

XL

"ETHEL, THE NURSE?" Paul Donnelly asked. "Sure, I remember her. Soft hands. Gave a good bath."

Prosecutor James Page turned his attention from Paul Donnelly to Nell Donnelly. She refused to rise to the bait Paul had thrown out and remained silent.

"I may call you, may not," Page said to Paul. "I've got Browning and Detective Cole. I think we've got enough to send her to prison. She and her husband can exchange notes from behind bars."

"Is this the last one?" Nell asked. "The last time I'll have to testify? I want to help, but how many times now have I had to give the same testimony?"

"Gets your name in the papers," Paul said, sounding quite pleased about it. "I'll testify if you need me," he told Page. "Be happy to."

"I don't think you can add anything," Page told him.

"I want to help," Nell said. She looked at Paul who seemed to be enjoying the situation. "But I've got other things to do before the end of the year and here it is September already."

Ten minutes after Page left the house, Nell was in the "Dog Run," between the Donnelly home and the Reed home. A few minutes after she led her German Shepherd along the path between flowering bushes, Reed joined her, minus his shepherd. She recounted her meeting with Page and again expressed her desire to, "Get it over with."

"I'm filing the papers before January," she said. He knew what she was talking about, what papers she referred to.

"I can't do the same, you know that," Reed said.

"I understand," she said. "I hate to ask about Lura's health as if I was wishing she would die or something."

"Not good," he told her. "They think it's pneumonia."

They walked in silence until Reed said, "Forty-five years we've been married. She's eighty-eight now and failing."

"A long time to be married," she said. "You promised her and you stuck to it. Something I can't do. But, then, she never threw an ash tray at you or threatened to shoot herself. I took another pistol away from him two days ago. Dropped it down the elevator shaft at the plant and heard it hit the bottom. Makes thirty-two if I counted them right."

"You have reason. I can't complain about Lura except we haven't had sex for over twenty years. Or more, maybe, I've lost count. She's always said I was never at home, which I wasn't."

"Someday," Nell said, "and don't get me wrong, I'm not wishing her demise, that would be tacky of me, but it would be nice if you didn't have to sneak into the house late at night while Paul's down on Twelfth Street or I didn't have to have George drive me to the Telephone building and wait in the car while you're instructing your secretary not to interrupt us."

"Hmmph," his reply.

"And besides, remember, you said you would never marry an Irishwoman." She laughed and he joined her.

"Man can say anything. Said I would never vote for a Roosevelt, too."

"About the nurse," she said, switching subjects. "Will they convict her? I can't testify against her, I honestly don't remember her and I never saw her while they were holding me, so I don't think I can say she was a part of it."

"You want them to send her to prison?"

"Yes, I do. I want everyone involved to be punished. That's the only way this terrible crime of kidnapping someone is going to stop."

"This Browning guy is trying to work a plea deal with Page for testifying against her. He wants to retract his plea of guilty and go to trial. The jury acquitted Scheidt, so he thinks they would acquit him."

"I didn't want him to get off and I don't want her to get off," Nell said.

"Then we'll see to it," he said confidently. "We'll send the nurse to jail. She's been there for eight months, now. A few more months would be a good message to would-be kidnappers."

FORTY-SEVEN MEMBERS of a potential jury to hear the state's charges against Ethel Depew for the kidnapping of Nell Donnelly was passed by her lawyers, George Charno and William Drummond and by the assistant prosecutor M.W. O'Hern without a strikeoff. The individual questioning of the jurors began with Mrs. Depew's attorneys objecting to the inclusion of Lacy Browning as a possible witness against her.

Nell Donnelly sat in the rear of the courtroom, along with her secretary Rose Hughes, as the jurors on the 47-member panel were questioned. Knowing that she would be Prosecutor James Page's first witness, she wanted to know who would be on the jury listening to her as she, once again, related the incidents of her kidnapping and that of her chauffeur, George Blair.

Defense Attorney Charno asked members of the jury panel if any of them had formed an opinion about the case or a semi-opinion. Page objected to the use of the term, 'semi-opinion.'

"I don't know what he means by semi-opinion," Page told the judge.

"I don't care what you know or don't know," Charno retorted. "That question was directed at the gentlemen on the panel and I am sure they understand even if you don't."

While the questioning of the panel was taking place, Rose Hughes came forward and took a seat alongside Ethel Depew. Charno objected to her being there and she was asked if the paper she held was a list of jury panel members. She said it was and Page complained that Charno was merely trying to embarrass Miss Hughes. She left her seat and returned to the one beside Nell Donnelly.

The next day, the first day of Ethel Depew's trial with the possibility of her receiving the maximum penalty of death by hanging, the defendant, dressed in a green silk dress with white lace cuffs, black hat, beige hose and black shoes, wept openly and copiously as Page read the charges against her to the jury. The courtroom was filled with a crowd of onlookers with women in the majority. When Nell Donnelly was called to testify, Ethel Depew's sobbing increased and she could be observed and heard throughout the courtroom.

"Damn," Page thought to himself, "another Myrtle Bennett," thinking of how the woman had cried—along with her attorney, Senator James Reed—when she was being tried for shooting her husband when he played the wrong card in a bridge game.

Nell Donnelly started her testimony with the strange auto-mobile blocking her driveway on that fateful December evening and told the long story she had told so many times before, the man with a gun forcing his way into her Lincoln convertible, the man forcing her to the floor of the automobile, the drive along Brookside Boulevard toward Kansas, the awful house she was forced into, the notes she was forced to write for the $75,000 ransom, the threats of killing the chauffeur and blinding her, the conversation with Martin Depew (whom she had identified from photographs) about why he kidnapped a woman—Ethel Depew's sobbing increasing in this part of the testimony—and how Nell and her chauffeur were finally rescued by some men she did not recognize.

Before finishing her testimony, Nell was interrupted by Prosecutor Page asking about how her lip was cut and made to bleed. She told how the man she had identified as Charles Mele had cut her lip when he tried to silence her and made it bleed.

The audience in the courtroom as well as the twelve men on the jury listened intently to her retelling of the incident.

Page asked her if she knew Ethel Depew or Ethel Deputy. Attorney Drummond leaped to his feet with a loud objection to Page using the name of Deputy.

"He has no right to use that name," Drummond said. "The defendant was charged under the name of Depew and the use of any other name is merely an attempt by the prosecutor to prejudice the jury."

Judge Ben Terte cautioned Page not to use other names to identify the defendant unless testimony showed her to use other names.

Nell said she knew the defendant as Ethel Depew and that she had been a nurse to her husband, Paul Donnelly, during Christmas week in 1930 and left before January.

"THE DEFENDANT WAS PRESENT," William Lacy Browning said. "On December 15, the day before the actual abduction, she and her husband, Martin Depew, were in the automobile with me discussing how the Italians Depew or someone had brought into town would grab Mrs. Donnelly and hold her for ransom. I wasn't taking any part in that end of it so I don't know what went wrong. I heard the Italians didn't show up or something. But she was there so she knew about the plan."

Defense Attorney Warren Drummond objected. "That doesn't prove she had any part in the actual kidnapping," he told the court.

Judge Terte overruled the objection and Drummond asked Browning why he had offered to testify for the prosecution.

"Didn't you expect to be rewarded by reducing your sentence?" he asked Browning.

"I'm here because by telling what I know of the case I would not have to serve my full time," Browning said.

Page put Kansas City Detective Robert Cole on the stand next. Cole told of the several different stories Ethel Depew had told him when he went to Pennsylvania where he had placed her under arrest.

A surprise witness, Lawrence Hagen, a general contractor, was the first witness for the defense the next day. Hagen said he had been arrested and placed in jail the month before for disturbing the peace and assault with the intent to kill after his

wife had filed charges against him with the purpose of sober-
ing him up.

He said that in the jail he had been placed under the "Key
man," who was Lacy Browning. He said Browning explained to
him who he was and how his picture had been in all the newspapers covering the Nell Donnelly kidnapping. He said Browning told him he was dickering with Prosecutor Page to reduce
his 25-year sentence for testifying against Ethel Depew.

"I asked him if she was guilty and he said she was as innocent as I was," Hagen told the jury. "I went home and told my
wife about it and I said I was going to tell Mrs. Depew's attorneys about it, but she talked me out of it saying there would be
too much notoriety. But when I read where Browning had testified and learned what he had told on the witness stand I
called her lawyers whose names I had seen in the newspaper."

On cross examination, Page asked Hagen if he had ever
been in the penitentiary. Hagen said he had, but that he had
been pardoned by the governor when he learned Hagen was
innocent.

"You tried to kill your wife, didn't you?" Page asked.

Hagen emphatically denied the accusation.

"You tried to cut your wife's throat, didn't you?" Page
charged.

"No, sir," Hagen said as Drummond objected.

Judge Terte told Page that he would have to confirm his
accusation in court records.

Hagen was followed by several witnesses for Ethel Depew, all testifying she was of good character.

The prosecution and the attorneys for the defense gave
rousing speeches to the jury in their arguments during sum-

mation of the case. Assistant Prosecutor O'Hern drew mur-
mured complaints from the audience who now seemed to be in
sympathy with Ethel Depew.

Drummond filed a demurrer, saying the prosecution had
failed to prove their charges and Judge Terte recessed the
court to consider his motion.

Opening court the next day, Judge Terte overruled the
demurrer and sent the jury into deliberation. Thirty-six minutes later the buzzer rang signifying the jury had reached a
verdict and Ethel Depew went into hysterics. As jury foreman
Leroy Cooper read their decision, "Not Guilty," she sobbed
uncontrollably. Wiping away the tears she rose to thank the
jurors.

The press closed in on Mrs. Depew and she appeared ea-
ger to talk with them.

"I waived extradition with promises that I would be able to
have an audience with the prosecutor, Mr. Page. I never saw
him until yesterday. I was promised I could see Mrs. Donnelly
but she has never spoken a word to me. They did not permit
me to go before the Grand Jury before they indicted me and I
had no chance for bond. I've been held in jail for eight months
and nothing to support that.

"First, I want to see my husband in the county jail here."

Minutes later she and Martin Depew were in each other's
arms. "You'll be released in a few years," she assured him.
"No one got hurt."

Nell Donnelly would not have agreed with her.

Little more than a month later the Jackson County Parole
Board voted to parole William Lacy Browning who was to have
served twenty-five years after pleading guilty for kidnapping.

Of the six people charged in the kidnapping scheme, three were serving prison sentences, two were acquitted and one paroled.

"It's over," she said to Jim Reed that evening. "Thank God, that part of my life has ended."

Another part of her life was about to begin. Lura Reed died at the age of eighty-eight. "I feel awful," she said to him. "It's as if I had wished her death."

"No," he said by way of comfort. "You had nothing to do with it. We have to get on with our lives."

And she did.

XLI

NOVEMBER 15, 1932, one week after Franklin Roosevelt was elected President of the United States, Nell Quinlan Donnelly wrote out a check for one million dollars, handed it to Paul Donnelly, then went to Jackson County Circuit Court before Judge Brown Harris and testified that Paul Donnelly had told her repeatedly that he had ceased to care for her and had inflicted indignities upon her that included absences from the home without explanation, making her uncomfortable before friends and similar circumstances.

She was granted an immediate divorce. She now had 100 percent of the Donnelly Garment Company and was no longer married to a man she did not care for.

Life, however, had not simplified for the Snyders. Robert, anxious over the appeal in the United States Circuit Court of Appeals now scheduled to commence on December 15, found scant comfort in his growing, massive collection of manuscripts and all forms of printed material about the middle of the country. The brothers, Kenneth and LeRoy had returned to their places of employment and the sons were engaged in schooling and journalism. Mary, equally busy, joined him in perusing their gathering documents, always with that look on her face of impending disaster. He knew a way to dispel her fears and concerns and those of his sons and his brothers: get rid of Hahatonka or lease it out. But, he was not at that point, yet. And maybe never would be. The place he loved, the place his father loved, his family loved. To give it up now meant that the electric company and his former friend, Louis Egan would win and the most scenic and beautiful site in the state would forever be awash in muddy, brown river water.

Senator Reed assured him the electric company had thin standing with their 100 alleged errors in the nine week trial in federal court in Jefferson City.

"We shouldn't have to go through this again," Reed had told him. "Why does one judge have more insight into the law than another? Reeves is no friend of ours. He's a sworn enemy of the Pendergasts and associates me with them, yet he gave us a fair trial. What gives three judges on the appeal bench better knowledge than he has?"

The testimony had already been given in the first trial. If the appeals court upheld any of the 100 reasons offered by the electric company there would be a second trial. What further proof could they offer a jury? Who would be on a second jury, city dwellers? Men who had never seen nor heard of Haha-tonka? Men who held small value for natural wonders? What would a new and different jury think of Gutzon Borglum, a world renown sculptor who was now carving the likeness of past presidents in a granite-faced mountain in the wilds of South Dakota.

As the time approached, Robert's health declined. The trial had already claimed one victim, Sid Roach. Robert kept in touch with the Roach family checking on Sid, but the news was not encouraging. Robert realized the value of the assistance Sid had given Reed at the trial, remembered his rousing speech to the jury on the day he collapsed following his last day in court.

He vowed not to succumb to the rigors of another trial the way Sid Roach had to the first trial.

Life, however, is uncertain.

He walked down the steep incline from the house across from the old post office and came out near the mill run where the electric company had burned the century-old mill house. Someone, probably LeRoy or one of the caretakers, had rigged a temporary bridge across the rapidly-moving, icy-blue water running from the spring. Robert walked across to the island and made his way up the rocky trail to the top of the island where the balanced rock still stood. He looked down on the spring, marveling at the rush of water shooting from the ground. His eyes followed it around the island, under the massive cliff and the magnificent castle above. He saw the clear blue water fade into the muddy, murky brown water from the river and the scene put a lump in his throat that caught and held his breath.

One thing the electric company and all their high-priced lawyers could not do was erase the beauty from his mind of the blue water he had looked down upon from atop that cliff as he stood by his father and listened to him tell what a glorious view they would have when the big house was finished. And the words his father had spoken to him.

"It's ours, Bobby. And it will always be ours. No one can take it from us."

But they had.

XLII

THREE APPEALS JUDGES, Kenyon, Gardner and Sanborn gave their attention to Senator Reed imploring them to overlook any, "Supposed," mistakes in the nine-week trial in Jefferson City almost a year ago.

"Common sense tells the court that a reversal in this case would be a tragedy," he proclaimed. "We should not be forced to go over this matter again through some supposedly trivial error. If anything is wrong it is the size of the verdict awarded to the estate."

As he spoke, Reed seemed to be addressing Union Electric Company President Louis Egan and Mrs. Egan who sat close by in the audience focusing their attention on Reed.

Reed pointed to the 4 foot by 7 foot relief map standing before the judges.

"One hundred and sixty acres, 6000 native trees cut, forty-five miles of muddy, slimy fetid water overflowing the most incredible wonderland in the state—even the entire country—in the words of world famous Gutzon Borglum who has seen the wonders of the world. Those are the errors committed here, all by this national corporation worth hundreds of millions of dollars. Those errors are not trivial words as their counsel would have you believe. They have destroyed something that took thousands of years for nature to form and they destroyed it in a few hours."

The electric company's Walter Walne saw it differently. "This engineering marvel that has been created has put the largest man-formed lake in the whole country—maybe even the world—in the middle of the state and has greatly enhanced the value of the Snyder estate. Hundreds, even thousands, will be able to access these wonders now. The main conflict in evidence is whether the beauty was enhanced or not."

Walne argued that Judge Albert Reeves had erred in allowing evidence of the financial setup of the Union Electric company and its holding company, the North American company with $900,000,000 of assets.

Reed argued that, "What errors crept in, if they did, were brought in by opposing counsel himself and were against us."

Reed presented photographs of Hahatonka's wonders to the judges and expounded on its beauty, the spring, the blue waters, the ancient mill house, the natural bridge and the caves, the dam across the small lake.

"Irreparable damage," he said. "All that beauty gone or damaged, never to be replaced. Half a million dollars was invested in the estate and old offers of sale for $300,000 are not germane now when we have good roads. When Mr. Snyder gathered this estate together, it took him a day and a half to drive to it. Now you can get there in a couple of hours by automobile.

"The tract may have at one time been offered to the state at modest amounts, but it was done in an effort by the Snyder heirs to found a monument to their father."

Concerning the charges by the electric company that the estate had been assessed for taxes in Camden County at $40,000, then raised to $60,000 when the Snyders had protested, Reed said, "Whoever heard of a man's property value being fixed by his protests against taxes?"

Reed's final pleading left the vision of mud flats, mosquito swarms, dead grass and decaying tree stumps bordering a debris-layered muddy lake in the judges' minds.

Walne's pleading left the images of dollar signs in their minds.

Which vision would be the winner?

IN MARY BOWEN SNYDER'S kitchen where the three sisters-in-law often gathered, Lillian Ethel said, "It's April already. The appeals court met in December, why haven't they made a decision?"

"Each side had to file what they called supplemental briefs," Mary Bowen Snyder said. "Justice moves slowly in the courts."

"And sometimes not at all," Mary Louise Snyder said. "I don't feel very confident about this."

"Nor me," Lillian said.

"Well, I do," Mary Bowen said. "We've been through so much and it has taken such a toll on Bob that I can't even think of going through it all again. God have mercy."

"Would Senator Reed represent us again as he did in the hearing?" Lillian asked.

"Of course," Mary Bowen said. "He's the best. If we have to go to trial again, he's the best attorney we could find."

A pause, then, "He's very expensive, however."

"What about the electric company?" Mary Louise asked. "I read in the newspaper that they had fifty lawyers working on our case. We had three."

"And one ended up with a heart attack," Lillian added.

"Sid Roach, yes," Mary Bowen said. "He's not doing well, either. A shame, I liked Sid."

A few days later, on April 24, 1933, Judge A.K. Gardner of the United States Court of Appeals issued that court's opinion on the nine-week trial held in Jefferson City, MO. All three wives read about that decision in the *Kansas City Star* along with the three Snyder brothers. Their opinions about the decision were the same: disappointment. Judge Albert Reeves had erred, said the three judges on the appeals bench, in his instructions to the jury and on allowing what they considered prejudicial testimony that Union Electric Light and Power Company was owned by a national corporation worth hundreds of millions of dollars.

A new trial was ordered by the court.

"YOUR LITTLE SON is two years old," Nell Donnelly told Jim Reed. "When are we going to make this official and move into the same house and you can adopt your own son?"

"Soon," he said. "Give the papers time to forget about the kidnapping, the divorce and how you adopted your son."

"They won't ever forget," Nell said. "It's good for Nelly Don dresses, but I resent all the press coverage. Let's set a date so I can prepare."

"I would rather not set a public date," he said. "Sometime towards the end of the year let's just elope."

She found that humorous. "I'll make a plan for us. I'm good at making plans, remember? I do it all day long at the factory."

"Speaking of the factory, I hear rumors from the communist labor organizers that they want to move in on you."

"Not a chance," she said. "I pay better than the union does, I have benefits they can't offer and my employees would turn down any effort to put a union in our shop."

"Just watch out for the damn communists that run the damn unions. They don't give a damn about your employees, it's power they're after."

"Changing subjects, what about this trial for the Snyders? What happens now that the courts overturned the one you just got through with up in Jefferson City?"

"I think it's quite a ways off. Egan and the electric company are trying to postpone it as much as they can so they don't have to pay the money the first trial gave to the Snyders. They've signed Brewster and let Walne go. Brewster is the man who ran for Senate against me and lost. Damn Republican. He's the one who got Coolidge to appoint Merrill Otis to the federal court."

"So you think this Judge Otis is going to be the judge in the new trial?"

"Seems likely. He won't be on our side, that's for sure, but neither was Reeves and he was fair."

She said, "You're not worried about the judge, then?"

"Some. It's the jury we have to convince, not the judge. He won't be much of a factor.

Even Senator Reed could be overconfident.

XLIII

DECEMBER 13 of that year, 1933, twenty guests, including a federal judge, were invited to the Reed home on Cherry Street. After passing out a wedding invitation to the guests, they were asked to rise and bear witness to the marriage of Nell Quinlan Donnelly and James Alexander Reed. As the judge performed the ceremony, the guests rose, surprised and somewhat shocked at what was taking place.

Nell felt a new life was beginning for her. Reed, 72 years old, was supremely happy, adoring his 44 year-old bride. Following a honeymoon, Reed processed paperwork to adopt his son, two year old David.

THE YEAR 1934 did not bring the Snyders back into court. Union Electric successfully delayed the retrial—allowing them to hang onto the $350,000 the jury in Jefferson City had awarded the Snyders. Reed worked at organizing a team of attorneys. He retained John Wilson of Kansas City who had helped in the first trial and added Henry Bundschu and Leon Bailey, both of Kansas City.

When Sid Roach died in June, the former congressman from Linn Creek, MO, who had collapsed following his summation in the first trial, his death became the first of three that year that would affect both the Snyders and the Reeds.

In early morning, July 10, two gunmen ambushed Johnny Lazia outside his apartment at Park Central Hotel in downtown Kansas City and shot him eight times. He died twelve hours later. Nell Reed looked at his photograph in the newspaper and told her husband that she thought she had seen the man before.

"I think he was the man who rescued me from the gang in the Bonner Springs house. He was so well dressed and the real gentleman," she said.

Reed, remembering the last meeting he had ever held with Lazia, told her about that meeting.

"So it wasn't just Depew and Mele and the rest of the gang that turned us loose because of the publicity the case was receiving in the newspapers," Nell observed.

"I think that may have been a factor," Reed said, not wanting to emphasize his close ties to Pendergast and the reputed criminal gang leader in the city. "There was a great deal of turmoil in the North Side. Lazia was getting pushed by people who wanted in on the easy money of gambling and bootlegging."

Nell looked again at the photograph. "Yes, I'm sure it was Johnny Lazia who ran off the gang and set me free that morning. Maybe we should attend the funeral."

"Why not, everybody in Kansas City who's anybody will be there. Think about whether you want your name and your picture in the *Kansas City Star* again or not."

She didn't.

On September 7, Paul Donnelly in one of his manic-depressive moods, put a rope around his neck in Hartford, Connecticut and strangled himself. After the divorce he had taken a new wife, a young woman named Virginia George, to Broadway in New York and squandered the million dollars Nell had paid him for his share in the business. The young wife was not successful on Broadway despite the money Paul put into her failed career and Paul grew morose and unhappy.

Nell read the news about Paul with sadness. "I wasn't there to take away his pistol or his rope," she told Reed. "I guess I can just say it was inevitable, but sad nevertheless."

XLIV

ALTHOUGH THE RETRIAL did not get started until February of the next year, 1935, the tension from all the legal wrangling did not leave Robert Jr's psyche. His manuscript collection allowed him to push aside—always temporarily—the planning and contemplation needed for the additional days in court.

As did his occasions with his family and days spent in the splendors of Hahatonka.

When court opened on the 4th of the month in the Central Division of the Federal District under Judge Merrill Otis, the judge ran into the first of a number of controversies concerning the jury. David Alpert of Kansas City, an underwriter for the Business Mens Assurance company, told the judge during the *voir dire* (a legal term for the judge's questioning prospective jurors) said that another underwriter for the same company, David Lashley, had approached him about the trial.

"What did he say to you?" Judge Otis asked.

"He told me that he had learned that I was on the jury panel and suggested the possibility that he might be able to help me get excused from jury duty."

The judge immediately ordered that the incident be referred to the district attorney's office, changed his mind after questioning Alpert and decided the whole incident did not merit a contempt citation against Lashley.

Judge Otis called attorneys from both sides into his chambers before seating the jury and told them that George Jackson had come to him and said that a man had approached him after he had been summoned for jury duty and told him that Senator Reed had been critical of President Roosevelt. Receiving no objections from either side, Jackson was named to the jury and was later elected foreman.

That would not be the last of complications with the jury. Other jury members, Fred Andersen, W.J. Mariner and Henry Tempel would earn a time with the judge and Senator Reed.

Robert's wife Mary asked LeRoy to take over the family's responsibilities for the trial.

"Robert's health is declining. Tell him that you'll watch over things so that maybe he can relax a bit."

"Sure," LeRoy said. He volunteered to be the first of the brothers to be a witness for the defense, which, this time was the Snyder Estate.

"Give you a chance to straighten out all the lies I tell," he joked with Robert. "After I get through bumbling through my testimony I'll make you look good."

He would follow Ernest Howard, an engineer who had testified in the first trial about the, "Drawdown," caused by the vast difference in flood levels and how it would damage Hahatonka with mud flats and other undesirable incursions from lake waters.

Robert Jr spoke to the jury for the next two days, emphasizing the improvements the Snyders had made to the property, the massive stone house along with numerous other buildings and over four miles of gravel roads.

Frank DeCou, a former game and fish official, and James King who was a foreman for the Snyders when they remodeled the large mansion in 1922, told the jury about the large Rainbow trout they had caught in Hahatonka lake before the dam waters overflowed it and killed off the trout.

Karl Krueger, director of the Kansas City Philharmonic orchestra, told about a visit to the estate and the muddy beaches he found there.

Thaddeus Seeley, a Michigan real estate man, estimated that Hahatonka had been devalued by at least seventy-five percent by the lake created by Bagnell Dam. Dwight Ford testified that its value had been reduced to $100,000 from $1.6 million.

The displays, exhibits and documentary evidence from the first trial was on display during the second. Ward Gifford, a Kansas City realtor, was the defense's last witness before the closing arguments on February 20.

Mary Bowen Snyder met Senator Reed on his way into the courtroom on the day of final arguments.

"Senator," she said, a hand on his arm carrying a brief-case, "We overheard some people in the hallway discussing the case. They said the Snyders were not going to get over $200,000."

"Who were they?" Reed asked.

"I don't know. They weren't members of the jury, I would have recognized them."

"Would you know them again?"

"I'm not sure. Mostly we just saw their backs. Robert heard them, too. He's upset about it."

"Rumors. Speculation," Reed told her, trying to reassure her of success in the trial. "But I will mention it to the judge."

Henry Bundschu for the Snyders told the jury, "There is no place in America, probably in the world, that holds the natural features and historic interest of Hahatonka. It has been shown during the course of this trial that the Snyder brothers have spent $517,000 in improvements upon the estate.

"It is a serious thing and a terrible thing to contemplate that this company came in to destroy the wonders gathered there, wonders that should have been enjoyed forever. You look down from the mansion now on an unsightly scene. Instead of rushing cascade there is scum.

"We ask for damages in the sum of one million dollars."

Edgar Shook, leading the argument for the plaintiff, Union Electric Light and Power Company, said, "The only damages to be considered are those of a central tract. Outlying land, of which there is more than four thousand acres, had been held by the Snyders for thirty years waiting for some sucker to come along and buy it.

"It has not been damaged and our witnesses testified the land was worth from $2.50 to $5 an acre. The central tract of six or seven hundred acres contains the natural wonders, and not a single acre of that tract was touched by the flood. It is high above the condemnation lines.

"You have heard about six thousand trees being cut down. To take that seriously would be like offering a drink of water to a drowning man. If there is anything the estate is crowded with, it is trees."

Judge Otis took an hour and a half instructing the jury then sent them into deliberation. They retired at five that afternoon and did not resume until nine the next day.

Before resuming, however, the next jury problem developed.

XLV

"I BELIEVE MR. MARINER is ill," jury Foreman Jackson told the judge in his chambers. "He seems kind of out of it and every time before we start on a ballot he says he wants to figure something."

Judge Otis called both counsels into chambers again. Before the trial, both sides had agreed that they would accept a jury decision on ten or eleven members if it became necessary in order to avoid the possibility of a mistrial. When the judge advised them of the information he had received from the jury foreman about juror Mariner, both sides agreed to the dismissal of Mariner from the jury and deliberations continued.

When juror Mariner sought to collect his check for duty, he asked that the name be changed to W.J. Mariner instead of C.L. Mariner. He said that C.L. Mariner was his brother and he had moved to California, so W.J. Mariner answered the summons sent to his brother. He told the judge he had advised a bailiff of his name before the trial, but none of the bailiffs said they had been advised.

Deliberations continued in the jury room until after eleven o'clock when they announced they had agreed on a decision by eleven jurors.

"We the jury award damages to the defendant in the amount of $200,000," Foreman Jackson announced.

Robert Snyder Jr received the news with vast disappointment once again.

Senator Reed was on his feet. "We will appeal the decision," he announced.

"Will it ever end?" Mary Bowen Snyder thought.

XLVI

NEARLY A YEAR AND A HALF expired before counsel on both sides and Judge Merrill Otis were able to reach an agreement on a date for the court to hear arguments by the defense to set aside a decision by the eleven-man jury to reduce the award by the electric company from the $350,000 decided by the first jury three years before to an award of $200,000.

Senator Reed and wife, Nell Donnelly, had spent time on a ranch they had purchased in Michigan, hunting and fishing and Robert Snyder Jr along with his wife, Mary, and his brothers' families spent time agonizing over the legal entanglements thrust upon them by Union Electric Light and Power Company.

"Louis Egan said he would keep us in court for seven years," Robert said, "and he has done just that."

"And we're out a pile of money," LeRoy said. "We don't get the check from them until this is settled, if it ever is settled."

"We'll take it to the Supreme Court of the United States if we have to," Robert said. "No one can just come in and build a dam and flood your property and destroy it."

Mary Snyder had serious doubts about her husband's ability to get through another trial. What could she say, what could she do to persuade him to forget about the damage to Hahatonka. There was no way to remedy the situation with the dirty water overrunning what was once a beautiful setting.

"Let's just build a dam of our own and keep the water out," Kenneth suggested. "Be cheaper than paying for another trial."

"In order to do that we would have to have the permission of the government and they would have to have the permission of Union Electric," Robert said. "Figure the odds of getting their permission."

"What are the odds on this hearing before the judge on the sixteenth of May," LeRoy asked.

"There were problems with the jury," Robert said. "More than just the man who tried to take his brother's place. Remember the rumor we overheard in the hallway about the award being $200,000? Someone had inside information about the jury. Maybe Senator Reed can turn the problems into a new trial."

May 16, 1936, Judge Otis called George Jackson to testify that a man had approached him after he had been summoned as a juror and had attempted to discuss the case with him.

The man was Frank Collins, an employee in the city license commissioner's office, Jackson said. Collins had visited him twice according to Jackson.

"I see you're one of the jurors in the Hahatonka case," Collins was said to have told Jackson. Collins went on to ask Jackson his religion and his politics. Jackson told Collins he voted for whom he liked.

Looking at Reed, Jackson said, "I have voted for and against you, Senator."

Reed had to wait for the audience to finish laughing at Jackson's remark.

Collins concluded, Jackson said, by saying, "Jim Reed is bad to our President. He talks awful bad."

"That's Jim's business," Jackson said he told Collins.

"Are you sure Collins was the man?" Reed asked.

"There are two men here who favor him, but I pick Collins," Jackson said.

When Collins was placed on the stand, he admitted to having visited Jackson twice at his home but not in connection with the trial.

"The first time, I think it was in the fall of 1934, I was polling for an election. The second time was about a year ago when I asked him to sign a petition for a playground for children. He said I was a man who had visited him twice and had mentioned some case he was connected with."

"You said you were the man?" Reed asked.

"No, I did not."

"Didn't Jackson say he was a juror and you mustn't talk to him about the case?" Reed asked.

"I don't recall any such conversation. The case may have been mentioned, but if it was, it was Jackson who mentioned it."

"Isn't it a fact that he asked you to leave his house?"

"No," Collins said emphatically. "I'm not the man he asked to leave his house. I have no idea who that was. No one has ever discussed the case with me."

"Was there any mention of James A. Reed in connection with the case?" Reed asked.

"He might have recalled you were an attorney in the case, I don't know."

"Did you say to him, Reed is in the Hahatonka case and he speaks bad of our President?"

"No, absolutely not."

Jackson was called back to the stand to testify about two other jurors, Mariner and Fred Andersen. Jackson said he felt sorry for Mariner and went to talk with the judge about him.

About Andersen, Jackson said, "He wanted to award the Snyders $25,000. He said Hahatonka was pretty, but that the property had not been damaged by the construction of Bagnell dam."

Jackson said Andersen had served as clerk for the jury, but, "He couldn't keep track of the ballots. After we discussed it and got up to $100,000, that's when Andersen told about a dream he'd had and he voted for the $25,000."

When Andersen took the witness stand he answered Reed's question about being to the Lake of the Ozarks.

"I told the jury I had never been there except to Warsaw, Missouri," Andersen said.

"Did you tell the jury about a dream you had about flying over the Lake in an airplane."

"I said I had a dream where I flew over the Lake of the Ozarks, looked at the property there and flew back."

"Are you a student of Baron Munchausen (a minor celebrity for telling outrageous tall tales based on his military service)?" Senator Reed asked.

"I am not. And I did not vote for a $25,000 award after telling the dream. I voted for $50,000 on the first vote and never voted for less than $25,000."

"Did you pass out your business card in the jury room?" Reed asked.

"Yes, I represented an appraisal firm at the time."

"Did you pass out your business card to the others to leave the impression that your opinion on property value was better than the others'?"

"No, absolutely not," Andersen replied firmly.

"So the appraisal firm you represented appraised property at the Lake of the Ozarks."

"No, not at the Lake of the Ozarks. Perhaps some in Southern Missouri."

"Did you tell the other jurors that there was no water power at the Lake of the Ozarks?"

"No."

Henry Tempel of Higginsville, Missouri, was next called as a witness. Tempel told of how he rode his horse over five miles of Lafayette County muddy roads then walked three miles on railroad ties before meeting his son-in-law who drove him to Higginsville to catch a train at five a.m. for Kansas City.

Tempel testified that a man attempted three times to talk with him about the case before jury deliberation.

"I went out a side door of the courtroom one day," he said, "and saw the man heading for another door. We met in the hallway and he asked, 'How much do they want?' I told him I was a juror and could not discuss the case. I met him later in the hallway and he asked, 'How much did they get the other time?' I told him again I could not discuss the case. When I met him the third time I began to look for someone to call. He left and I haven't seen him since."

"Why do you think he attempted to talk with you?" Reed asked.

"It could have been idle curiosity or maybe he wanted to influence my vote," Tempel said.

Edgar Shook, attorney for Union Electric asked, "What this man said could not have influenced you one way or the other, could it?"

"No, sir," Tempel said.

Tempel was asked about the conduct of Fred Andersen in the jury room.

"Andersen passed out a business calling card to all the jury," Tempel replied. "Next, he rose from his chair and said he had taken an airplane over the Hahatonka estate in Camden County, that he had stayed overnight down there and the next day flew over the property again. He said it was as beautiful as ever. He described the castle, springs and all. He painted a beautiful picture of it. Then, he told us it was all a dream he had had the night before. Andersen was good at that. He said it was not damaged. He wound up by saying, 'In view of these facts, my vote is backed down to $25,000.' I told him the case would have to be decided on the evidence.

"And, as the clerk, he miscounted the ballots."

"How many ballots were taken?" Shook asked.

"Approximately one hundred," Tempel told him.

"How many times did he miscount the ballots?"

"Once, but I don't think any particular attention was attracted to that. He was a difficult man to understand. We got up to $100,000 and after telling about some dream he had, he voted for $25,000.

Tempel said the jurors were urged to bring in a speedy verdict because of the illness of George Jackson, the foreman.

Jackson from the witness stand said that after the verdict he had visited his doctor who gave him 48 hours to live. Jackson, 73 years old, said, "I was a very sick man. If I had been in good health I would still be in that jury room trying to get a larger verdict."

Jackson said he had told the jury that his vote was for one-half million and he would be willing to give three-quarters of a million dollars. He said some of the jurors were in favor of giving the full million dollars asked by the Snyders.

After the hearing, Fred Snyder asked Foreman Jackson about the testimony and what he had found important.

"I believed Mr. Robert Snyder, what he said about the property. He was the most believable of all the witnesses. Mr. Snyder would tell the truth if it hurt him."

That was a compliment about his father that Fred treasured. It did little to dispel the worries he had about his father's health, however.

1936 WAS A DRY YEAR. On a visit to Hahatonka in June, the Snyders were able to see the beaches again and to see some of the brown, muddy water decline allowing the spring to undue some of the damage the river water from the Niangua did. In June, Judge Merrill Otis made his ruling on the Snyders' request to set aside the decision of the jury in the second trial.

Judge Otis wrote, "Inquiry touching the jury when it began looked to larger matters than the two relatively insignificant things which actually were developed."

He referred to the juror Mariner who had answered the summons sent to his brother: "After Mariner was excused and before the verdict was reached by the jury, it was learned by the judge, by marshal and by counsel of both parties that Mariner was not the C.L Mariner who had been summoned.

"Although counsel for the defense (the Snyders) knew this fact before the verdict, they took no action based on the knowledge that Mr. Mariner was not the person who had been called for jury duty.

"If it was too late to make the objection after Mariner was excused and before the verdict, it is clearly too late to make the objection after the verdict."

Judge Otis gave no importance to Reed's contention that juror Andersen had unduly influenced the jury.

"Apparently," he wrote, "it was juror Andersen who held the verdict down. Possibly, even probably, except for Andersen the jury would have agreed to a larger verdict. It can scarcely be said, however, that he was unreasonably obdurate. To meet the views of his associates he raised his estimate of damages from $25,000 to $200,000, the amount on which the jurors finally agreed.

"Counsel argues that they would have challenged Andersen if they had known he was an expert land and personal property appraiser. But that basis for argument disappears when we consider that Andersen was not himself an appraiser of properties at all. He was a mere solicitor for an appraisal company, one who painted rosy pictures of the value of his employer's services . . . As Mr. Hyde, solicitor of appraisal contracts, he was as likely to truly value a golden sunset or a poet's dream as when he was Dr. Jekyll, seller of stocks and bonds.

"In conclusion, it should be said that in the opinion of the trial judge, from a consideration of all the evidence, the amount of damages found by the jury was most liberal to the Snyders. A verdict for a smaller amount would have been fully justified and more consistent with the most credible and convincing testimony in the case."

In plainer words, Judge Otis considered the Snyders for-
tunate to have received a verdict of $200,000. It was his opin-
ion they were entitled to less.

When the appeals court ruled that Judge Albert Reeves
erred in allowing the corporate structure of Union Electric
Light and Power Company to be introduced to the jury, they
also said Judge Reeves erred when he ruled that the waters of
Hahatonka Bay were private waters and were not navigable to
the public. This reversal, upheld by Judge Otis's ruling in the
second trial, would now allow the public to enter the original
Hahatonka Lake in their boats.

As it turned out, those would be the last official words on
the trial of Hahatonka.

On February 9, 1937, completely exhausted by the seven
year battle with his old friend Louis Egan, Robert Snyder Jr,
died.

Later that year, the Big House became a hotel and Hahatonka became a resort.

EPILOGUE

MARY BOWEN SNYDER lived out her life in Springfield, MO, dying in 1967 at the age of 85. She became an expert on rare books and had helped her husband gather his immense collection of manuscripts and books. She mourned the loss of her husband and his determination never to give up on the terrible wrong he felt the building of Bagnell Dam did to Hahatonka.

ROBERT JR'S collection of 14,000 items was sold to William Volker who donated the entire set to Kansas City University—which became the University of Missouri, Kansas City (UMKC)—and Clarence Decker, the future president of the university, brought the collection to Kansas City from the Hahatonka library just a few days before fire destroyed the huge mansion in 1942. Included in the 14,000 manuscripts and books are the 19th century history of the Trans-Mississippi west, Native Americans, Mormons, the cattle trade, frontier religions, transportation and maps.

LEROY SNYDER purchased the heavily mortgaged shares of Hahatonka owned by Mary Bowen Snyder and Kenneth Snyder in the 1940's following the destructive fire. With other investors he attempted to subdivide Hahatonka into building lots and to form a social "Village Club," resort, but the project failed when one of the investors was prosecuted by the Internal Revenue Service for fraud. LeRoy died in 1966 as a result of a fall in his home, leaving his estate to his wife Lillian Ethel, "Provided that she survived at least 30 days after his death," according to terms in his will. LeRoy was engaged in the oil business.

KENNETH SNYDER died in 1969 from a stroke. He was survived by his wife, Mary Louise and two daughters. He was active in amateur theatrical and musical productions.

HAHATONKA. In 1937 the family leased the large mansion out for use as a hotel, something the family had wanted to do for some time, but Robert Jr resisted. Mrs. Josephine Ellis of Jefferson City, MO, became the manager. Maxine Williams worked in the hotel for $1 per day and room and board following her graduation from high school.

"It was beautiful," she recalled about the mansion.

In 1942 the castle and the stables were destroyed by fire.

Betty Majors, an eighth-grader recalled watching the fire.

"We used to go out there on Sundays," she recalled.

Following the fire, Hahatonka fell into disrepair. LeRoy's failure to turn the estate area into a resort left it to the weather to affect, which it did. In 1978 the State of Missouri purchased the area from an investment company and it became a state park. The state cleared trails through the park and brought the remnants of the castle into a receptive area for visitors. The park was now referred to as Ha Ha Tonka.

At the dedication of the state park June 10, 1979, an Osage chieftian dressed in tribal regalia made a speech saying, "The land you dedicated today is Osage land. It was purchased from a country having no right to sell it (France) which had taken it from a country having no right to give it (Spain) and no treaty nor sale had ever been made with the rightful owners, the Osage."

ELLEN "NELL" QUINLAN DONNELLY REED, the designer of Nelly Don fashions, owner and manager of Donnelly Garment Company and victim of a kidnapping scheme in 1931, married former senator James A. Reed in 1933. They spent time in a large Michigan ranch where he taught her hunting and fishing. In 1952 she donated 731 acres of southern Jackson County land to the Missouri Department of Conversation where it became the James A. Reed Memorial Wildlife Area. The "Nelly Don" label, became one of the largest garment manufacturing companies in the United States. The generous benefits the company paid to its employees inspired the workers to reject efforts in an attempt to unionize the plant. In the 1950's the plant averaged earnings of $14 million per year. She sold the plant in 1956 and it became Nelly Don Inc. The company eventually filed for bankruptcy because of decreasing sales which Nell blamed on the company selling both garments and fabric, something she would never do when she was the owner. "Sell one or the other," she advised, "never both."

Nell Reed died in 1991 at the age of 102.

SENATOR JAMES ALEXANDER REED continued to oppose the policies of President Franklin Delano Roosevelt and to practice his law business. After his marriage to Nell Donnelly he adopted his natural son, David Quinlan Reed. En route to Oklahoma to argue a case, the light plane in which he was riding crashed on landing and he spent the rest of his life using a cane. He loved hunting and fishing, having to hunt from the back seat of an open car after the accident. He died at the age of eighty-two in 1944 and was eulogized in the House of Representatives by fellow Missourian Clarence Cannon.

GEORGE SEATON BLAIR, served for 48 years as Nell's chauffeur, butler and close confidant. George's Methodist parents were sharecroppers near Charleston, Arkansas. He was the ninth of 12 children. George died in 1977 at the Reed ranch in Michigan.

LOUIS EGAN, the former friend of Robert Snyder Jr, who many in the Snyder family held responsible for Robert's demise, was involved in a violation of federal law and was arrested at his Clayton, MO, home after conviction in a Union Electric $600,000 slush fund scandal. Egan lost a 2 year legal fight to escape imprisonment and in December 1943, was sent to federal prison. He died in 1950 at the age of 69.

MARTIN DEPEW or MARSHALL DEPUTY, sentenced to life in the Missouri State Prison in 1932 for engineering the kidnapping of Nell Donnelly, was set free in January, 1947 by the parole board who said that Depew had been one of the best workers the prison ever had. Depew was 52 at the time.

CHARLES MELE, sentenced to 35 years in prison for the kidnapping of Nell Donnelly in October 1932, was freed by the parole board in February 1947.

WALTER WERNER, sentenced in June 1932 to life in prison for his involvement in the kidnapping, was freed by the parole board in October 1947.

NOTES

ABBREVIATIONS USED IN THE
NOTES

KCS   Kansas City Star

KCT   Kansas City Times

KCJ-P   Kansas City Journal-Post

JCCN   Jefferson City Capital News

NYT   New York Times

JCHS   Jackson County (MO) Historical Society, Box 20F17, folder 6a, Robert McClure Snyder, His Life, by Suzee Oberg

CCH-XII Camden County Historian, Volume XII, The History of Ha Ha Tonka, Bill Snyder's Story, Ha Ha Tonka, A Personal History, Published by the Camden County (MO) Historical Society

SB   *Strange Bedfellows*, Prepared by Missouri Valley Special Collection, Kansas City Public Library

SD   Startling Detective Magazine, April, 1932, *The Gangsters Solved the Donnelly Kidnaping*, Leon N. Hatfield

LT   *Leavenworth Times* (Leavenworth, Kansas), July 31, 2014, Ted Stillwell, *Portraits of the Past: The Nelly Don Kidnapping Sensation.*

DT   The Devil's Tickets, A NIGHT OF BRIDGE, A FATAL HAND, AND A NEW AMERICAN AGE, Gary M. Pomeranz, 2009, Crown Publishers, ISBN 978-1-4000-5162-5

DMB , *Dictionary of Missourian Biographys*, University of Missouri Press, 1998

NOTES
I

page

13. . .**left his office**: *KCS*, October 28, 1906

13. . .**Snyder's green Royal Tourists**: JCHS, page 10

13. . .**the gas situation. He'd been working that**: From *"Kansas City, Missouri: Its History and Its People, 1800-1908", by Carrie Westlake Whitney, published by the S. J. Clarke Publishing Co., Chicago, 1908, pages 332-335:*

14. . .**—Carey, once again accused**: JCHS, page 9

15. . .**he took a bit of boyish joy**: *NYT,* October 28, 1906

13. . .**From catching the largest tarpon**: JCHS, page 8

14. . .**what seemed like days ago**: JCHS, page 9

14. . .**Hahatonka, what a joy**: JCHS, page 8

15. . .**Frank Schroeder, struck with shock and terror**: *KCS,* October 28, 1906

16. . .**Richard Andrew watched**: *KCS,* October 28,1906

17. . .**While Snyder was being rushed**: *KCS,* October 28, 1906

19. . .**Snyder was buried**: JCHS, page 12

II

20. . .**Kenneth Snyder handed***: KCT, April 22, 1929*

21. . . **"Yes, I know Louis Egan"**:*CCH-XII*, page 64

III

22. . .**large rainbow trou**t: *JCCN,* December 30, 1931, *CCHS-XII*, page 62

22. . .**began sawing the trunks**: CCHS-XII, page 64

22 . . .**Lakeside was the name**: CCHS-XII, page 62

23 . . . **"He's the one—"**:CCHS-XII, page 61

24 . . . **"the court appointed three commissioners"** CCHS-XII, page 64, *KCS*, November 28, 1931

24 . . . **"offered twenty-eight thousand—"**:CCHS- XII, page 64

24 . . . **"A hundred and forty-some thousand—"**: CCHS-XII, page 64

25 . . . **"When he was the prosecutor—"**: DT page 76

26 . . .**"he threatened to keep us in court for seven years,"**:CCHS-XII, page 64

26 . . . **"Did you see it?"**: *KCS*, November 28, 1931

IV

29 . . . **"They put the thing together—"**: *National Register of Historic Places* Registration Form, 1998; prepared by Laura Johnson, Preservationist, with Benjamin Cawthra, Historian.

30 . . . **"All those damn property owners—"**: *Ameren UE History of Bagnell Dam* by William E. Turner; *Minutes of the Public Service Commission*, State of Missouri, December 23, 1925 meeting.

31 . . . **"We're burning the houses—"**: *Before The Dam Waters, Story and Pictures of Old Linn Creek, Ha Ha Tonka and Camden County,* T. Victor Jeffries, 2nd Printing, 1980, page 22

31 . . . **"Judge named Skinker—"**: JCCN May 11, 1930; *Miller County Autogram,* May 15, 1930

V

41 . . . **"I'm planning a trip to Europe—"**: DT 205; *Nelly
        Don: A Stitch in Time*, Terrence Michael O'Malley, First
        Edition, 2006, page 50
42. . . **"being against the right of women to vote:** DT page 72
43 . . . **"I'm pregnant."**: DT page 204; Kansas City Public Li
        brary, Missouri Valley Special Collections, *Strange
        Bedfellows.*

VI

44 . . .**lawyer had threatened to punch***:* DT page 186
44 . . . **"primarily a business trip:** *Springfield Daily News,*
        Springfield, MO, March 18, 1931
46 . . .**which got him barred:** DT page 72
49 . . . **"—every governor since father died"**: JCCN
        December 23, 1931

VII

53 . . . **"Mr. Page said, let's pause—"**: DT page 111
54 . . . **"Tell us again—"**: DT page 64

VIII

58 . . . **"Here's the way it can go,"—***:* *Nelly Don: A Stitch in
        Time*, Terrence Michael O'Malley, First Edition, 2006,
        page 50
62. . **"Tom's going to back me—"***:* *Pendergast,* by Lawrence
        Larson and Nancy Hulston, 1997, University of Mis
        souri Press, Columbia, Missouri, page 91; KCJ-P Janu
        ary 10, 1932

IX

65. . . **"father had been the one"***: CCH-XII page 58

66. . . .**Reeves was a known adversary:** *Pendergast,* by Lawrence Larson and Nancy Hulston, 1997, University of Missouri Press, Columbia, Missouri, page 178; *Dictionary of Missouri Biography, 1998,* University of Missouri Press, Columbia, Missouri, page 643

68. . . .**Sid's list, five farmers**: KCS February 3, 1932

70. . . .**"This condemnation suit—":** KCS December 2, 1931

71. . . .**"The utility company says it is the United—":** KCS December 2, 1931

72. . . .**"And, gentlemen, they proceed to improve—":** Ibid

73. . . . **"There was in this country—"***: KCS December 2, 1931

X

75. . . .**each of the forty pictures:** KCS December 3, 1931

75 . .**Howard told the jurors how**—Ibid

79. . . .**bust of Robert E. Lee that he never***: PBS American Experience, *The Carving of Stone Mountain,* Retreived, September 1, 2015

79. . . . **"One and a half million dollars,":** KCS December 7, 1931

81. . . . **"That beautiful spot is killed—"***: Ibid

82. . . . **"Have you ever been—"***: Ibid

83. . . .**The movies were "before and after":** Ibid

XI

84. . . . **"—operating a steam shovel—"***: KCJ-P December 22, 1931

XII

89. . . **"I'm going to give the history—"**: KCS December 21, *1931*

90. . . **"What is the document?"**: KCS December 9, 1931

91. . . **"In contemplating the destruction—"**: Ibid

92. . . **He started the names"**: Ibid

XIII

95. . . **"—grab some rich guy—"**: KCJ-P December 22, 1931

96. . . **"You get seventy-five hundred—"**: Ibid

98. . . **"Why don't you grab him?"**: KCJ-P Sept. 9, 1932

99. . . **"Let's drive over and tell Browning."**: Ibid

XIV

101. . .**The first date he quoted—**: CCH-XII page 55

101. . .**Lewis and Clark sent a messenger**: Ibid

102. . .**the tale of the counterfeiters**: CCH-XII pages 56, 57

103. . .**old men of the Osage nation**: CCH-XII page 54

103. . . **"—it is the bills that is the best—"**: JCCN December 23, 1931

105. . .**Nell Donnelly noticed the automobile—**: KCJ-P December 18, 1931; KCS December 18, 1931

106. . .**he opened the door where Blair sat**: Ibid

107. . .**Nell felt the man hit her**: KCS December 18, 1931

108. . . **"Got my Irish up—"**: KCS December 18, 1931

109. . .**the time on her watch was 7:15—**: KCS December 18, 1931

110. . . **"I don't have that much money—"**: Ibid

111. . . **"Write what I tell you—"**: Ibid

XV

112. . .**A telephone call his wife**—SD page 48; KCS December 17, 1931; LT July 31, 2014

113 . .**SHORTLY AFTER court resumed**—SD page 46; KCS December 18, 1931

115. . **"I got a call—"** SD page 45; KCS December 17, 1931

116. . **"I'M POLICE CHIEF SIEGFRIED**—SD page 46

117. .**The line of the note**—SD page 46

117. .**Taylor handed him the note**—SD page 46; KCS December 17, 1931

120. .**—recovered Mrs. Donnelly's Lincoln**—SD page 47

121. .**the kidnapers can have**—SD page 47, *Called to Courage, Four Women in Missouri History*, Margot Ford McMillen and Heather Roberson, University of Missouri Press, Columbia, MO, page 110, Nell Donnelly Reed.

121 . . **"Says her name is Madame Peri**—*Tom's Town,* page 196, by William Reddig, First Edition, 1947, Lippincott Publishing, Philadelphia and New York; KCJ-P December 18, 1931

123. .**George Blair's wife, Savannah**—KCJ-P December 18, 1931

126. . **"I will take a half-hour's time—"** DT page 206; KCJ-P December 21, 1931; *Leavenworth Times*, Leavenworth, Kansas, *Portraits of the Past,* Ted Stillwell, July 31, 2014; *Nelly Don: A Stitch in Time*, Terrence Michael O'Malley, First Edition, 2006, page 53

127. .**THE VOICE ON THE RADIO**—KCS December 18, 1931

130. .John Lazia looked a bit out of place—SD page 47

XVI

132. .PAUL DONNELLY paced the floor—KCJ-P De - cember 18, 1931

XVII

139. . "Friends," the man answered—LT; MA

141 . . "Wait three minutes—KCJ-P December 18, 1931

142. .. came to a lighted cafe—KCJ-P December 18, 1931

143. .."Is this the chief?"—SD page 47; KCJ-P December 18, 1931; KCS December 18, 1931

146. . . "Are you Mrs. Donnelly?"—SD page 48;

146. . . "Are you all right?"—SD page 48; KCS December 18, 1931

XVIII

152. . .Kansas City master architect Adrian Van Brunt—CCHS-XII, page 59

154. . .the testimony of Stone and Webster's—KCS- December 18, 1931

155. . "some photographs of the estate—" Ibid

159. .Mary, deeply concerned about her husband— CCHS-XII, page 67

XIX

162 . .**began describing the dining room**—KCJ-P
December 26, 1931

163. . **"Oh, the towel,"**—KCJ-P December 22, 1931; SD
page 49

165. . .**Lazia told us to get out of town**—KCJ-P December
22, 1931

166. . . **"thing is, the man was sick**—" KCJ-P December
22, 1931

XX

168. . .**Carey had become involved**—JCHS page 9

169. . . **"—a damn piece in the Hutchinson—"** *Hutchinson News,* Hutchinson, Kansas, December 22, 1931,
"UNDERWORLD WAYS"

171. . .**that's how Robert Jr wrote it**—NYT, February 16,
1902

XXI

173. .**where the figure came from**—JCCN December 21,
1931

175. .**laundry that might have handled the towel**—SD
page 49; KCJ-P Dec 26, 1931

176. . .**Goodhue agreed with the sheriff**—Ibid

179. . **"—Paul Scheidt. He lives here—"**Ibid

182. . .**Scheidt didn't answer right away**—Ibid

184. . .**person following the chief. Nell Donnelly**—Ibid

185. . . **"—Lacy Browning brought this man—"** Ibid

189. . .**looked at her husband and immediately**—KCJ-P
December 22, 1931

XXII

191... **"—was actually a summer resort—"** KCT
December 23, 1931

194... **"—outstanding place to see things—"** KCS
December 23, 1931

195... **"—That's him," Nell Donnelly said.**—SD page
50; *Decatur Daily Review*, December 23, 1931, Decatur, IL; *Macon Chronicle Herald,* December 23, 1931,
Macon, MO

XXIII

198. .**The bus trip to Chicago**—KCJ-P December 26,
1931

201. .**SENATOR JAMES REED pulled**—KCJ-P January
10, 1932

XXIV

205... **Sheriff Arthur Rabb drove up**— KCJ-P January
10, 1932

XXV

209... **Dr. Walter Williams, president of the University**— KCS December 29, 1931

212... **Walne repeated his request**—Ibid

213... **Mrs. Donnelly identified him**—SD page 50; KCS
February 2, 1932

XXVI

215... **E.L. Williams, a hydraulic engineer**—KCS
December 30, 1931

217... **the electric company's first**—KCS December 31,
1931

XXVII

222. . . **"there would be sand and gravel beaches—"** KCT January 1, 1932

224. . . **"Tell me, Mr. Rudolph—"** JCCN January 2, 1932

227. . .**laid the paper in front of Circuit** —KCJ-P January 4, 1932

231. . .**George Mann, said he had lived—** JCCN January 8, 1932

XXVIII

233. . .**For two hours the former senator** — KCJ-P January 9, 1932

235, . .**Senator Reed had returned and**—JCCN January 14, 1932

XXIX

238. . .**JOHN T. WOODRUFF, Springfield attor ney**—JCCN January 27, 1932

239. . .**Former U.S. Congressman**—JCCN January 25, 1932

240. . .**Louis Egan was introduced**—Ibid

XXX

249. . . **"—HEART ATTACK," Mary Bowen Sny-der**—KCS January 26, 1932

XXXI

250. . . **"ANYONE MAKING ANY DEMONSTRA-TION—"** JCCN January 27, 1932

XXXII

257. . . "Now they can hire a smiling and fat—" JCCN
January 27, 1932

XXXIII

258. . .AT 10:30 ON FEBRUARY 3, 1932—KCS January
3, 1932

XXXIV

261. . .JACKSON COUNTY PROSECUTOR— KCJ-P
February 15, 1932

262. . . "—the wrong charge—" KCJ-P February 16,
1932; KCS February 16, 1932

263. . .Nell Donnelly sat impassively—KCS February 16,
1932

268. . .At noon the next day—KCS February 18,1932

XXXV

270. . . "Let me get this straight," KCJ-P July 14, 1932;
Southeast Missourian, Cape Girardeau, Missouri, July
13, 1932

XXXVI

273. . . "Tell me what you wrote about your father—"
NYT February 16, 1902, *"ROBERT M. SNYDER IN
DICTED"*; NYT October 3, 1902, *"ST. LOUIS CITY SCAN
DAL"—"American State Trials, Volume IX*, John Davi
son, LL.D Editor, F.H. Thomas, Law Book Company. *In
the St. Louis Circuit Court, Criminal Division, Judge
Ryan O'Neil*

277. . . **"Two years later—"** NYT May 27, 1906, *"AFTER R.M. SNYDER AGAIN"*

277. . . **"We'll have the trial postponed—"** KCS February 22, 1932

279. . .**an editorial by Nell Quinlan Donnelly**—KCS, KCJ-P, JCCN, Associated Press, March 4, 1932

XXXVII

281. . .**"Yeah, that's where they got him—"** *Macon Chronicle Herald*, April 25, 1932, Macon, MO

284. . .**JUDGE BEN TERTE, behind the bench—** JCCN June 17, 1932

286. . . **"'Well, boys, I did it,'"** *Palm Beach Post*, Palm Beach, Florida, June 13, 1932

XXXVIII

288. . .**THE DEMOCRATIC NATIONAL CONVENTION**—NYT, May 14, 2007, *F.D.R.'S ROUGH ROAD TO NOMINATION,* by Jean Edward Smith

291. . .**The fourth ballot**—DT page 206; —*Tom's Town,* page 196, by William Reddig, First Edition, 1947, Lippincott Publishing, Philadelphia and New York

XXXIX

293. . .**She told her story**—*Southeast Missourian,* Cape Girardeau, MO, July 13, 1932

297. . .**C.C. Franklin, assistant to Lasson**—*Southeast Missourian,* Cape Girardeau, MO, July 14, 1932

299. . .**When the buzzer sounded**—KCS July 19, 1932

XL

304...**FORTY-SEVEN MEMBERS**—KCJ-P September 6, 1932

307...**A surprise witness**—KCJ-P, September 9, 1932

309...**Opening court the next day**—KCJ-P September 10, 1932; *Gettysburg Times*, Gettysburg, PA, September 10, 1932; *Reading Eagle*, Reading, PA, September 10, 1932; *Lawrence Journal-World*, Lawrence, KS, September 10, 1932

309...**Little more than a month later**— *Lawrence Journal-World*, Lawrence, KS, October 21, 1932

XLI

311..**NOVEMBER 15, 1932**—*Macon Chronicle Herald*, Macon, MO, November 16, 1932; DT page 207; DMB page 644

XLII

314..**THREE APPEALS JUDGES**—KCS April 24, 1933, KCJ-P April 24, 1933; DMB page 644

318.. **"Brewster is the man—"** CCHS-XII, page 67

XLIII

320..**On September 7, 1934, Paul Donnelly**—*Lawrence Journal-World*, Lawrence, KS, September 8, 1934, DT page 208

XLIV

322..**first of a number of controversies**—KCJ-P February 4, 1935

323...**He volunteered to be the first**—KCJ-P February 6, 1935

324.. **"We overheard some people**—CCHS-XII, page 67

XLV

326. . "I BELIEVE MR. MARINER IS ILL—" KCS
February 22, 1935; KCJ-P February 22,1935

XLVI

329. .Jackson was called back—KCS May 16, 1936,
KCJ-P May 17, 1936

333 . .Judge Merrill Otis made his ruling—KCJ-P June
17, 1936, KCS June 17, 1936

EPILOGUE

336 . . . MARY BOWEN SNYDER: KCT April 8, 1967

336 . . .ROBERT JR's collection: JCHS page 13

336 . . .LEROY SNYDER: KCT June 30, 1966

337 . . .KENNETH SNYDER: KCS December 9, 1969

337 . . .Maxine Williams worked: Lake Sun Leader, Sept
24, 2014

337 . . .Betty Majors, an eighth-grader: Ibid

337 . . .LeRoy's failure:CCH—XII page 69

337 . . . "The land you dedicated—" CCHS-XII page 2,
Indians and Ha Ha Tonka, Neva O. Crane

338 . . .the generous benefits: *Nelly Don: A Stitch in Time,*
Terrence Michael O'Malley, First Edition, 2006, page
69

338 . . .en route to Oklahoma: DMB page 643

338 . . .GEORGE SEATON BLAIR: *Nelly Don: A Stitch
in Time,* Terrence Michael O'Malley, First Edition,
2006, page 85

339 . . .LOUIS EAGAN:*Time* magazine, July 29, 1940, *St.
Louis Sunday Tribune,* December 30, 1943

339 . . .MARTIN DEPEW:*Jeffersonian,* Jefferstown, KY,
March 14, 1947

339 . . .**CHARLES MELE**:Missouri State Archives, Missouri State Penitentiary, Volume 2, pages 183-184

339 . . .**WALTER WERNER**:Ibid

Made in the USA
Charleston, SC
15 November 2015